Courier of Death

A SPENCER & REID MYSTERY
BOOK THREE

CARA DEVLIN

Edited by Jennifer Wargula

ISBN paperback: 979-8-992305722

Chapter One

London
May 1884

Leonora Spencer hurried through the busy corridor at Scotland Yard, determined to be invisible. It was a risk for her to be within its walls, and in the middle of the day, at that. But there had been no messenger boy hanging about, waiting to be hailed, near the Spring Street Morgue, and the deadline for unidentified corpse descriptions for *The Police Gazette* was noon sharp. As the top of the hour had neared and her agitation increased, Leo determined she would simply have to deliver the latest description to Constable Elias Murray at the news office herself.

It wasn't the constable whom she was attempting to avoid, even though a few months ago, he'd confessed to being the anonymous reporter who'd profiled her in *The*

Illustrated Police News. They'd dined out once while he'd pretended to have a romantic interest in her, but he'd only been gathering information for his article. It had been disappointing to realize he'd had an ulterior motive, but she no longer carried a grudge against him. Elias Murray hadn't wounded her irrevocably.

Unlike someone else. A man she'd once trusted beyond measure.

However, discovering the identity of the Jane Doe lying in her uncle's morgue took precedence over her own discomfort, so Leo had gathered her mettle and set out for the Metropolitan Police headquarters herself.

At the front desk, Constable Woodhouse greeted her with some surprise before allowing her to pass through to whichever part of the building she intended to go. If the startled glances she received in the narrow corridor and stairwell were any evidence, her recent absence from the Yard had been noted.

Constable Murray shot to his feet when she knocked upon the open door to his cramped office. "Miss Spencer." His lips gaped. "I…I didn't expect to see you."

Leo overlooked his disconcerted state and handed him the typed description: a woman in her late sixties, found on the mudflats under Westminster Bridge. Her neatly trimmed nails, expensive silk petticoats, and velvet dress from a high-end boutique on Oxford Street had led Leo to believe that she was a woman whom someone, somewhere would be missing.

"There was no messenger boy today, or you wouldn't have seen me," she replied. It was honest, if somewhat rude. With Constable Murray, she no longer cared to be polite.

He took the typed description. "Thank you. You know, twelve bodies have been identified since we started running these descriptions in the *Gazette*."

"That's wonderful." The positive outcome was worth a bit of awkwardness, she supposed.

With a glance toward the wall clock, the sensation of ants crawling up her legs jolted her. Leo had been in the building for five whole minutes. Every additional minute she remained was another in which she might be seen by the one person she'd vowed never to see or speak to again. It was a vow she was determined to keep.

"Until the next John or Jane Doe then," Leo said before retreating into the corridor.

Unfortunately, Constable Murray followed. "Miss Spencer, I wanted to express to you again how sorry I am for my dishonesty. I think I convinced myself that ultimately the article would be of assistance to you, a way to shine some light on your stimulating work." He still gripped the typed description of the Jane Doe in his hand, but in his nervousness, he had crumpled it. "However, I've come to accept that I was merely doing a service for myself—and I genuinely regret it."

A few months ago, had she not been so disconcerted by Constable Murray's unexpected interest in her, she might have guessed at the truth. He'd expressed a far greater interest in newspaper reporting than in policing, which should have been a glaring clue. However, her resentment toward him had long since fizzled out. Even the handful of additional articles printed about her in various London newspapers, describing the role Leonora Spencer, *'the female morgue worker-turned-detective,'* had played in solving a murder inquiry a few months ago—of which Constable Murray swore he had no hand in writing—had failed to truly distress her.

"Thank you, Constable. Let's call a truce, shall we? Now, I really must go," she said and again turned to leave.

The longer she lingered, the greater the chance that she would cross paths with a certain detective inspector she'd been sidestepping since early March, when she'd learned he wasn't who he'd claimed to be for the sixteen years she'd known him.

Jasper Reid was not even his real name.

Because of her unusual memory, which captured images in minute detail and allowed her to return to them no matter how much time had passed, the sharp details never fading, Leo repeatedly had experienced the world-bending moment in which he'd confirmed her suspicion. The blade of his betrayal slipped between her ribs and into her heart again and again, taking her breath away each time.

His given name was James. James Carter. His family—his real family—ran the notorious organized crime syndicate known as the East Rips. And sixteen years ago, on the night Leo's family had been brutally murdered in their home on Red Lion Street, *he* had been the boy who'd come into the darkened attic looking for her. *Jasper* had been the shadowy figure she'd puzzled over ever since that night, half believing he was a figment of her imagination. Because instead of killing her, he'd hidden her in a steamer trunk to save her life.

"You seem particularly rushed today," Constable Murray observed.

Leo gritted her molars. He had followed her toward the stairs.

"Is it the date?" he asked.

The question was curious enough for her to stop and peer at him. "What is important about the thirtieth of May?"

"The way you're rushing to leave, I presumed you knew about the warning Clan na Gael sent back in the autumn. We're to be on alert today."

Leo didn't like the sound of that. Clan na Gael had come to power a few years ago when the Fenian Brotherhood, a militant political group seeking Irish independence from Britain, disbanded. The two groups were essentially the same, however, and they, along with the Irish Republican Brotherhood, had been waging a dynamite war on London for the last decade, attempting to instill terror among the British. In the previous year alone, there had been explosions at various government offices at Whitehall Place, at *The Times*, and at Paddington station, where dozens of people had been injured.

"What warning was this?" Leo asked.

He gave a small shrug. "Nothing to take very seriously, I'm sure. They threaten to bomb the city all the time but hardly ever carry out the blasts. I won't trouble you further with it." He tipped the brim of his hat. "Good afternoon, Miss Spencer."

Unsatisfied with his response, Leo watched him return to his office. Men's voices echoed up the stairs and along the corridor, giving her what felt like a nudge in the back. She descended the stairs, her fingers clenched as she hoped to clear the building without seeing Jasper—or James, if that was how she should be thinking of him now. That name felt entirely wrong though, as did the cinch of her stomach and the ache of her heart whenever she thought about him. Paired with the boiling of her blood, the mixed emotions never ceased to confuse her.

He had tried to speak to her several times since that morning two months ago, when Leo let herself into his home on Charles Street. She'd surreptitiously entered his bedroom to view the old scar on his chest, of which she'd caught a glimpse the night before, after Jasper had been injured in an explosion at a wallpaper factory. Only after a sleepless night had Leo realized why the scar bothered her so deeply. The shape of it perfectly matched the shape of the porcelain shard broken off from her old china doll's leg, the very shard a young Leo had used to stab the mysterious boy who'd found her in the attic the night of the murders. It was how she had received a pair of parallel scars on the palm of her right hand.

Jasper had followed her from his room after she'd stormed out, a bedsheet clutched around his waist—the only thing concealing the rest of his naked body. But Leo had not paid any attention to his undressed state. It was a minor scandal compared to what he had just admitted to her.

"Wait, Leo. Wait, please, let me explain." He'd taken the stairs after her but abruptly stopped when she'd opened the front door. For her to be seen leaving his house just past dawn would have spurred rumors. For Jasper to potentially be seen in nothing but a bedsheet coming after her would cement Leo's ruin.

She had not allowed him to explain, as he'd begged, and had slammed the door behind her. Predictably, he'd come to her home on Duke Street later that morning, but she'd instructed her Uncle Claude to send him away. The next day, Jasper had shown up at the morgue. Leo told him that unless he left the premises right then, she'd upend a bucket collecting run-off from one of the autopsy tables all over his shoes.

When Jasper met her on the pavement outside her home the following day, he'd asked whether she would at least give him five minutes to hear him out. She'd held her temper and calmly stated, *"I cannot even look at you right now. Please, just give me space."*

Reluctantly, he'd nodded and left.

She hadn't spoken to him since.

Not thinking about Jasper—or James—hadn't been as easy as avoiding him. Unless she occupied her time with other things, all she found herself doing was thinking of his lies and all the unanswered questions that cluttered her brain but were too unwieldy to unpack.

So, when her friend Nivedita Brooks invited her to a meeting of the Women's Equality Alliance, she'd jumped at the chance. Not only did Leo believe in the cause, but focusing on the dearth of women's rights in England, especially the right to vote, gave her another injustice toward which to direct her anger. One that had nothing to do with Jasper Reid.

The women at the WEA meetings were forward-thinking and bright, and most had accepted Leo even after learning she worked as an assistant in her uncle's city morgue. Some, of course, kept their distance, choosing another row in which to sit, but it hadn't offended her much, and it hadn't bothered Dita at all. Most of the WEA members, including their president, Mrs. Geraldine Stewart, were welcoming. In the past few months while she'd been attending meetings, her uncle had supportively pointed out that it was good for her to be a part of something that wasn't connected to either the morgue or the Metropolitan Police.

As she reached the doors to the entrance lobby, Leo turned her mind to the WEA meeting that she and Dita were to attend that week. But as one of the doors opened, her legs and heart came to an abrupt stop.

Detective Inspector Jasper Reid and Detective Sergeant Roy Lewis entered the lobby of Scotland Yard together. Jasper locked eyes with Leo, and whatever he was in the middle of saying to the detective sergeant fell off. He stopped moving. Leo's throat cinched as she took in the sight of him. His hooded, dark green eyes, his slightly rumpled clothing, and the dark blond stubble on his cheeks and chin. He'd either forgotten to shave that morning, or he was beginning to grow a beard. A sense of helpless misery pierced her chest.

Sergeant Lewis tipped the brim of his hat to her before moving past them and further into the building. At the clearing of Constable Woodhouse's throat from where he stood behind the reception desk, Leo's sudden paralysis lifted. Her heart thrashed against her ribs as she averted her welling eyes and stepped forward again.

"Leo, wait."

"I'm in a hurry, Inspector."

"I suspect you're only in a hurry to avoid me."

The accusatory tone brought her to a standstill. She whipped around, the coals of her temper stoked to life. "Yes, I am, although that turns out to have been a complete failure."

Jasper glanced toward Constable Woodhouse, who was openly listening to their exchange, then stepped toward Leo and lowered his voice. "It has been months, Leo. We need to talk."

She squared her shoulders as fury prickled under her skin. "I'm not ready."

The muscles along Jasper's jaw tensed. "I didn't think it possible to underestimate your propensity to be mulish, but it seems I have."

Her lips parted on a gust of disbelief. "You have no right to be upset."

She barely suppressed kicking him in the shin before she turned for the doors again.

"Leo," Jasper pleaded. "I'm asking you to stop."

She didn't know why she complied. Maybe it was because, as furious as she was with him, as intent as she'd been to uphold her vow to never speak to him again...she missed him, which only made her more upset. Although this time, with *herself*.

He whisked off his bowler and, more quietly than before, said, "I think it is high time we spoke. Not here, of course—"

"No, not here." Leo struggled to keep her voice equally soft but managed to whisper, "If anyone here found out why I haven't spoken to you in two months, you'd be sacked, wouldn't you? You've lied to everyone, not just to me."

He pressed his lips thin, his expression injured and subdued. Her eyes, already brimming with tears, began to sting. *Blast!* She needed to get out of there before they fell.

Leo rushed outside into the courtyard behind the building. She filled her lungs with warm, late spring air and blinked back hot tears. What she'd said was true: Jasper hadn't just lied to her. He was related to one of the most powerful crime families in London, and surely, if anyone within the Met were to learn of it, he'd be released from duty at once. How Jasper had managed to come face-to-face with Andrew Carter in March during the investigation into the murder of his wife, Gabriela, and not be recognized was beyond her comprehension. Had Andrew known who he was? Or had Jasper changed so drastically since the age of thirteen that his own relative did not know him?

It was just one of the dozens of questions she'd been stewing over. Another was whether the late Chief Superintendent Gregory Reid had known the truth about him. The Inspector had rescued Leo from the attic and taken her in as a ward while searching for her aunt and uncle, Flora and Claude Feldman. At that time, Jasper had been a runaway from the East End, who'd been arrested for thievery. But after a show of heroics at Scotland Yard—stopping a drunkard from colliding with nine-year-old Leo—he piqued the Inspector's interest, and Gregory Reid had taken in Jasper as well.

He welcomed Jasper into his home, into his life, and loved him like a son. Leo couldn't bear the thought that Jasper might have lied to the Inspector too.

The courtyard buzzed with commotion. Officers, both in uniform and plain clothes, were arriving and departing, and hansom cabs were lined up, ready for hire. Scotland Yard was a hub of activity, and in the past, she had always felt a pinch more alive whenever she was there. Now, however, it was a place she only wished to evade. Jasper was the reason, and she bitterly held it against him. Leo increased her pace, eager to return to the morgue. There, the next postmortem report would distract her, and she could push Jasper and his lies from her mind. For a little while, at least.

Up ahead, a familiar constable crossed under the arch that led into the courtyard behind headquarters. For several months, Police Constable John Lloyd had been courting Dita, and Leo would often join them when they went across the river to Striker's Wharf, a nightclub and dance hall. John was an affable fellow and usually had a smile for Leo whenever he saw her. But now, as she walked toward him, tension creased his brow.

A fresh bruise discolored his swollen left eye, and gashes on his cheek and bottom lip were crusted with dried blood. Oddly enough, he wasn't wearing his policeman's uniform. His civilian clothes appeared rumpled, and in his left hand, he carried a brown leather valise. Leo slowed. It looked to be a lady's valise, trimmed with floral embroidery. Only about ten or fifteen yards separated them, but Constable Lloyd had yet to see her. Leo lifted her arm to hail him, and his attention clapped onto her.

He stopped walking as abruptly as if he'd smacked into a wall. Then, he spun on his heel and started away in the direction from which he'd come.

"Constable Lloyd!" she called, worry mixing with curiosity. What on earth was he doing?

Beyond the archway that led into the yard, a man wearing a brown wool cap pushed off from the iron hitching post he'd been leaning against and stood to attention. His scowl was fierce, Leo noticed, and he seemed to be directing it straight at Constable Lloyd. The man shook his head, as if to say, "*Don't.*"

Before she could think twice about the man, a pulse of light blinded her. A violent, crushing blast lifted her feet from the ground. Heat raced over her skin and through her hair, and the brutal percussion of an explosion thudded through her chest. The strike of it emptied Leo's lungs even before she landed hard on her back, cracking her head against the ground.

The world went dark and still and silent.

She came to—how much later she was unable to tell—with a shrill chime filling her ears, followed by a burrowing pain. Slowly, she lifted her hand to her throbbing left ear. Acrid smoke filled her nose and throat, and she coughed as her eyes fluttered open. A river of smoke flowed over her, with pockets of blue sky cutting through it, then disappearing again as the black haze blotted them out.

Bomb.

It was a bomb.

Muted shouts filtered through the strident ringing in her ears. And then, Jasper was hovering over her. He was all she could see, his lips forming her name, his dark green eyes filled with stark panic. She tried to sit up but found it impossible. In the next second, she was in the air again, this time firmly locked in Jasper's arms. As he carried her back toward the building, her vision swam, and a surge of nausea gripped her. For over his shoulder, sprawled upon the ground, lay Police Constable John Lloyd.

Or what remained of him.

Chapter Two

Chaos swarmed the lobby as Jasper passed Constable Woodhouse's now abandoned reception desk. Jasper's pulse pumped hard, and his breaths came in short puffs. Leo batted at his shoulder with feeble pats and mumbled for him to put her down.

"I can walk," she wheezed. Her lungs probably hadn't yet filled back up with air; the force of the explosion would have driven it right out of her.

"Just let me carry you. You're bleeding," he said as he continued toward the detective department.

She kicked her legs in objection to his command, albeit weakly. "This is embarrassing. Put me down."

When he'd heard the explosion, he'd sprinted for the yard, praying Leo had stormed away from him and their brief altercation fast enough to have cleared the bomb. But there she'd been, visible through the thick, gunpowder smoke, sprawled on her back and unconscious.

Jasper hadn't drawn breath again until he saw her

lashes fluttering, her brow pinching in pain, and her head moving side to side. Blood trickled from her left ear, the blast rupturing her eardrum.

Men were running in every direction, and beyond the walls of the building, there was a cacophony of shouts and screams. It appeared Clan na Gael had followed through with the bombing. They'd sent the first warning months ago, informing them that police headquarters and a few other significant places in London would be bombed. Several letters like it had arrived every month, but prior threats had never been seen through. As such, no one had taken the warning letter for the thirtieth of May too seriously. Jasper certainly hadn't.

He brought Leo into his office and lowered her gently onto a chair. She pressed a hand to her bleeding ear and winced.

"Where else are you injured?" He knelt on the floor before her, checking for more blood, from the crown of her head to the soles of her boots. She'd lost her hat in the blast, and her sable hair had come loose from its pins.

"Nowhere. I'm just sore," she insisted, speaking loudly to account for the temporary loss of hearing in her ear. She tried to stand but then wobbled and sat back down. "It was John."

Jasper stood, his breathing returning to its normal cadence now that he was sure she wasn't badly injured. "John?"

"PC Lloyd. Dita's beau. *Oh no*...Dita." She tried to stand again, and he gripped her arm to keep her from tottering to the side. After momentarily allowing him to steady her, she wrenched free of his grasp.

"Don't." Leo shrunk away from him.

Jasper backed up, trying to deflect the sharp stab of insult. Of course, she wouldn't want his help. She'd made it perfectly clear that she despised him. And he couldn't entirely blame her.

The last two months had been hell. He'd tried to come to terms with the fact that Leo might never forgive him, that she might never speak to him again, just as she'd promised. That early morning when he'd awoken to find her in his bedroom on Charles Street still felt surreal. At first, Jasper hadn't trusted he was awake. A part of him believed he was asleep and dreaming as she came silently to the side of his bed. It wouldn't have been the first time he'd succumbed to a nighttime fantasy about Leonora Spencer, even though he'd wake from the unbidden dreams with a guilty conscience to some degree, anyway.

But that morning, when she'd pressed her fingers to the scar on his chest, her hazel eyes round with realization, he'd known it was no dream. It was the moment he'd feared for sixteen years.

"Are you certain it was PC Lloyd?" he asked as raised voices in the detective department escalated.

Leo nodded, then winced again. She'd probably hit her head on the ground when she'd been thrown back in the blast. "Yes, I saw him just moments before—" She turned for the open door. "We can't let Dita go out there."

She staggered and leaned against the doorjamb just as Sergeant Lewis came through.

"Where is the doctor?" Jasper asked him.

"Treating another man outside," he answered. Then, after eyeing Leo's bloody ear and disheveled state, he asked, "Should I fetch him?"

"I don't need a doctor," she insisted, though she still

clung to the jamb. "I need to find Matron Brooks. Have you seen her?"

Leo's friend, Dita, was a matron at the Yard, assigned to search and guard female suspects as well as young children when they were brought in for questioning or held for arrest. She would have likely been in the building at the time of the explosion.

"Tomlin has her in an interview room," Lewis answered in a low voice.

"Already?" Jasper asked, astounded by the rapidity with which the Special Irish Branch detective inspector had summoned her.

"He is questioning her?" Leo released her grip on the doorjamb and started across the department toward the collection of desks assigned to Tomlin and his detectives. From there, a corridor led to a few interview rooms.

"You cannot just barge into an interview, Leo," Jasper told her, staying on her heels, but she didn't slow.

Detective Inspector Bruce Tomlin and his team of investigators were not only assigned to every case that involved Irish terrorists plaguing the city, but they also worked to infiltrate and subdue political militant groups before they could wreak havoc. Undercover detectives would go so far as to assume false identities to join gangs and run with known Fenians, all to gain insight into their operations. Sometimes, they would foil a planned attack because of the intelligence they'd gathered.

Tomlin would not handle this attack against the Yard well. Especially since a Met constable appeared to have been behind it.

Lewis kept pace with Jasper. "They're saying it was PC Lloyd. That he's with Clan na Gael."

"That isn't true." Leo threw a scolding glance over her shoulder, but it put her off balance. She shot out a hand to grip a nearby chair to steady herself.

Instinctively, Jasper reached for her to help keep her upright. But again, she shrugged him off. "I don't need your assistance," she snapped.

Lewis raised a brow. He and some other officers had noticed Leo's recent absence, though the detective sergeant hadn't commented beyond a few prodding inquiries such as *How is Miss Spencer these days?* and *Did Miss Spencer deliver that postmortem report yet?*

Jasper fielded her current rejection of him by biting his tongue and gesturing for her to continue toward the interview rooms. Tomlin wasn't going to take kindly to her interrupting him, but she was too bloody stubborn to be persuaded to leave off.

The corridor was mobbed with detectives speaking to people who appeared to have witnessed the blast. Some were bloodied, pressing handkerchiefs to their wounded heads; others looked unharmed but were wide-eyed with shock.

Leo staggered to a stop outside the first interview room. The door was shut, and a pane of frosted glass obscured the people inside for privacy.

"Leo—" Jasper began, but she twisted the knob without so much as a knock.

He groaned as she swept inside. Inspector Tomlin was standing next to Miss Brooks's chair, looming over her. Detective Sergeant LaChance was seated at the small table across from Miss Brooks, who shot to her feet. Her eyes were red-rimmed, her cheeks wet.

"They're saying it was John," Miss Brooks said as she

and Leo gravitated toward each other and then embraced. “I can’t believe it. I don’t believe it.”

“I’m so sorry,” Leo said as the matron sobbed fresh tears.

Inspector Tomlin directed his outrage toward Jasper. “Reid, get this woman out of my interview room.”

Bruce Tomlin was roughly forty years of age, with boot-black hair and an established beard cut through with gray. Standing at over six feet, he’d likely used his height to intimidate the matron into giving up anything she might know about the blast.

“Miss Spencer was injured in the explosion,” Jasper said, “and was concerned for her friend. I’m sure now that she sees Miss Brooks is well—”

She peeled away from Leo, distraught. “You’re injured?”

“Not significantly. A ruptured eardrum, which will mend,” she replied.

“Well, do hear this, Miss Spencer,” Tomlin said, his voice rising. “You will wait outside this room until I have finished questioning Matron Brooks.”

“They think John is a Fenian,” the matron said, still clinging to Leo’s arms. “But he would never have done this.”

“Dita, had you seen him at all today? Did you notice his injuries?” Leo asked.

Tomlin growled, “I am the one asking the questions here.”

“Then you should inquire if Miss Brooks knows how PC Lloyd received the black eye and gashes to his face that I noticed just before the explosion,” Leo suggested in a clipped voice.

Jasper exhaled, bracing himself for Tomlin's wrath. He was accustomed to fielding Leo's insolence, but Tomlin wasn't. Slowly, Lewis backed out of the doorway and made himself scarce. *Lucky bastard.*

"I will ask the questions *I* decide are important," the inspector replied sharply. "Wiley!"

Several moments later, the Criminal Investigation Department's desk constable shot into the small interview room, his chest puffed up and his cheeks red. When he saw Leo, his expression changed instantly to one of derision. She and Horace Wiley were at constant odds, and though Jasper generally disliked the constable, he chose to overlook him whenever possible. Leo, however, chose to needle him.

"Escort Miss Spencer out of the building," Tomlin ordered Wiley.

A smug glint of pleasure crossed Wiley's expression, and he reached for Leo's arm. Jasper intercepted, clasping the constable's forearm before he could touch her. "Don't," was all he said, though even to his own ears, the sound of his voice was as menacing as pond ice splintering underfoot.

Wiley wrenched his arm away and glared daggers at him but didn't try to take her arm again.

"Someone, escort her out of here," Tomlin demanded, a vein that cut through his forehead becoming more visible by the second.

"He was carrying a valise." Leo's comment severed the growing tension. "Constable Lloyd was about ten or fifteen paces away from me when I saw him. He appeared unsettled. Nervous. He looked to be fresh from a fist fight, and he was carrying a brown leather valise."

"A leather case housed the bomb," Sergeant LaChance confirmed. "We've found remnants of it near Lloyd's body."

Miss Brooks let out a small wail and returned to her seat, her trembling hands clasped over her mouth.

Jasper clenched his hands into fists. *Christ.* Ten or fifteen paces? Any closer, and Leo would have surely been killed.

"The valise wasn't his," she continued.

"How could you possibly know that?" Tomlin asked. "Did you speak to him?"

"No," she answered. "In fact, when he saw me, he turned and started walking away from the Yard. But I'd already seen that it was a woman's valise. The leather was heavily embroidered and embellished down the center with a floral pattern. When he stopped and turned, I believe I saw a monogram embroidered on it too. Why would he have had a lady's case when he lived alone in bachelor's rooms? And by his visible apprehension, I think it's possible he—"

"You've suffered an injury, Miss Spencer. Hit your head in the blast, it looks like," Tomlin interrupted. "Go home. If I need more of a statement from you, you will be summoned. This isn't a request." He glared at Jasper with an unspoken order to remove her at once.

Jasper held the inspector's glare, but he had no standing to object. This would be Tomlin's case, not his. That rationale didn't stop him from feeling stymied, however, as he stood aside and gestured for Leo to leave the room. She did, albeit unhappily.

"That man is a bully," she seethed, once the door had slammed shut behind them.

"That may be, but as this is a bombing, he'll be leading the investigation into it."

"Do you think Constable Lloyd's remains will be brought to Spring Street?" she asked as they wove back through the busy department.

As it was the closest morgue, Jasper suspected the remains would indeed be delivered there. No autopsy would be ordered, as cause of death was more than evident. But there could be more to learn from the man's remains.

"Perhaps you shouldn't assist Claude with this one," Jasper said. Leo wasn't affected by dead bodies, but John Lloyd had been an acquaintance. Not to mention, she'd seen him die.

"I'll decide that for myself, thank you." She picked up her speed, walking toward the department's exit.

He overtook her to block her path. "I know what you are thinking, but this is not an investigation you can force your way into."

"He was Dita's beau. They were about to become engaged to marry. He wouldn't have done this willingly," she said, ignoring him as she was wont to do.

"Then let Inspector Tomlin and his men find out what really happened. You need to stay out of it this time."

It was a mistake; he knew it the second the order flew off his tongue. Leo drew her shoulders back, her eyes glazing over with impenetrable hardness.

"You don't get to tell me what to do anymore, Inspector Reid."

She pushed past him and strode away.

He sighed, letting her go. "I never got to tell you what to do to begin with," he muttered.

Behind him, Lewis let out a low whistle from his desk, where he'd retreated earlier. "I don't know what you did, guv, but I wouldn't hold my breath for mercy."

Jasper raked his fingers through his hair and, without responding to the detective sergeant, returned to his office.

Chapter Three

Leo never would have admitted it to a soul, but halfway through Claude's examination of Constable Lloyd's remains, she considered that Jasper might have been correct: She should have sat this one out.

A rash of heat lit her skin, and a swell of nausea gripped her. Leo clutched the clipboard and pencil tighter in her sweaty hands while recording her uncle's observations as he made them aloud. Her head swam, the words blurring on the paper as she wrote them. The acrid odor of gunpowder clung to the mangled body, and it filled the back of her mouth with every breath.

"I'm sorry, Uncle Claude. What was it you just said?" Leo asked, her hearing still muffled from the blast. It would take weeks for her ruptured eardrum to heal. She could only hope the incessant ringing would be gone much sooner than that.

"Complete separation of the aortic valve." Her uncle lowered his spectacles, the thick glass heavily magnified, and peered at Leo. "My dear, you are most assuredly concussed. I insist you go home to rest."

He meant well, but retreating to their terrace house on Duke Street would do little to settle her. Leo didn't like to be there without her uncle, and that was entirely due to her aunt, Flora Feldman. It was cowardly of her to avoid her elderly aunt, but lately, Flora's outbursts had been more random and hostile—at least, toward Leo. No one else seemed to inspire her eruptions of temper and nonsensical accusations. Thankfully, her aunt had taken well to her newest nurse, Mrs. Boardman, and with Claude, she was as complacent as a cat curled up by a fire. Had Jasper been in her presence over the last two months, Flora would have doted on him too, as she always had. But not Leo. For some illogical reason, Flora blamed her for the Spencer family murders, even though she'd been just a child at the time.

A strange comment Flora had made in March about letters she'd received from her sister, Andromeda—Leo's mother—and some sort of *bloody, bloody business* had intrigued Leo. But Claude hadn't known anything about the letters, and a search of the house hadn't turned them up either.

"My head feels fine. I'd much rather keep busy," Leo told her uncle, swiping at her brow before writing down the postmortem finding.

As the aorta was the main vessel for distributing oxygen-rich blood to the body, a complete separation of the valve from the heart would mean Constable Lloyd died almost instantly. The excessive damage to the rest of his torso and limbs from the explosion would have been excruciatingly painful had he lived, even for a short while.

There was some comfort in knowing he hadn't suffered long, if at all.

However, why he'd been carrying a bomb toward Scotland Yard continued to dumbfound her. Leo hadn't known him well, but she'd never have believed he was mixed up with the militant Irish in London. In fact, she *didn't* believe it.

Jasper had told her to keep out of Inspector Tomlin's way, and she knew she couldn't interfere directly with the investigation. But that didn't stop her mind from combing over the handful of seconds between when she'd first spotted John Lloyd and when the bomb detonated.

"Hmm. This is peculiar," Claude said, having returned to his examination of the body.

Leo looked up from her notes to see her uncle holding the constable's left wrist. The right hand—along with much of his forearm—had been severed completely in the blast. Those remains hadn't been salvageable.

"What have you found?"

"Ligature marks. See here?" Claude pointed to a thin line of bruising on top of the constable's wrist. Though gunpowder residue coated him, a closer look showed reddened skin, still partially visible. She ran the tip of her finger over the chafed red line, which was a few millimeters wide.

Claude peered at the underside of the wrist, but there weren't any ligature marks there.

"His wrists were bound together, the undersides pressed together," Leo said.

Had the right wrist not been blown to pieces, she suspected it would have shown a matching red line.

"It looks to be that way," her uncle agreed. "And as the

bruising is still red, I estimate the marks were inflicted less than twenty-four hours before death."

Leo quickly scribbled the finding down, her nausea beginning to clear. Claude had already noted the contusions near Constable Lloyd's left eye, and the gash on his cheek below the bruise. While much of his lower jaw had been decimated, the upper half of his cheek remained intact. Still, it would certainly be a closed-casket funeral.

"You've also determined he was struck in the face less than twenty-four hours ago," she said.

Black eyes weren't uncommon among police officers. Plenty of them got into scrapes while performing their duties, especially with men they were attempting to arrest. But the ligature marks on his wrist couldn't be misconstrued: John Lloyd had been bound and beaten just hours before he'd approached Scotland Yard with a bomb.

The man she'd seen standing outside the arch, who had scowled fiercely when John turned around and started away from the building, sprang to Leo's mind.

"It's not conclusive that the victim received this ligature mark at the same time as he did the injuries to his face," her uncle said firmly, as if knowing the determination she'd reached.

"But surely, the likelihood is high."

If he had been held against his will and abused, then there was a story of violence behind John's actions. One that might explain why he'd done what he had. It might account for his distraction and expression of fear when Leo had seen him. She also wondered if that scowling man had anything to do with the bomb being brought to Scotland Yard.

"The report must only include known medical facts and evidence."

Claude needn't have reminded her. She'd been transcribing her uncle's examinations and typing his post-mortem reports for nearly five years. Conjecture was not tolerated, nor should it be.

With every death inquest, Mr. Pritchard, the deputy coroner, presented Claude's postmortem findings at the coroner's court. The jurors who were present at these inquests were given the medical findings, and it was paramount they reach a verdict based on facts, not speculation.

"The facts," Leo began, "are that the victim sustained bruising consistent with a fistfight or beating and a ligature mark on his left wrist consistent with being bound by a thin rope, less than twenty-four hours before his death."

Claude assented with a nod. "That is correct."

And that would be what she wrote in the report. But her own mind was hers to fill with as much speculation as she wished.

She tapped the tip of her pencil to the paper, thinking. Claude had cut the clothing from the body first thing, and Leo had gone through the pockets, noting the contents in the morgue's possessions register. Besides his policeman's warrant card, there was nothing but a single coin in John Lloyd's pockets. It was unlike any coin Leo had seen before. The circle of brass had been stamped with the image of a fox and a crane standing together. It was a token of some sort, though she didn't know for what. Asking Dita would have been the most direct way to find an answer. But as she was grieving, Leo didn't wish to bother her friend.

Just then, Tibia, the morgue cat, leaped agilely onto a vacant autopsy table next to the constable's corpse and began to purr, seeking attention. Or more likely, her lunch. The gray tabby lived in the morgue, and though she was welcome to wander the postmortem room, she preferred bedding down under the desk in the back office, where Leo kept a small coal brazier stoked to warm her feet in the colder months.

The cat's paw instantly found the odd token on the table and batted at it, sending the round of brass to the floor.

"Tibby, no," Leo said, leaning down to retrieve it. Her ruptured eardrum throbbed as she bent, sending a flash of pain through her head. And then, the pealing of a bell joined the ringing in her ears. Someone had arrived through the morgue's front door and entered the lobby.

Wincing, she put the token into her pocket. "I'll go see—"

Raised voices cut her off. There was a sign on the postmortem room door, asking visitors to please wait to be welcomed. However, the agitated tones of a man's deep tenor and the pleading one of a woman were worrisome. There were some who, in their grief and panic, would ignore the sign and barge straight in—only to be traumatized by what they found. Currently, there were three corpses on tables whose examinations Claude had put on hold to address the police constable's postmortem.

She set her clipboard down and started for the lobby. But her concern had been warranted as a young man pushed his way into the postmortem room, his eyes red and wild.

"Sir, please wait outside," Leo said as Claude hurried to lift a sheet over the constable's remains.

The man paid Leo no attention and stalked forward, ripping his hat from his head. "Is that him? Is it our Johnny?"

Oh no. Constable Lloyd's family had arrived.

"Family must wait in the lobby," Leo tried again as a woman entered the room on the man's heels. Her face crumpled, even though Claude had successfully covered John's ruined body.

"Where is he?" she asked, voice trembling, her hands clasping her handbag to her chest in trepidation. "They're saying he had a bomb, that he set it off!"

The man arrived at the table, his eyes riveted to the sheeted body.

"Sir, please, this isn't something loved ones should see," Claude said, but the man, who was most likely a brother of John's, was oblivious to their warnings. He tore back the top portion of the sheet. Leo had already seen the remains, of course, but now she seemed to look upon them with fresh eyes. It was truly horrific what the blast had done to his body. The woman's scream and the grief-stricken moan that came from the man made the moment even more wretched.

Claude drew the sheet back up as the man staggered away, and Leo attended to the woman, whose legs were going soft. She placed an arm around her shoulders and led her back into the lobby, depositing her into the nearest chair. Appearing to be about fifty years of age, Leo presumed she was John's mother. The man came into the lobby next, guided by Claude. The coroner exchanged a quick glance with his niece before retreating and closing the door to the postmortem room behind him.

"Can I fetch you some tea, Mrs. Lloyd?" Leo asked, sitting in the chair next to her. "You are Constable Lloyd's mother, correct?"

She sniffled, her eyes closed and a stream of tears flowing past her lashes. "I am," she gasped. Then, she shook her head. "No tea, thank you."

"I knew he would get into trouble," the man said as he began to pace the small lobby. The grieving tended to do one of these two things: either sit still in bereft shock or explode with restless energy and fury.

Leo focused on the man. He wasn't much older than John, and they shared similar physical features. "You are his brother?"

"He should've come with me to my shop instead of joining the bloody, no-good police," he said as though he hadn't heard her question.

"What is your work, Mr. Lloyd?" Leo asked. At this seemingly offhand question, the man slowed his pacing. He blinked as he looked at her, acknowledging her for the first time.

"I'm a carpenter," he answered. "Like our father, but Johnny, he wanted to be a bobby. Always wanted to be a bobby."

John had said something like this to Leo once. However, it was apparent his brother hadn't supported his decision to join the police force.

"Mr. Lloyd, you said you knew your brother would get into trouble." Leo's heart began to sink. "Do you mean to say that you suspected this would happen?"

He slammed to a halt across the room and stared at her, aghast. "You mean with a bomb? No, never. Johnny couldn't have had anything to do with that."

She kept quiet. John had been carrying the bomb, so he must have had *something* to do with it.

"What kind of trouble did you mean then?"

It wasn't customary to ask the family members any questions about the deceased other than what arrangements they would like to make for the body. But she conceded that this wasn't a customary situation.

"I meant about the gambling," the constable's brother replied readily enough.

"Charlie, don't speak ill of your brother when he can't defend himself," Mrs. Lloyd pleaded, pressing a hankie to her wet cheeks.

Leo recalled the brass token, now in her apron pocket. It might be a gambling marker of some kind.

"You know it's true, Mum," Charlie replied. "Either that, or he was on the take."

"Stop!" Mrs. Lloyd burst into more tears.

"How else do you explain the posh boots, the better threads he kept buying, and the hats. Christ a'mighty, he had a closet full of them," Charlie went on.

The times Leo, Dita, and John had gone to Striker's Wharf together, she hadn't noted the extravagance of his clothing. Perhaps that was simply because she was accustomed to seeing him in police blues.

"How long had your brother been bettering himself?" she asked.

Charlie snorted. "Bettering himself. Ha! He was hanging about with the wrong sort, telling me to stop my worrying and mind my own business. I told him, I said he would trip up, be sorry…" He closed his fist and pounded it against his forehead twice, as if to stop his mind from going back over what had been said between them. "And now look what's happened."

Leo tried but failed to make the correlation between a vice of gambling and the decision to carry a bomb in a valise. However, the token in his pocket could very well indicate that John had been at some gambling casino shortly before his arrival at the Yard. Had that been where he'd received the bruising on his face?

"Have you spoken with anyone from Scotland Yard yet?" Leo asked. It seemed strange that Inspector Tomlin would not have rounded up the constable's family for questioning as immediately as he had Dita.

Mrs. Lloyd shook her head. "I was at home when Charlie came to tell me what had happened. We went straight to Scotland Yard, but a constable outside told us the body had already been brought here."

"And how did you learn of the explosion, Mr. Lloyd?" Leo asked.

He'd quit pacing, his restlessness transforming to melancholy in the blink of an eye. "A friend came to my shop. Drives a hansom, keeps it near Whitehall. Said he saw the whole thing, Johnny walking toward the Yard, the bomb exploding, and…"

Charlie's explanation fell off as rapidly as his temper had. If he was angry with his brother, Leo suspected it had more to do with misplaced feelings of loss than with anything else. Anger so often preceded despair, and John's brother seemed to be closing in on the latter.

The bell chimed on the front door as a pair of uniformed police constables entered the morgue lobby.

Leo stood to greet Constables Warnock and Drake, who doffed their helmets. "We heard you were sent here," Drake said, speaking to Mrs. Lloyd and her son. "We're to bring you to the Yard. The lead inspector has some questions to put to you."

Charlie's ire flared to life again. "I got nothing to say except my brother is innocent. He wouldn't have done this. He loved his job, respected his mates!"

Mrs. Lloyd, perhaps sensing that the two constables weren't going to leave without escorting them to Scotland Yard, got to her feet. "Miss," she said, addressing Leo. "I'll have my boy collected as soon as I can manage it."

Her chin wobbled, and then she put her head down and left. Drake went with her, while Warnock waited for Charlie to come along. He did, although with reluctance.

Leo exhaled, tension dissolving from her back and shoulders as she returned to the postmortem room. Claude handed her the clipboard with her notes. "As soon as you're finished typing, my dear, you're to go home."

At twenty-five, Leo didn't enjoy being told what to do, even if her uncle was only trying to show his care and worry. But she agreed and started for the office and her typewriter. After speaking with John's family, however, home would not be her first destination.

Chapter Four

It wasn't the right night to attend the theatre. Jasper had known it before collecting Miss Constance Hayes from her boardinghouse, and when she appeared on her doorstep, dressed in a glittering dark maroon gown, he wished he'd sent her a note earlier, bowing out.

He wasn't in the mood for lively entertainment. The Rising Sun, the pub across the street from the Yard, would be full of fellow officers tonight. He should be there, commiserating and drinking with them until he blacked out. The bombing and Constable Lloyd's death had cast a pall over the central offices for the rest of the day, as they would for many days to come. Not only had one of their own been killed, but by all appearances, he'd intended to do harm to other officers as well.

Confusion swirled all afternoon at the Yard about Lloyd's hidden connections to Clan na Gael and the Irish Republican Brotherhood. They'd all been on edge, waiting for more reports of bombs exploding throughout the city, as the letter had warned months ago when it arrived. But no additional blasts had occurred.

Arriving at the Adelphi, Jasper strove to push the chaos of the day to the back of his mind and focus on the young woman he'd been courting for nearly six months. It wasn't easy, especially when they settled into their seats, and Constance had yet to inquire about the bombing. Employed at *The Times* as a typist for the society pages, she would have almost certainly been privy to the news. Or perhaps she hadn't been paying any attention beyond the gossip columns.

Her seeming lack of acknowledgement, however, grated on him, and he'd grown more discomfited as the first act, then the second played out on stage. At last, after the final curtain, they hired a cab to return Constance to her lodgings. Once they'd settled into the enclosed bench seat, the driver perched high behind them, Jasper at last broached the subject.

"Did you hear about the bombing at Scotland Yard today?" He tried to keep his tone conversational.

She twisted in the seat next to him as the small cab bore them away from the busy street outside the theatre. She was strikingly pretty, with blonde hair, large and expressive blue eyes, and a figure that turned men's heads. As the daughter of a viscount's younger brother, she wasn't titled, but she was still an aristocrat. She was also Oliver Hayes's cousin, which was how Jasper had been introduced to her back in the autumn. Oliver, the Viscount Hayes, and Jasper and Constance often went out on the town together. It was easy to sit back and let the two of them do all the talking—all the laughing and socializing too.

Constance's lips popped open, but instead of noticing the rosy fullness of them, he noted how she suddenly appeared remorseful.

"Oh, yes, I had heard. A man was killed, wasn't he?"

It wasn't the answer he'd wanted. An aloof claim to this being the first she'd heard of it wouldn't have fallen through him as hollowly. She'd known about the attack, that a fellow officer had died, and yet she hadn't thought to ask him about any of it.

"A police constable, yes," he replied solemnly.

Constance slipped her arm through his. "Is it true that he was trying to bring the bomb into your building?"

"Allegedly."

The remnants of the suitcase Lloyd had been carrying, which Leo had been certain belonged to a woman, had been inspected by Her Majesty's Inspector of Explosives, Colonel Derring Majendie. Highly esteemed as the country's best bomb analyst, he'd been called to the Yard to investigate the remains of the leather case. Jasper had gotten it from Lewis, who'd heard from Detective Sergeant LaChance, that the case did appear to belong to a woman. Some of the pink and white striped silk interior cloth remained on the strips of leather after the blast, and when pieced together, it was embellished with floral embroidery, along with a partial monogram: GL.

"Well then, I'm not sorry he's dead," Constance said. "If he intended to kill other officers, he deserves what happened to him."

Jasper stiffened at the unfeeling, pejorative comment. It wasn't the first of its kind that she'd made to him. The more he'd come to know her, the more she'd begun to express them. While she was usually merry and brisk with a laugh or observation, there were times when she appeared to lack deeper feeling or concern. He'd been brushing off these moments for a few months now, explaining them away as a product of her privileged and sheltered upbringing. But they were becoming more and more difficult to dismiss.

She laid her head against his shoulder. "I'm glad you weren't injured."

While he appreciated the belated remark, no inquiry was made about other possible victims or injuries. Leo came to mind.

All day, he'd bristled with stifled fury when he thought of how close she had been to Lloyd when the bomb detonated. Had Jasper not detained her in the lobby and kept her from leaving for another minute, she might have been right next to the constable at the time of the blast. She might have been killed.

Jasper had wanted to stop by the morgue on his way home to be sure she was recovering well. But after some vacillating, he decided to stay away. She had made it clear she didn't want to see him or accept his help.

Leo had always claimed to have no recollection of the awful night when her family had been slain. She'd certainly never revealed that she'd received help during the ordeal. But Jasper always suspected that it was a lie. She had a perfect memory, and yet the night of February 16, 1867, as well as much of her life before then, was a blur to her. Jasper had been left to wonder what would happen if she ever did work out that it had been *him* in the attic. That he was related to her family's killers. He'd assumed it would be total excommunication, and he'd been correct. A part of him had also questioned if she would be angry enough to reveal who he truly was to other people—Scotland Yard, specifically. But so far, she hadn't.

Constance's hand settled upon his, lifting him from his thoughts. She wove her fingers through his. Softly, she said, "Why don't you tell the cabbie to take us to Charles Street instead of my boardinghouse?"

Jasper went rigid in his seat. When the urge to remove her hand from his struck, he knew the problems he'd been acknowledging lately, then dismissing, could no longer be ignored.

"I don't think that would be a good idea," he replied.

This last month, she'd become more forward in her affections, and with some guilt, he'd willingly received them. More ardent kisses, a few salacious explorations with her hands. Nothing so bold that she would be ruined or debased, but these moments certainly all pointed toward an official betrothal in the near future. In two weeks, her parents and younger brother were due to arrive in London, and though she hadn't expressly said it, Constance expected Jasper to ask her father for her hand in marriage.

The man Jasper thought of as his father, Gregory Reid, had married well above his station too. The Honorable Emmaline Cowper, the daughter of a viscount, had gone against her family's wishes and married a police inspector.

Given his own career at Scotland Yard and his courtship with a lady of status, Jasper seemed to be walking in his father's footsteps. But there was a significant difference between them, one that Jasper could no longer deny. Gregory Reid had been desperately in love with Emmaline. Jasper simply did not feel the same way for Constance.

"You know I am a thoroughly modern woman," she said with a small laugh. "So modern, in fact, that I plan to tell my parents all about my job at the paper. I no longer care what they will do. I am a woman who makes her own decisions."

And her decision that they should go to his home on Charles Street wasn't something that could be misconstrued. As much as he'd enjoy a tumble in bed—it had been a hell of a long time since he'd been with a woman—he couldn't do it. After that, he'd have no choice but to propose. He'd have to marry her.

Hell.

"I've been needing to speak to you about something, Constance," he said, haltingly. "I should have long before now."

He'd been selfish to allow their relationship to go on. Part of him had hoped that with time, the certainty that she was right for him would come. It hadn't. And he could no longer pretend that it would.

Constance peeled herself from his side with evident apprehension. After weeks and weeks of suppressing his doubts and avoiding a decision, it arrived in an unfettered rush.

"I'm sorry. The last thing I want to do is hurt you," he began, "but this needs to end."

She held still a moment, staring at him in disbelief. Then, in horror. She shot backward along the seat, away from him entirely. "You…you no longer wish to court me?"

Christ. He was a sodding bastard.

"I care for you, Constance, and I thought our courtship was what I wanted, but…"

"How long have you known you would not propose?"

No longer stunned, she now appeared furious. As she had every right to be. And when he swallowed the honest answer to her question—*for some time now*—Jasper knew he was low and vile, and everything he despised in certain types of men. A type he'd never considered himself to be. Shame consumed him.

He didn't reply, but no doubt Constance heard the answer in his silence. She sat tall, her body rigid, as she faced forward through the cab's open front.

"What we have isn't enough on which to base a marriage," he said. He owed her some semblance of an explanation, at least.

She pursed her lips, still staring ahead. "Is it because of *her*?"

The carriage wheels lurched and fell, jostling them. Without needing to think, Jasper knew to whom Constance referred. Nonetheless, he bit his tongue, refusing to acknowledge it.

Constance twisted suddenly to spear him with a hateful glare. "Is it because of your precious *Leo*?" She spat the name with unabashed animosity. She'd never uttered Leonora's nickname before, and without so many words, she made it clear that she disapproved of Jasper's use of it. And that she suspected he felt more for Leo than he claimed.

"Tell me you aren't throwing me over for a bizarre woman who works in a deadhouse!"

He was indisputably at fault for disappointing Constance, for possibly even breaking her heart—though he couldn't quite convince himself she felt as deeply as that for him. But her outburst kindled his temper.

"She has nothing to do with my decision to end things."

"Spare me your lies. I'm not a fool," she snapped. "Although perhaps I have been. I wanted to believe you only felt obliged to tolerate her because of your father."

She scoffed as the hansom pulled alongside the pavement outside her boardinghouse. She gathered her wrap closer around her shoulders. "Oliver warned me."

Jasper peered at her, dismayed. "Warned you about what?"

"That you would never be free of her. That you didn't truly wish to be."

The driver stepped down to open the cab door. *Free of Leo?* As if she had some hold on him, or he was under some spell of hers.

"Leave Leonora out of this," he rasped.

The door opened, and Constance poised herself to leap down. Glancing over her shoulder at him, she hissed, "I'm only grateful I won't ever have to hear about her again."

She continued to her boardinghouse door without a second backward glance. Jasper scrubbed his jaw and, aware the cabbie was waiting for a new destination, directed, "Scotland Yard."

He'd go where he ought to have gone in the first place.

The Rising Sun would still be busy, and there would be some coppers there he could have a pint with. He could make a start at forgetting the last few hours and easing the knot in his gut. It hadn't formed because he'd just ended things with Constance. It was her comments about Leo that bothered him. She'd made it sound as though he rattled off at the mouth all the time about her. It wasn't so. In fact, over the past two months, he hadn't spoken her name at all. He'd thought of her though. Perhaps too much.

Jasper yearned to just *talk* to Leo. He'd happily endure an interrogation from her about his deception for the chance to explain himself. She hadn't asked him a single question about his past, and knowing her mind, she must have dozens of them. Jasper wanted to have it out with her, and afterward, if she still despised him, then so be it.

The cabbie dropped him off outside Number 4 Whitehall Place, between the front façade of Scotland Yard headquarters and the Rising Sun public house. As he'd hoped, the tavern was a lively spot, with gasoliers inside spilling their warm, yellow light through the windows lining the street. Inside, he wasn't surprised not to see Lewis, who would be at home with his wife and their two young sons by now. But he spotted PC Warnock and DS LaChance seated at a table near a window. Unlike Tomlin, LaChance did not imagine a rivalry between the larger CID and the Special Irish Branch and would often socialize with constables from the other departments. Warnock and LaChance hailed Jasper to join them.

He hadn't taken four strides in their direction when a rumbling shook the floorboards. Then, an explosion and a bright ball of flame lit the darkened street outside. Glass blew inward as the windows of the tavern shattered.

Jasper hit the floor, arms up over his head to shield himself from the gust of the blast and the cutting shards.

An uproar of voices immediately followed the blast, and Jasper got to his feet and joined the surge of men as they hurried into the street. Flames burned in a field of debris scattered before them, and one corner of the wall at Scotland Yard headquarters lay in a pile of rubble.

Another bomb had detonated.

Chapter Five

Two more bombs, both planted at St. James's Square, exploded roughly around the same time as the one at Scotland Yard. The blasts came one after the other, the first at a gentleman's club and the next just outside the home of a Tory member of Parliament. By some miracle, no one was dead, though numerous injuries had been reported, and a horse that had been attached to an unmanned carriage had been killed.

It was near to midnight by the time Jasper was able to return home. The shallow cuts along his cheeks and forehead from the shattering windows at the Rising Sun had started to throb. The wounds were minor compared to the deeper slices Warnock and LaChance—and anyone else seated nearer to the windows—had received. He'd barely felt them at all as gawkers and news reporters surged into Whitehall Place. The fire brigade arrived within minutes to douse the scattered flaming debris, which included desks, chairs, and filing cabinets and their contents from the offices of the CID and Special Irish

Branch. The two departments had received the brunt of the damage, and it seemed to have been intentionally so. The timer-set device that had detonated the dynamite was found in the cellar of Scotland Yard, directly underneath the Special Irish Branch section.

How it had been placed there, and when, had yet to be determined.

As it was so late, Jasper expected Mrs. Zhao to be abed when he let himself in through the front door at 23 Charles Street. He shed his coat and hat, envisioning the heavy pour of whisky he'd toss back before tending to his cuts.

"Mister Jasper?" Mrs. Zhao appeared at the back of the entrance hall, near the corridor to the kitchen. The sixty-something Chinese woman had worked for his father for nearly thirty years, and though her official role here was housekeeper, she was more of a grandmother or kindly aunt to Jasper. She came toward him quickly.

"You were hurt in the bombs." Her eyes, framed by fine lines, widened with concern. "We heard them from here when they went off at the square. We went and saw men stumbling around with bloodied faces, but you weren't there."

He held up a palm to calm her. "I was at Scotland Yard. There was an explosion there as well."

Two bombs in one day at Scotland Yard seemed an odd choice for Clan na Gael. Especially since three had detonated around the same time that night, while the fourth, the one that killed Constable Lloyd, had occurred earlier in the afternoon. It was possible that the bomb Lloyd had carried accidentally went off before he could plant it, fouling the plan and requiring another bomb to be brought in. But how had it been done? Security around headquarters had been impermeable after the explosion that afternoon. No one would have made it inside with a suspicious package. And then there was the discrepancy between the construction of Lloyd's bomb and the twisted remains of the one found in the cellar of the Yard: Lloyd's had been made using gunpowder, whereas the clockwork-timed device in the cellar seemed to have been rigged with dynamite.

Jasper rubbed his forehead, then winced when a small cut reopened.

Belatedly, he considered what Mrs. Zhao had said to him. "You said *we* heard the explosions?"

Motion at the top of the stairs drew his eyes. Leo stood there, her hand gripping the newel post. "There was another bombing at headquarters?" she asked.

The stutter of his heart and the instantaneous burst of pleasure that followed anchored his boots to the faded burgundy carpet. The physical reaction brought forward Constance's voice, accusing him of ending things because of his "precious Leo."

Shit.

"Miss Leo arrived earlier," Mrs. Zhao explained as Jasper forced his heart rate to even out. "I didn't think you would mind her waiting in the study."

He came to his senses and started up the stairs. "Of course not."

Leo stood aside at the landing, inspecting him as he ascended. She noted the blood on his face but said nothing. He looked her over too. The blood from her left ear had been cleaned away, her hair re-pinned. But she still wore the same dress as earlier, and she carried with her the barest odor of gunpowder.

He started toward the study, and she followed.

"How bad was it?" she asked.

"There's a new door to my office," he quipped, thinking of the hole, roughly twenty feet in diameter, that had been blown into the corner of the building.

She didn't laugh. "Was it another suitcase bomb?"

He shook his head. "This one was a clockwork-timed bomb, constructed with dynamite. The damage to the Yard was much more severe this evening."

"Were people harmed?"

"Luckily, the front offices were already closed for the day, and the men in the other departments were far enough away from the blast to go unharmed."

"Then how did you get those cuts?" she asked.

"I was at the Rising Sun, near the windows, when the blast occurred."

"Mrs. Zhao told me you'd gone to the theatre this evening," Leo said as she entered the study on his heels.

There was evidence that she'd already made herself at home—a fire burning in the coal brazier, the wide, leather swivel chair behind the Inspector's desk pushed aside, unsolved case files spread out on the blotter, and a crystal cordial glass with a sip of cherry liqueur left at the bottom. Seeing it all loosened a kink in his stomach that he'd grown accustomed to in her absence.

Hell, he didn't want to have missed her as much as he had.

Jasper walked toward the decanters and the whisky he'd been dreaming of for the last few hours. "I was at the theatre earlier. Then, I went to the public house," he explained. He didn't mention Constance.

"I've only come because I need to tell you about what happened during the postmortem examination for Constable Lloyd." Leo kept her tone direct and businesslike. Jasper swallowed the smoky spirits and grimaced.

"It isn't my case," he reminded her.

"As I am very well aware," she said. "However, there is something more that happened at the morgue, which I couldn't include in the postmortem report, and Inspector Tomlin will most certainly never listen to me should I try to tell him."

Jasper fought the sparks of intrigue that she'd successfully stoked. "What makes you think he'll listen to me?"

"You're a fellow detective; he must listen to you."

He chuckled, then took another sip of whisky. Tomlin was a pompous prig who not only believed the main CID was inferior to the Special Irish Branch but that it was poorly managed. After today's fiasco with Leo barging into his interview with Miss Brooks, he would likely dismiss Jasper just as quickly as he would have her.

When he didn't reply, Leo let out an exasperated sigh and hurried back to the desk.

"I knew I shouldn't have come," she huffed as she pulled the folders she'd brought out from the Inspector's drawer into a messy pile. She stuffed them away again and slammed the drawer shut.

The unsolved cases stored there were ones that had haunted Gregory Reid. Whenever he started to feel particularly melancholy, he would take them out and read through them again, hoping for some new stroke of inspiration. No case had been more important to him than the Spencer family murders. That thick folder, however, was no longer in the desk. As one of his father's final requests, Leo had taken it with her to review when she felt ready.

"Leo," he said softly, but she tossed back the rest of the cherry cordial she and his father had loved, then set the glass down on the desk.

"Don't concern yourself, Inspector. I thought you might help by passing this information along to Inspector Tomlin, but that's a mistake I won't make again." She started for the door.

"Stop. Leo, please." He moved to intercept her, but she was too far away. She would reach the door first. "All right, if it is that important, tell me what happened with Lloyd's postmortem."

If it would get her to stay, then he would concede. She stilled, though she appeared disgruntled when she turned and crossed her arms over her middle. "If I didn't think it was important, I wouldn't have come. There is no other reason I am here."

He sighed, thinking that she had looked at least a little concerned for him when she'd stood at the top of the stairs, inspecting him for injuries. But now, he kept his mouth shut and gestured with a wave of his hand for her to get on with it.

She did.

"When Constable Lloyd's family arrived at the morgue, his brother commented that he'd suspected his brother would get himself into trouble. He said John was mixed up with the wrong sort."

"The wrong sort being Clan na Gael?" Jasper shook his head. "Lloyd wasn't Irish."

She let her arms fall back to her sides, and her combative edge softened. "No. I don't think he was involved with them directly. His brother said that John had recently begun buying new clothing, posh hats, and boots. Things he couldn't have purchased on a police constable's wages."

A man couldn't purchase much more than necessities on a constable's wages, Jasper knew. He had lived sparely for some time, too, until he'd been promoted to detective inspector and received a raise in his income. It still wouldn't be enough to keep a house located on as affluent a street as this, nor a housekeeper. But now wasn't the time to worry about those things.

"He thought Lloyd was on the take?" Jasper guessed.

"He did. But I also found this." As she came toward him, Leo reached into her skirt pocket. She opened her palm, revealing what appeared, at first glance, to be a coin. "It was the only item in his pockets. Other than his warrant card."

It was mandatory for every officer to have their warrant card, enclosed in a black leather case, on hand, even when off duty. Jasper took the coin from her palm. But it wasn't money. "It's a gaming marker."

"I thought it might be," Leo said. "If Constable Lloyd's vice was gambling, perhaps that is where he became involved with the wrong sort, as his brother put it."

Jasper held up the marker. "This is evidence. Why was it in your pocket?"

She lifted a shoulder. "I wanted you to have a look and

confirm what it was. You can give it to Inspector Tomlin when you speak to him."

He was already dreading that conversation. "All right. So he gambled," Jasper said, dropping the brass marker into his trouser pocket. "That doesn't account for why he'd be carrying a bomb toward headquarters."

"Claude found ligature marks on his remaining wrist," Leo said.

Jasper exhaled, understanding the unspoken detail: The constable's other arm had been blown to atoms. It turned his stomach.

"Paired with his bruised eye, and the gash on his cheek and upper lip, it's accurate to say he'd been beaten and bound within twenty-four hours of his death."

Jasper finished his whisky. "You think he was coerced into bringing the bomb to the Yard."

She pushed down her shoulders and nodded. "I do. And I might have seen someone who was part of the plot. A man in a brown wool cap was standing just outside the arch. When Constable Lloyd saw me, he turned around as if to leave the courtyard. This other man wasn't happy. He shook his head as if in warning."

Jasper clenched his fists. "Did this man see you?"

"I don't think so. That's not the point. I'm saying there might be other people behind Constable Lloyd's actions."

He trusted that she'd indeed seen someone there besides Lloyd. In the recent past, during a few other investigations in which she'd been involved, she'd proved herself to be remarkably perceptive. Her deductive reasoning was sound, and if Jasper were being honest with himself, she would have made a damn good detective had she been born a man. Some women were employed in civilian positions at the Met, like Miss Brooks, and in smaller constabularies, the wives of station chiefs would sometimes assist their husbands. Right now, however, the criticisms and excuses for why women were not employed in any official capacity by the Metropolitan Police as officers weren't the only reasons why Leo could not be involved with this case.

"Your closest friend has lost the man she loves, and he is being accused of something truly horrific and dishonorable. You have an agenda. You want to prove his innocence," Jasper said.

"That isn't what I'm doing," she insisted. "You didn't see John's face. The man was terrified. It wasn't the face of someone with deadly intent."

He stopped himself from asking just how often she'd seen the faces of men with deadly intent. As he well knew, she had, and on more than one occasion.

"The fact remains that Constable Lloyd *was* carrying a bomb toward Scotland Yard."

"But don't you want to understand why?" she asked, her bad mood seeming to intensify.

He returned to the decanter of whisky and poured himself another. "Of course, I do, but for the last time, Leo, it is not my place to interfere with Tomlin's investigation. He'll read the postmortem report, and he can deduce for himself if the bruising and ligature marks are related to the incident or if they are not."

Silence ensued, hinting at her displeasure from being thwarted. Turning around, he saw that she did look disappointed. In *him*.

She cast her eyes away from his. "I'll go then." The fire

had been snuffed from her tone. Instead of storming toward the door, she merely walked.

"Can't you stay?" he heard himself asking. It was what he wanted, though he hadn't known he was going to voice it.

Leo stood stock-still by the door without looking at him. "We'll only shout at each other," she murmured.

"Good."

She spun to look at him, flummoxed.

"I want you to shout at me," he explained, walking slowly toward her. "Scream at me. Hell, if you want to hit me, I'll stand here and let you. I just need you to talk to me, Leo."

She peered at him with skepticism, as if he'd lost his mind. "I don't have anything to say."

"Bollocks. You have plenty to say. You must have a thousand questions scuttling about in that brain of yours."

Her eyes, a striking fusion of pale brown and gold, flared. "Even if I were to ask you questions, how can I trust you'll answer with the truth? You've done nothing but lie to me for sixteen years."

"Trust me or don't, Leo, but I have nothing else to hide from you. Now, stop running away and face me, dammit!"

The tenuous hold on his temper had slipped, and when she stared at him with seething resentment, he expected her to turn and leave. *Again*. Her chest rose and fell with angry breaths. But she held still.

"Did he know?" she asked, her voice barely audible. "Did the Inspector know?"

Jasper exhaled. "He knew who I was, yes. A few weeks after I met the Inspector, my aunt came to the Yard, searching for me." He gazed into his whisky glass, remembering his father's confession shortly before he'd died. "She had a photograph of me."

Gregory Reid, knowing the Carters for who and what they were, had not wanted to send Jasper back to them. Considering the way he'd arrived at the Yard, battered and bruised, the Inspector had correctly assumed the beating had been inflicted by Robert Carter, his so-called uncle. They were, in fact, second cousins, but he'd insisted Jasper address them as Uncle Robert and Aunt Myra. It hadn't mattered. No label could have erased his hatred for Robert or the subsequent repulsion he felt for Myra.

The Inspector had shown Myra the body of a drowned young boy about Jasper's size and age, though bloated beyond recognition. He'd deceived her by placing Jasper's old clothing and the rosary Myra knew to be his with the corpse. However, Jasper told Leo none of this now. What she really wanted to know was if the Inspector had known the Carters had killed her family. That Jasper had been there in the attic with her.

"He didn't know it was the Carters at your house that night. I never told him."

His father had suspected the East Rips were involved, of course. They were known for violence. But he'd never spoken to Jasper about it. In all their years together, he never indicated that he knew who Jasper's blood relations were at all. Not until that last confession, just prior to his death.

"Why…" Leo squeezed her eyes shut and released a tremulous breath. "Why did your family kill mine?"

It was one of the questions he'd anticipated if she ever did speak to him again. It was also perhaps the easiest to answer.

"Punishment for a betrayal," he replied. "I don't know what your father did; I wasn't old enough to be privy to that conversation. But he betrayed the East Rips somehow, and they wanted to make an example of him."

Leo's glistening eyes blinked. "My father *betrayed* them? But...how did he even know them?"

After months of wanting to explain to her, he now understood that telling her the truth might feel worse than her avoidance of him had. He knew the answer would be a blow to her. He licked his lips, then answered reluctantly, "He worked for them."

Shock melted the tension on her brow. She shook her head. "No. You're wrong. You're lying. My father wasn't an East Rip."

"Not everyone who works for the Carters is an East Rip," he said quietly, hoping to calm her. "They have a wide network of associates and allies. Hell, not even every Carter is an East Rip. My own father wasn't. He was Patrick Carter's cousin. He wasn't involved, and neither was I until...well, until after he died."

Leo breathed evenly, shaking her head. "My father was an accountant, not a criminal."

He didn't need to tell her outright what she would soon grasp on her own: that her father had been keeping the books for one of the Carters' many businesses. Some were legitimate. Others, less so.

Leo pressed her fingers to her left ear, as if it was causing her pain. Her chin quivered. "I need to go. I wasn't ready." She turned for the door.

"Let me flag you a cab," he offered, starting forward. She held up her hand.

"I'll flag one on my own," she said. "Goodnight, Inspector."

It prickled, Leo calling him that. "I wish you would call me Jasper again."

"That isn't your name though, is it?" She stepped into the hall, and before he could object, she walked away.

Chapter Six

Dawn painted the walls of Leo's bedroom orange and pink. Since returning from Jasper's home, she'd lain abed with her mind churning, sleep a distant prospect. Her father had worked for the East Rips. Or at least, Jasper believed he had. Was it possible that he was remembering things incorrectly? He'd been thirteen at the time, after all. Essentially, a child still.

But as night ticked closer toward daylight, Leo couldn't quite convince herself that he was mistaken. As much as it pained her to admit it, Jasper likely remembered that night just as vividly as she did. It wouldn't matter that they'd been on opposite sides of the horror.

If the Carter family had decided to punish Leonard Spencer to such an extent, his betrayal must have been extraordinary. The nature of that betrayal could very well have been described in the letters her mother had written to Aunt Flora. *The bloody, bloody business,* her aunt had mumbled one night, although at the time, Leo hadn't fully understood to what she was referring.

Leo and Claude had looked through Flora's things for any letters she'd kept from Andromeda Spencer. They'd searched a cedar chest, the closet, and boxes into which Flora had tucked trinkets she thought special enough to cherish: a baby's bonnet, yellowed by time; an empty glass atomizer that still smelled faintly of perfume; and a brooch Claude believed to have belonged to Leo's grandmother. But there had been nothing at all from Andromeda.

Restless to begin the day, Leo got out of bed and dressed. Claude joined her in the kitchen shortly after she'd finished cooking the eggs and sausages, both of which emerged from the hob barely charred this time. As her uncle had been asleep at the time of the three bombings the night before, she informed him after they'd sat down to eat. Just as Leo had, he thought the different timing of the bombs and the differences in their construction peculiar.

"Might the two explosions at the Yard be unrelated?" he mused as he added a handful of watercress to his eggs, perhaps to make them more palatable. "At any rate, I'm glad Inspector Reid was unharmed. Am I to assume the two of you are no longer quarreling?"

Claude had given her privacy and hadn't addressed the distance she'd kept from Jasper over the last few months, but he'd surely noticed it. Especially since whenever Jasper had come to the morgue to discuss postmortem findings with Claude, Leo would close herself in the office or quickly leave on an errand.

"We weren't quarreling." To admit they had been would lead her uncle to ask why. The reason wasn't something she wished to speak of to anyone.

Though Jasper had hurt and betrayed her, and she had moments of wanting to lash out and injure him just as deeply, she couldn't bring herself to unmask Jasper. Not only would it destroy his career, but it might also draw the attention of the Carters back to him. Somehow, Jasper had come face-to-face with Andrew Carter in March, and the East Rip hadn't recognized him as any kind of relation. The Carter family tree had roots that were broad and deep in London, with numerous brothers, cousins and uncles. From what he'd said last night, his own father had been a cousin to Patrick and Robert Carter, with Jasper and his mother only being taken in by the East Rips Carters after his father had died. Then, when his mother was killed—something he had only recently revealed during their investigation into Gabriela Carter's murder —he'd been left alone to stay with his aunt and uncle. What that must have been like for him as a boy was one of the many questions taking up residence in Leo's mind.

But the answers to the questions she'd asked last night had disillusioned her, and now she wasn't sure she wanted to ask any more at all.

"Uncle Claude," she said, piercing her sausage with the tines of her fork. "I've been thinking about the letters my mother wrote to Aunt Flora."

"I do wish we had found them, my dear," he said.

It wasn't just the contents of the letters Leo longed to read. She also yearned for the opportunity to see her mother's handwriting. To hold something that her mother had once touched.

Not long after the murders, Gregory Reid had brought her a few things he'd collected from her family's home on Red Lion Street: framed photographs, some clothing, her sister Agnes's rag doll, and Jacob's pocket watch. Things the Inspector had thought she might want or would eventually come to cherish. At the time, as a little girl who had just lost her family, Leo hadn't cared about the home itself or anything within it. To her mind, the house was a place of pain, of heartbreak and fear, and she was only grateful to know that she never had to step foot inside it again.

A handful of years passed before she thought to ask Claude what had become of her family's belongings. He replied that as soon as he and Flora had arrived in London, he'd relinquished the premises back to the leaseholder, along with most of the furnishings. Leo hadn't been upset. What meaning could sofas and chairs, mirrors and bedsteads possibly have compared to the family members she'd lost?

Now, however, after searching through Flora's things for her mother's letters without success, a new thought struck her: What had happened to her family's possessions that the leaseholder wouldn't have wanted? Things like mementos, papers, letters, and diaries? She posed the question to Claude, who lowered his fork and wrinkled his brow.

"I haven't given those things a thought in years."

"Did you burn them?" she asked.

"My goodness, no," he answered swiftly. "I couldn't decide what to do with them, so after Inspector Reid went through them and then returned them to me, I put them in boxes and set them aside. Forgot about them entirely."

"Set them aside where?"

"The morgue's crypt." He winced as if in apology and lifted a shoulder. "There wasn't space here."

She gaped. The crypt was a storage facility of sorts,

holding not only old items from the morgue's previous iteration as a church, but also the unclaimed possessions of the dead. Families would sometimes leave their loved ones' things behind, either accidentally or intentionally. Or when an unidentified and unclaimed body was taken away to be buried in a pauper's grave, the person's items were left to be stored in the crypt. Leo had gone into the vast space countless times over the years.

And now, her uncle was saying her own family's things were down there too.

"Why have you never told me this?" she asked.

Remorse pulled at the corners of his lips. "As I said, I haven't thought of those boxes in years. And earlier, well, I couldn't allow a child to rummage through her parents' personal things." He paused, cocking his head. "I hope you're not too upset with me."

There was no reason for her to be upset. He was right to have kept them from her when she was younger. She wouldn't have wanted to see them then. And how could she be vexed that the boxes had slipped his mind after all these years? He was nearly seventy years old, after all.

"Not in the least," she assured him, reaching to cover his hand on the table with her own. "But I would like to see them now."

Although Leo and her uncle hadn't found her mother's letters to Aunt Flora, it was possible that her mother might have kept letters Flora sent to her and were now stored in the boxes in the crypt. Within them, there could very well be information about what Leonard Spencer had been doing. If that proved to be the case, Leo hoped she was ready for whatever she might learn.

Before his death, the Inspector had given her the

extensive record he'd compiled on the Spencer family murders and asked that she be ready before opening the file. She thought she had been. But after viewing a foggy, over-exposed crime scene photograph of her father, lying on his side on the sitting room carpet, a dark blood stain on the front of his shirt, Leo had slammed the folder shut, her stomach convulsing with a surge of nausea. She hadn't yet tried opening the file a second time.

At the sounds of his wife stirring from her slumber upstairs, Claude got to his feet and promised Leo that he would look for the boxes later that day. She left for Scotland Yard before Flora could come down for breakfast. She'd once told her uncle that she wasn't avoiding her aunt deliberately, but now she wasn't certain that was true anymore.

With a pinch of guilt, she walked swiftly toward Great Scotland Yard. Most mornings, Dita would come to Duke Street on her way into work, and she and Leo would walk there together. However, last evening, before going to Charles Street, Leo stopped by Dita's home in Covent Garden. Distraught over John's death, she'd told Leo she wouldn't be going in to work for a few days.

"I don't know if I'll ever be able to walk into that building again without thinking of him," she'd said, her eyes swollen from ceaseless tears.

Leo had merely kept her arm around Dita, saying nothing of the precise image she would always have of Constable Lloyd in the moments before that flash of light had blinded her. She was just grateful her friend would not have the same memory imprinted on her brain in perpetuity.

Activity swarmed the Metropolitan Police's central

offices as Leo walked through Great Scotland Yard. Rubble from the brick exterior of the building still cluttered the street. The remains of a carriage sat outside the Rising Sun, the latter of which had born the blast relatively well, beyond its shattered windows. Leo thought of Jasper. He'd been inside the public house when the bomb detonated. What if he'd been outside? Standing near that carriage?

The leaden drop of her stomach angered her. Why couldn't she despise him enough not to care?

Officers in uniform and in plain clothes, as well as citizens and reporters, were standing about, gazing upon the damage. As Jasper had jested, he did indeed have a new door to his office—an enormous hole in the front corner of the building. She could see straight inside the CID and partially into the offices on the floor above it. Had the bomb detonated during the day, any number of people might have been killed. But if the bomb had been set to explode using a timer, as the morning newspapers were saying, then the intent had not been to kill but rather to terrorize, as Clan na Gael and the Irish Republican Brotherhood tended to do.

It's what made the suitcase bomb John Lloyd had been carrying earlier yesterday so strange. It had been constructed using gunpowder, while the others, as Jasper had revealed, had employed dynamite. Why would they have used two different types of explosives?

Leo continued toward Spring Street. While she was curious what Inspector Tomlin had thought of John Lloyd's postmortem report delivered via messenger the previous evening, she knew better than to think he might discuss it with her. At the morgue, a curious influx of bodies kept Claude and Leo occupied, and when it came time for tea, she told her uncle to sit and rest rather than descend into the crypt to search for the boxes of Spencer family belongings, as he'd promised to do. It had been sixteen years. It could wait another day.

At last, evening rolled in, and Claude began his nightly cleaning of the postmortem room. Leo was seated at the desk, typing notes when her uncle called, "You'll be late for your meeting if you don't leave soon."

Her fingers stalled, and her eyes rolled toward the ceiling. She had completely forgotten. On the first and third Wednesdays of every month, Mrs. Geraldine Stewart hosted the Women's Equality Alliance at her home on Carlisle Street. Leo and Dita had gone to the last several meetings together, and the previous night, Dita had implored Leo to still attend, even if she would not be able to join her. The truth was she'd have much rather skipped the meeting, but as it was important to Dita, she resolved to go.

Leo set aside the postmortem report and gathered her coat and hat.

"Thank you for remembering," she said to her uncle as he was scrubbing down an autopsy table. She stopped to kiss his cheek, and he chuckled as if the affectionate display equally delighted and embarrassed him.

Leo went to the nearest cabstand on Trafalgar Square and rode an omnibus toward Piccadilly Circus, a route beleaguered by traffic and several more cabstand stops. It was nearly a half hour later when she arrived at the Stewarts' fine home. Through the front windows, a crush of people could be seen, and when a maid opened the door to allow her entry, a low thrum of voices flowed out into the night.

The maid took Leo's coat and gloves and indicated that she was to join the others in the large front sitting room. At least a dozen more people than usual filled the space, with chairs lined up in rows facing the far end of the room, where a grand marble fireplace dominated the wall. It was then that she remembered: They were to have a guest speaker that evening, a member of Parliament sympathetic to the vote for women.

Some ladies stood and mingled, while others had already taken the seats positioned closest to the front. A few women, whom Leo recognized from past meetings, cast her assessing looks. Without greeting her, they continued with their conversations. The women here were a mix of classes, though most were wealthy and dressed in the finest fashions of the day—certainly far better than what Leo wore. Her dark, blue-and-black pin-striped skirt and matching short coat hadn't a single frill or flare. As she wended her way toward one of the middle rows, nodding hello here and there to those who acknowledged her, she noticed their strained expressions. The hushed conversations too.

She lowered herself into a cane back chair, curious as to the mood of the room.

A woman seated two chairs over peered at her. "You are Miss Brooks's friend."

"Yes, I'm Leonora Spencer," she said, reminding the woman of her name. They had already been introduced twice before, but while she recalled Mrs. Emma Bates well, the widowed sister-in-law of Mrs. Stewart, their hostess, apparently could not say the same for Leo.

It wasn't too much of an insult. Mrs. Bates seemed to be an aloof sort, and Leo suspected hers wasn't the only name the woman couldn't hang on to. In her middle thirties or so, she had the appealing features of a much younger woman. Tall with a full bosom, narrow waist, supple, unlined skin, and glossy blonde hair.

"Ah yes, I remember now. You are the woman from the morgue."

Leo couldn't quite tell if Mrs. Bates was disapproving. It sounded more like an observation than a judgment. She decided not to waste time discovering which it was.

"I am here alone tonight, as Miss Brooks was feeling unwell," Leo said, moving on.

If Dita ever wished to confide in any of the WEA ladies about her former beau, that would be her choice. However, Leo imagined it would be a struggle for anyone to claim connection to a police constable who had been planning to bomb Scotland Yard. Even Dita.

"It is just as well for your friend," Mrs. Bates said with a heavy sigh that lifted her generous bosom with theatrical flair. "Sir Elliot isn't coming."

"The guest speaker?" Leo asked with a twinge of disappointment. It was immediately followed by hope that the meeting might disperse early. She felt a little guilty, but it had been a very long day. As fiercely as she believed in the rights of women in politics, she also longed for something to eat and a chance to put up her feet.

"A messenger just arrived with the news. My sister-in-law is quite wounded," the other woman said, her eyes searching the room for Geraldine Stewart. "She was assured of Sir Elliot's support."

Her eyes came to a rest, and Leo followed the direction of her gaze. Mrs. Stewart and her husband stood within the entrance to an adjoining room. She was a formidably tall woman of about thirty years. Unlike some of the women she'd met at the WEA meetings, Mrs. Stewart hadn't been put off by Leo's work. In fact, she'd seemed impressed by it. She had the slightly unnerving habit of maintaining unblinking eye contact while in conversation, though now, with her brow knit in distress, she didn't appear so intimidating.

Mr. Stewart took his wife's hand and pressed his lips to her knuckles. It was an intimate display. One of support and mutual concern for the disappointing turn of events. The last few meetings Leo had attended, he'd been present as well.

"Mrs. Stewart is fortunate to have a husband who supports her cause," Leo said.

The topic of women's suffrage, in general, wasn't popular among men. For the bulk of history, men had been accustomed to leading the world of business, education, and politics, all of which seemed to revolve solely around them, with women relegated to being their caretakers as wives, mothers, sisters, or daughters. However, there were changes afoot, with more and more women beginning to enter the workforce and delaying marriage. Much like herself, she supposed.

"Geraldine captured herself a man of superior sensibility," Mrs. Bates agreed. "Porter truly is an exception to his sex."

Porter Stewart stood a half inch shorter than his wife, but that in no way made him diminutive. He was polished and self-possessed, with a pencil mustache and a benign grin. A striking man by every account.

Mrs. Bates gave another sigh, though this one was of a different variety. "It is why I doubt I shall ever remarry."

Leo shifted her attention from the Stewarts and peered at Mrs. Bates. She wasn't certain how to respond to such a statement, though it would be rude or dismissive to say nothing at all. She parted her lips to offer a banal "I hope that isn't so," but a rising commotion cut her off.

Twisting in her seat, Leo witnessed the throng of well-dressed ladies parting for several blue-uniformed Metropolitan Police officers. Detective Inspector Tomlin was at the head, his expression fixed in a pugnacious glower. Stunned, Leo got to her feet as Tomlin came to a stop in the center of the room. He was close to the row in which Leo stood, though he did not seem to see her.

"I am looking for Mrs. Geraldine Stewart," he said loudly.

Mr. Stewart stepped forward. "What is the meaning of this, officers?"

"Mrs. Stewart. Where is she?" Inspector Tomlin reiterated.

"I am right here," she said. "As my husband has just inquired, why have you and your men come?"

The inspector looked her over, his scowl deepening. Then, he signaled to the uniformed officers. They surged toward the WEA leader.

"Mrs. Stewart, I'm placing you under arrest in connection with the bombing at Scotland Yard yesterday afternoon and the death of Police Constable John Lloyd."

Gasps of alarm fired off throughout the room. Leo's jaw went slack as the constables reached for Mrs. Stewart.

"This is madness!" she cried.

Her husband came forward to block them. “I demand to know who you are, sir, and what evidence you have to make these wild accusations against my wife.”

“Step aside, or I will place you under arrest as well for obstructing an officer of the law in his official duties,” Tomlin shouted as more panic and confusion rumbled around the sitting room. A few ladies near the back pushed each other to flee the meeting altogether.

Mrs. Bates bumped into Leo as she shuffled past her in the row of seats. It jolted some sense into her, and she raised her voice to be heard above the din.

“Inspector Tomlin!”

He cocked his head at the sound of his name but was busy gesturing for the constables to put their suspect in handcuffs and to block Mr. Stewart from intervening.

Leo followed Mrs. Bates as she moved straight toward her sister- and brother-in-law.

“Think of the children, Porter,” she urged, taking Mr. Stewart’s arm and stepping between him and the officers to dissuade a second arrest.

“I am no murderer or bomber,” Mrs. Stewart declared loudly. “I demand to know your evidence against me.”

“You’ll hear all about it at Scotland Yard,” Tomlin replied with a goading grin.

“Detective Inspector Tomlin,” Leo said again, and this time, he turned his head. His mouth creased into another scowl.

“My God, woman, why am I not surprised to find you here?”

She ignored the turning heads and accusatory looks that she might know the man who’d so suddenly become their enemy. “The Women’s Equality Alliance is a peaceful group. It doesn't endorse or organize bombing campaigns, and neither does Mrs. Stewart."

The constables shuffled past, bringing the shocked WEA leader with them. "Porter!" she cried as they took her from the room.

"I'll summon our lawyer, darling! I'll put a stop to this!" he shouted.

Inspector Tomlin watched the arrest with a satisfied expression. It turned Leo's stomach. He then turned his smug grin toward her. "You're a member of this radical women's group, are you?"

"It is hardly radical to petition for the right to vote," she replied.

He ignored her and stuck his hands into his pockets. "Interesting how *you* were the one to suggest the suitcase PC Lloyd was carrying belonged to a woman. The crafter's mark was located on one of the remaining leather pieces, so we tracked the shop down and showed the owner the partial monogram that you yourself told us about."

A spike of warning darted into her stomach. He'd sweetened his tone, speaking to her as if she were a little girl with nothing but cotton fluff between her ears.

"The letters I saw were *GL*," Leo said.

"Indeed. A partial monogram. The shop owner recalled the valise well, including the lady for whom he'd made it. Geraldine Stewart. Any guesses as to her middle name, Miss Spencer?"

Mr. Stewart and Mrs. Bates were standing by, listening. Now, they both murmured their disbelief.

"Lynette," Mrs. Bates whispered, then clapped her

lace-gloved hand over her lips as if she'd just committed some mutiny.

"I don't believe it," Mr. Porter goggled. "I need to speak to my lawyer. Emma, will you see to the children?" he requested, turning to Mrs. Bates, who took his arm and led him from the room.

Leo turned back to the detective inspector, who was still quizzing her with a mean glare. "You know what else is strange, Miss Spencer? Lord Babbage was due to come to Scotland Yard yesterday for a meeting with the Commissioner. With your *connections* to the Yard being what they are," he said, unmistakably referring to Jasper, "might you have known about Babbage's appointment? Maybe even let it slip to Mrs. Stewart beforehand?"

Lord Babbage was a well-known conservative member of Parliament, and he was wholly against giving women the right to vote. She lifted her chin at his devious insinuation.

"Now, here you are, attending a meeting of this so-called *alliance*," he went on. "And you were near PC Lloyd when the bomb detonated."

The spike of warning she'd just had redoubled. "What are you suggesting, Inspector?"

He leaned forward, baring his teeth. "I'm suggesting you also come to headquarters so I can question you properly about your involvement."

She gaped at him. "I am not involved in any fashion."

Tomlin crooked his finger to the remaining constable at his side. "Put Miss Spencer in the back with our suspect. And don't forget the cuffs."

He stood aside, allowing the constable to come forward. "Hands, miss."

Humiliation and fury slid through her as she stared at the iron cuffs held up for her. She set her jaw, determined not to make a scene. Several ladies were still present, and they would spread the news of the double arrests with alacrity.

"Question me all you like, Inspector. I have nothing to hide," Leo declared as she held out her wrists.

Chapter Seven

Jasper cracked open his heavy eyelids and took in the state of Lord Oliver Hayes's library in the early dawn light. Someone had left the terrace doors open overnight, letting in the cold morning mist. He smelled dew on the air. It was fresh and clean—entirely the opposite of everything that had occurred the previous evening. The sight of empty whisky bottles on the carpet, a broken glass near the open French doors, a pair of men's shoes slung over the curved arm of a chandelier, and what looked to be Jasper's suit jacket pinned to the dartboard with a bone handle knife accompanied the painful throbbing of his temple.

It had been a long while since he'd traveled out of town and into Kensington for one of Oliver's soirees. They were always wild and slightly unhinged, but after a full day of sorting through the rubble at Scotland Yard, moving his office for the time being to the other half of Roy Lewis's desk, and assisting the Special Irish Branch detectives with interviewing witnesses to the bombings—

most of which were pointless and repetitive—an evening of highbrow intoxication and entertainment had been preferable to going home to drink and sleep alone.

Or enduring another late-night visit from Leo in which she recoiled from him in loathing.

The invitation to Hayes Manor had come a week ago, when Jasper had still been courting Constance. She had likely told her cousin all about their break-up, and as such, Jasper had gone to the soiree with the full knowledge that he might very well be turned out.

Oliver, however, had only clapped him on the shoulder as soon as he'd arrived. "You should know that Constance has asked me to call you out. But as I am a terrible shot, and as dueling is illegal and you could arrest me for issuing the challenge, I told her she'd have to settle for your utter humiliation in a sparring session at the boxing club. But first, let's drink."

And that had been that.

The promised sparring session had never come about, but the women, drink, and opium had been overflowing at the party. The lattermost vice was something Jasper had not touched and had turned a blind eye to. Drink, he'd indulged in. And though the attentions of a woman who went by the name of Azure—for her blue, erudite eyes, he imagined—had been bountiful, they'd left a hollowness within him that extended to every corner of his body. And more than once during the encounter, he'd needed to push any thought of Leo from his brain.

Your precious Leo.

Damn it all.

The incessant pounding in Jasper's skull and his sour stomach capped off a truth he did not want to acknowledge: His feelings for Leonora Spencer were becoming impossible to ignore. Coming here, giving in to his base desires, had only served to highlight them.

He shifted on the leather chaise longue where he'd ended the night, his back and neck stiff from having slept in an awkward position. Getting up with a groan, he felt the room spin.

While waiting for the dizzy spell to cease, muted shouts came through the open terrace doors from the garden. Oliver's voice and the deeper tenor of his butler, Riverton. Jasper staggered toward the dartboard and his wrecked coat. Thankfully, the shoes hanging from the chandelier belonged to another man; his boots were still on his feet. He'd just pulled the knife blade free from the board's cork when Oliver rushed inside from the terrace, heaving for breath.

"Jasper. Come quickly."

"Has a wife or two turned up?" he asked, inspecting the tears in his jacket. Vaguely, he recalled of one of Oliver's guests declaring that a jacket as ugly as his needed to be put out of its misery. Checking the coat pocket, Jasper found the pound note the man had stuffed inside after using it as target practice, telling him to buy a better one.

"No," Oliver said. "A body. In the duck pond."

Sobriety snapped up Jasper's spine, clearing his head in an instant. "One of your guests from last night?"

The young viscount had the washed-out, pallid complexion of a man who needed to vomit if he wanted to become sober again. "Follow me."

He turned and stumbled to the stone steps leading down to the clipped grass, a vibrant green carpet that a team of gardeners maintained. Past the garden bordered by a hedgerow, the lawn sloped toward the small pond, the edges thick with water lilies and bulrushes. Two other men present the night before were approaching the duck pond too. In their shirtsleeves and trousers, Lord Hastings and Sir Daniel Winthrop looked to have just risen from their stupors as well.

"Saw him from the window," Sir Daniel said. "Just floating there."

Riverton stood at the edge of the pond, his hands clasped behind his stiffened back, waiting. He turned to Oliver. "My lord, shall I fetch a footman to pull him out?"

Jasper held up a palm. "No, Riverton, not yet. Everyone, stay back."

A man wearing a long, black cape floated face down in the center of the pond.

"Be sensible, Reid. We cannot leave him in there," Hastings argued. He was an earl, Jasper recalled. They'd met last night, so everything was a bit hazy, but he did recall Hastings' belligerence even then.

"He is dead. It doesn't matter if he is in or out of the water just now." Jasper stepped forward, his eyes peeled on the ground. The lawn turned to marsh near the water's edge, and as he circled the perimeter of the small pond, he spotted boot prints.

"Has anyone been over here this morning?" he asked Oliver.

The viscount shook his head. "I don't believe so. Riverton?"

The butler shook his head. "No, my lord."

Jasper crouched for a better look at the prints. Two different sizes, it appeared. One pair could belong to the dead man, and the other to a second individual. Or two men could have been carrying the man's body.

"What is it you are doing?" Hastings queried.

"Looking for evidence. Before any of us mucks it up."

A fleck of white against the darker, marshy ground near the water's edge caught his attention. Jasper moved closer, plucking it from the wet ground where it had been crushed beneath a boot. A man's linen handkerchief, monogramed at the corner. *NLF*. He could not think of any man he'd met the previous evening with those initials. He would put the question to the others when he interviewed them. For now, Jasper folded the handkerchief and put it into his trouser pocket. After a thorough search of the pond's perimeter, he was satisfied. By then, two more guests and a few additional servants had descended on their group.

"All right, Riverton," Jasper announced to the forbearing butler, "you may have him pulled out."

Two footmen waded into the water, and Jasper turned to the gathered guests. "I need all of you to remain on the property for now. Are there any others still abed?"

Shrugged shoulders and dense expressions met him.

"Oliver, have your staff check all the rooms, not just the bedchambers. I'll also need to speak to the staff, so gather them as promptly as you can. As for the ladies who were here last night—"

"They were hardly ladies," Hastings snorted. Sir Daniel and the two newcomers joined him in sharing mischievous glances. Jasper tamped down the urge to box Hastings in the teeth.

"I will need their names and how to contact them," Jasper finished, ignoring the earl's smug grin.

Though he sincerely doubted the women who'd joined in the revelry last night had anything to do with the man's death, he couldn't overlook them. Most likely, he was a drunken guest who'd imbibed too much, stumbled out onto the darkened lawn, fallen into the water, and drowned.

Oliver came to stand beside Jasper as the footmen dragged the body toward shore. The pond wasn't deep; the footmen were only in up to their shoulders.

Jasper showed the viscount the handkerchief. "Are these initials familiar to you?"

Oliver peered at the mucky linen with the pale blue embroidered letters but only frowned. "I don't know whose they could be."

Jasper would ask again later. Oliver had smoked a fair amount of opium and consumed far more drink than Jasper had the previous night and was looking peaky. The footmen in their sopping clothes climbed out onto the marshy lawn, pulling the dead man's body by the arms. His legs had not even cleared the water before they dropped the poor sod and scuttled away, unnerved to have been handling a corpse. Jasper thought again of Leo and how she would have handled the task with enviable composure.

He crouched next to the man and rolled him over onto his back. As he'd suspected, the man had been young. Twenty-something, if Jasper were to guess. His drenched black cape, plastered to him, was reminiscent of what a barrister might wear, or a university student. His hair was brown, and a smattering of freckles crossed his fair-skinned face, now cast with an ashen blue pallor. A gash marred his left cheek, and his left eye was blackened from an altercation before his death.

"My God," Oliver gasped, then turned in haste to retch into the reeds. Jasper stayed crouched, observing the body and waiting for his friend to finish. When he did, he wiped his mouth and stared at the body. "It is Niles."

"Niles who?" Jasper asked.

"Foster. Niles Foster. A family friend."

"Was he here last night?" He had no memory of meeting this man at the soiree. Oliver shook his head. "No. I didn't invite him."

Jasper peered at the black cape. "Why is he wearing this?"

"He is—or rather, was—a parliamentary aide," Oliver answered, sounding distant and blinking rapidly, appearing to be in a mild state of shock.

Jasper moved to the body's feet and with some effort, thanks to the sopping laces, removed the man's left shoe.

He took it over to the boot prints he'd seen near the water's edge and tried to align it with either of the two sets. Neither matched. So long as Oliver and Riverton were correct, and no other guests had been at the pond that morning or the night before, it looked as though Niles Foster hadn't been alone when he'd gone into the water.

"Might he have arrived without an invitation?" Jasper asked after replacing the shoe and then searching the man's coat pockets. He found nothing in them, but with Foster's arms splayed wide at his sides, the cuffs of his sleeves had ridden up, exposing his wrists. Thin, matching bands of red bruised the skin on each wrist. Ligature marks.

Some color had come back into Oliver's cheeks after retching, and he slurred less when he answered, "No. I don't think so."

Jasper rose to his feet, his attention stuck on the ligature marks. "You say he was a family friend?"

"My father's best mate from Oxford was Niles's father," he answered, then frowned. "I just saw him last week. Niles, I mean. His father is dead."

Looking ill again, Oliver ran a hand down his face, gripping his chin. "We argued."

"What about?"

Oliver paled again. "I need to sit. Put something in my stomach. Can we discuss it inside?"

Residue from his own hangover felt like a greasy wash in Jasper's stomach. He wished like hell that he'd gone home the night before.

He turned to one of the waterlogged footmen. "Send word to the Kensington constabulary that there has been a suspected drowning at Hayes Manor. Let them know I'm present."

Jasper's attention shifted back toward Foster's blackened eye, cut cheek, and the ligature marks on his wrists. The injuries, at least on the surface, resembled those Leo had described as present on Constable Lloyd.

"Hastings," Jasper called. The earl had yet to drift back toward the manor with the others. "Help me carry the body to the house."

"You cannot be serious," he spluttered.

"Take his ankles," Jasper ordered. "Or you'll learn just how serious I am."

Seven men in all, including Jasper, had stayed the night at the viscount's soiree, though the ladies had disappeared sometime before dawn. Jasper wasn't as concerned about them; the footprints around the pond belonged to men, not women. The interviews with Oliver's remaining guests convinced him that none of the men still present were involved in the man's drowning; they were far too sloppy from an excess of liquor, and some were still addled from the effects of opium.

It was Oliver's interview, however, that interested Jasper the most. As he and the viscount sipped on a strong brew of coffee in the dining room, Oliver described his relationship to the victim.

"We never got on well," he said. "Had our fathers not been friends, I would have cut Niles loose years ago."

"What was the trouble with him?"

"He's the perpetually unfortunate sort. Never able to hang on to money, always getting into some twist or another. Depend on him, and you can count yourself a fool."

Jasper had known men like this before. Incurably unlucky, never able to make a good decision, opportunities slipping through their fingers at every turn.

"However, after his father passed, and then mine, I don't know...I suppose I felt a certain responsibility toward him," Oliver said with a shrug.

Jasper bit his tongue. Shortly after Gregory Reid had passed away, Oliver had been the one to tell Jasper that he should no longer feel any responsibility toward Leo. It had been Jasper's father who'd treated her like family, he'd said; Jasper needn't do the same. The advice had rubbed him the wrong way. Leo wasn't a burden he'd been saddled with upon the death of the Inspector.

Perhaps Oliver had merely been thinking about his own burden, Niles Foster, when he'd dispensed his advice back in March.

"You said you argued last week. What about?"

Oliver frowned. "Niles wanted money. He called it a 'loan', but as you might suspect, it was never a loan with him."

"You'd given him money before?"

The viscount nodded and sipped his coffee. "I cut him off after the first few loans were never repaid. That didn't stop him from asking, though. I tried to help in other ways. I thought if he could get some respectable work… So, I connected him with one of my friends in Parliament. Sir Elliot Payne."

Jasper didn't recognize the name. Then again, he didn't keep up with politics as Oliver did.

"He needed an aide, so I stuck my neck out for Niles." Oliver had the beleaguered look of someone who'd been disappointed again and again.

"Last week, you told him you wouldn't give him the loan, and he became upset?" Jasper asked.

Oliver raised a brow. "It wasn't like him to react the way he did." He rubbed his cheek, the dark bristle in dire need of a straight razor. "It was damn embarrassing. We were in public. At the bloody Houses of Parliament."

"What day last week, specifically?"

He took a moment to remember correctly, then said, "Monday. Or Tuesday. I can't be sure."

"Did he tell you what he needed the money for?"

"No, and I didn't want to know. He was a profligate at the gaming tables, so I imagine he'd suffered a loss."

"What was the requested amount?"

"Fifty pounds." Oliver laughed. "Can you imagine? The bloody stones on that man."

Jasper thought of the bruised eye and gashed cheek. "Did your quarrel become physical?"

The viscount slanted him a chastising glance. "If you mean to ask me if I'm the one who gave him that scuffed-up face, the answer is no. I maintained my temper, though only because we were in full view of several MPs of my acquaintance. Otherwise, I might have pummeled him." He suddenly looked ill. "Forgive me. I shouldn't have said that, not with him lying dead in my hunting room."

Shortly after the interview with Oliver ended, three constables arrived from Kensington station. Jasper informed them of the events of the morning and asked for the body to be sent to the Spring Street Morgue. There was a closer deadhouse, of course, but with the ligature marks and facial injuries, Jasper wanted Claude to have a look at the body. It didn't make sense for Niles Foster and Constable Lloyd to have the same injuries, yet he couldn't shake the similarities from his mind.

He accepted Oliver's offer of a driver to take him back to Scotland Yard, riding ahead of the wagon that trundled the body to its destination on Spring Street. It was just shy of nine o'clock when he arrived at the Yard—or as near to the building as he could get. The cleanup was still in progress, with sweating laborers piling what remained of the rubble from the bomb's blast into wagons to be hauled away. Already, men were erecting scaffolds to begin patching up the hole in the corner of the building. Inside, Jasper made his way toward the detective department, where sunlight streamed through the gaping hole in the office. Detective Sergeant Lewis saw Jasper approaching and kicked his boots down from where they'd been propped on the desk they would now be sharing.

"Has Chief Coughlan arrived yet?" Jasper asked, eyeing the dirt left behind on the blotter.

"Come and gone, though I'm sure he'll be back." Lewis grimaced and quirked his brow. "You look like shite."

The hammering and clinking of bricks and metal outside burrowed into Jasper's ears. "I am aware, thank you."

He started to shed his coat, belatedly recalling the knife holes in the back.

"Listen, guv, there's something you should know," Lewis began.

Jasper rubbed his temples. They throbbed, and a gnawing pit had replaced his stomach. It seemed the early morning commotion at Hayes Manor was finally catching up to him. As soon as the chief arrived, he'd inform him of Niles Foster's death and request to lead the investigation. Then, he'd go home, bathe, and feed his hangover with a finger of whisky. A little hair of the dog was the only thing that would work to steady him.

"Tomlin's made two arrests in the Lloyd bombing," Lewis continued.

Jasper nodded. "Good."

It wasn't his investigation, as he'd told Leo several times already. The apparent drowning at Hayes Manor, however, might be, if Coughlan thought him impartial enough.

“A suffragist,” Lewis said. That grabbed Jasper’s attention.

“Not a member of Clan na Gael?”

His sergeant grimaced as he shook his head. “Tomlin also nabbed someone else.” He squinted as if preparing to be dealt a blow to the face. “It’s Miss Spencer.”

Everything in Jasper went still. His hearing muffled as he tried to make sense of what Lewis had just said. Tomlin had arrested *Leo*?

For the second time that morning, the hangover he well deserved drained away to be replaced by clear-headedness and biting urgency.

“Where is she?”

Lewis turned his eyes toward the ceiling, indicating the upper floors where the matrons guarded the women and children being held at the Yard.

Bloody hell.

Jasper grabbed his coat and stalked from the room without another word.

Chapter Eight

Leo paced the pale blue carpet in the small room. Inside, it was stuffy and hot, the window having been nailed shut long ago as a preventative measure, though that seemed utterly absurd. No rational woman would jump to her freedom from three floors up, for heaven's sake. Her limbs ached with restlessness even as she moved, charting the room from one corner to another and back again. She'd been there all night and into the morning, and so far, she'd only been brought a single cup of water to quench her thirst. Her stomach rumbled fiercely, but her anger was doing well to snuff that out.

After being handcuffed in the Stewarts' home and led out to the back of the police wagon, she'd settled on the bench next to Geraldine. The woman had been stark white, her eyes round in disbelief. "They think I've murdered a man. That I set off a bomb!"

Leo had tried to ignore the cold, surprisingly heavy iron cuffs around her wrists. Inspector Tomlin would be forced to release her swiftly, she'd reasoned, as he had nothing to charge her with and no evidence at all to point to her involvement with the bombing. But Mrs. Stewart was facing a much more serious plight.

"Did you know Police Constable John Lloyd?" she asked the woman.

At the rapid shake of Geraldine's head, Leo explained what had unfolded the previous day and who the victim had been.

"Miss Brooks was to marry him?" At this, Mrs. Stewart's eyes shone with tears. "The poor dear. I'm so very sorry for what she is going through, but I had absolutely nothing to do with his death."

Leo believed her. However, there was the matter of the valise that John had been carrying. Inspector Tomlin had confirmed that it belonged to Mrs. Stewart, and when Leo described the case that had housed the device, the WEA leader had gaped.

"Yes. Yes! That is my valise. I've had it for a handful of years, ever since our trip to France after Porter and I married. But it should be in my attic, not blown to pieces by a bomb!"

Leo considered what Inspector Tomlin had said while making the arrest. "Lord Babbage was to visit Scotland Yard that afternoon. It seems they've concluded that he might have been the intended target. And you, Mrs. Stewart, have been quite vocal about your dislike for him."

"Of course I have been," she replied. "The man is infuriatingly prehistoric in his views of women. It is no secret we dislike each other, but I would not try to kill him!"

Babbage had recently been quoted in *The Times*, calling

Geraldine and all women like her "bratty shrews." They were no better than whining children who'd been given too many sweets before bedtime, he'd added.

"Besides," Mrs. Stewart continued, "we've gathered enough petition votes to bring a debate to the House floor in just two weeks. That is what Sir Elliot was to announce tonight before he sent word that he couldn't attend." She squeezed her eyes shut in apparent frustration. "It's what the WEA has been striving for. I would never jeopardize this opportunity with such violence."

Leo had signed the petition at her first meeting. A debate in the House would force members of Parliament to listen to the WEA's arguments, and with Sir Elliot's support, it could sway opinions. Now, however, that debate was unlikely to be held.

It was possible, Leo considered, that Geraldine Stewart was being set up to look like a radical, violent activist. It was precisely what someone like Lord Babbage would want.

The ride to Scotland Yard had been bumpy and rough, and the two women had felt the jolts keenly in the back of the police wagon. It wouldn't have been a shock to learn the driver had been instructed to aim the wagon's wheels for the largest holes in the cobblestones along the way.

"Why have they arrested you?" Mrs. Stewart asked after several minutes of silence had passed.

"The inspector isn't fond of me. I'm sure this is punishment for questioning him in public."

They arrived at the Yard, and Leo's heart rate increased in anticipation of crossing paths with Jasper. It would be humiliating to be seen in handcuffs, being led away like a common criminal. Thankfully, it was later in the evening, and she hadn't seen him. The constables brought her and Mrs. Stewart to the third-floor rooms, where they were given over to the care of the on-duty matron.

The room with the blue carpet that Leo had been treading for hours likely had been a servant's bedroom, back when the building existed within the Palace of Whitehall, a once grand structure with multiple wings used to house Scottish royalty and diplomats. Now, furnished with only a chair and footstool, and a small commode in which to empty her bladder, the room was spartan. She'd sat with her legs tucked up beneath her in the dark all night, nodding off a few times, waiting for Inspector Tomlin to come rail at her.

But he hadn't.

As the morning sun lifted above the rooftops outside, a knock landed on her door. Leaping to her feet, she was prepared to see Inspector Tomlin enter her quarters. Instead, Sergeant Lewis had entered, the matron standing in the open doorway to act as chaperone.

"Miss Spencer, I've just been informed of your arrest," he remarked matter-of-factly.

Heat suffused her cheeks. "I haven't been properly booked," she said to clarify.

"Shall I send for Inspector Reid?"

"No," she answered a little too eagerly. "No, please, it's not necessary. But could you send word to my uncle? He's sure to be worrying himself sick about where I've been all night."

"He was in looking for you just now. I assured him I'd make certain you were all right."

Leo exhaled, relieved. Yet also infuriated. How long

must she wait here before Inspector Tomlin decided he was ready to question her?

"How is Mrs. Stewart?" she asked. "Is she still being held?"

There had been little sound outside her small room that morning, and Sergeant Lewis's answer explained why.

"She's been taken to Holloway Prison to await official charges."

Leo's breath left her at the news, and she didn't regain it until after the sergeant bobbed his head in departure, the matron closing and locking the door behind him. Geraldine had already been taken to *prison*? How was that possible? Leo felt completely useless as she began pacing the room again.

Shortly afterward, the matron returned with a small bowl of gruel. The older woman had searched Leo upon her arrival the night before for any weapons or stolen items, turning a deaf ear to her assertions that she would find nothing of the sort on her person. This matron wasn't warm or smiling, however, as Dita would have been. Leo left the bowl of thin gruel untouched despite her grumbling belly. Where the devil was Inspector Tomlin? At least the handcuffs had been removed before he'd gone home last night, leaving her to stew.

She was standing at the window, watching the street below when she heard a gruff command from the corridor: "Open that door. Now, please."

Leo closed her eyes at Jasper's deep voice, her heart launching into her throat as a ring of keys rattled, and the lock turned.

This was going to be nearly as bad as when he found

her stuck in the open grave at All Saints Cemetery back in January.

Jasper stalked into the small room and came to an abrupt halt when he saw her at the window.

"Christ, Leo." He came forward, raking her from crown to toe with his smoldering green eyes. "Are you hurt at all?"

She stumbled at the question. It wasn't the one she'd expected. "I'm fine, I've just… I've been here all night. Inspector Tomlin put me here and never returned."

He swore an oath under his breath. "What has he charged you with?"

Leo sensed Jasper's temper was about to boil over. He was angry, but to her surprise, she didn't think it was with her. "Nothing. Yet."

He turned to the matron. "Miss Spencer is coming with me."

The woman's eyes widened. "But Inspector, I have orders to—"

"She is coming with me," Jasper said, more slowly this time. After biting her lip, the matron nodded. Jasper held out an arm, indicating for Leo to leave the room. She did so, with great relief.

"Go home," he said, passing her in the corridor on the way to the stairs. "I need to speak to Tomlin."

She caught his elbow to slow him. At her touch, he stopped moving, and his eyes lowered to her hand. With a dart of panic, she released him.

"Tomlin was out of line," he said, his voice tight.

"The man is galling," Leo said. "But I am fine. It is Mrs. Geraldine Stewart I'm more concerned about; he's arrested her for conspiracy in the bombing. The first bombing, that is, involving Constable Lloyd."

"The suffragist. Yes, I've heard." He grimaced and began down the stairs. "Are you really a part of that group?"

"Do you disagree that women should have the right to vote?" she shot back. "Am I not intelligent enough to decide for whom to cast my own ballot?"

Jasper stopped on the bottom step and turned, his arm still on the railing, barring her from passage. "I am not in disagreement. And I am well aware of your intelligence, Leo. But there *are* suffragists who are radical enough to plot a bombing."

"Not the WEA. Not Geraldine Stewart. She is being set up."

He sighed and turned to take the next set of stairs down. It was then that she noticed how disheveled and exhausted he appeared. Golden bristle on his jaw, in want of a razor; clothing, rumpled; and several holes in the back of his jacket.

"What happened to you?" She regretted the question right away. What he did wasn't a concern of hers. Not anymore.

"There was an incident this morning," he answered as he kept on toward the detective department. She followed, her stomach twisting with hunger again.

Police Constable Horace Wiley, whose desk guarded entry to the CID, sneered at Leo from his seat. "I understand you're here for booking."

"Miss Spencer is free to go," Jasper said.

"That's not what I've heard, Inspector."

"Well, you are hearing it now," he barked. For a change,

Leo held her tongue against provoking Wiley as she and Jasper swept past the tedious man.

She wanted to ask Jasper what the incident had been, but doing so would display an interest in his affairs, and she wasn't certain that would be wise. They came to a desk—Sergeant Lewis's. Currently without an office, Jasper seemed to be sharing the space with him.

"Tell me why you think Mrs. Stewart is being set up," Jasper said as he removed his holey coat and tossed it over the back of a chair.

She glanced over her shoulder toward Constable Wiley. He was watching and clearly trying to eavesdrop on their conversation.

"I wish you still had an office," she said.

"So do I." He scrubbed his scruffy jaw. "My shaving kit was in there."

Leo kept her voice low. "The valise belonged to Mrs. Stewart, but she says it had been in her attic for years. Why would she put a bomb in a suitcase that could so easily be traced back to her?"

"Maybe she thought it would be completely destroyed in the blast."

"Why take the chance, when she easily could have purchased a nondescript case from a secondhand shop and used that? And how could she have forced Constable Lloyd to deliver the bomb? She didn't even know him."

"Or so she says," Jasper argued.

Leo clenched her fists. "You agree with Tomlin then?"

Jasper leaned forward, bracing his hands on the desk. "Tomlin is a horse's arse, and I'd like to crack him in the jaw for arresting you and leaving you locked up all night for no reason." He took a breath, and Leo's fingers loosened. "But he is right to consider that Mrs. Stewart is lying. The valise belonged to her. It is evidence. And after the second wave of bombings that same night, he has no choice but to consider a link to Clan na Gael."

That notion hadn't yet crossed her mind. If possible, her worry for Geraldine increased. The Metropolitan Police would wish to solve the bombings swiftly, place the blame upon someone's shoulders, and laud their accomplishment to the press. Tomlin likely believed his investigation was now over.

"She isn't connected to that group," Leo said.

Jasper arched a brow. "Tomlin isn't a man to be trifled with, Leo. Don't give him a reason to look your way."

"I already have, it seems," she said with a lift of her arms. She had a thought. "Might I look through the prisoner albums?"

"What for?"

"The man in the brown cap I saw scowling at Constable Lloyd. I could look for him among the prisoner photographs, if he has a record."

Jasper gripped the back of his neck, the muscles along his jaw tensing. "Those albums can't leave the building, and I can't have you in here. So no, I'm sorry. Go home, Leo. I have things to see to here."

She tried not to let her aggravation show. "Right. The incident from this morning," she said.

He nodded, watching her with an expectant arch of his brow. When she said nothing more, he cocked his head. "You aren't going to inquire about it?"

"Is it any of my business?" she replied coolly.

"It will be when you arrive at the morgue."

A body, then.

"Murder?"

He looked around the room, then lowered his voice. "Possibly. He was found in Viscount Hayes's duck pond at dawn."

She looked him over again. "You were already there. For a gathering last night."

Jasper stood back and rolled a shoulder. "Why would you assume that?"

"Because you haven't shaved, your clothing appears to have been slept in, and you smell of whisky and cheap perfume."

Jasper frowned and sniffed his collar. He didn't deny it, and a prickle of irritation bothered her. Had Constance Hayes been present at this party? No, she wouldn't ask. Because she did not care.

"Who drowned? Another member of your party?" she asked instead.

"No. It was an acquaintance of Oliver's. Niles Foster, a parliamentary aide. Turned up at some point during the night, though by the footprints around the pond, he wasn't alone."

He rubbed his thumb along his cheek and chin in thought. There was something he wasn't telling her. Dragging it out of him would take too much effort, however, and after the night she'd endured upstairs, she was severely lacking in stamina.

"I need to find my uncle. I'm sure he'll be at the morgue," she said, turning to leave. Then hesitated. "Or perhaps I should stay and wait for Inspector Tomlin. I don't look forward to speaking to him, but I also don't want him to have me detained again."

Jasper crossed his arms. "I will deal with Tomlin. Go."

She nodded, grateful. And yet, she didn't *want* to feel grateful to him for anything. Discomfited, she again turned to leave just as Sergeant Lewis was coming toward his desk. "I found an address for Sir Elliot," he told Jasper, handing him a piece of paper.

Leo's attention piqued. "Sir Elliot?"

Jasper folded the paper and tucked it into his trouser pocket. "The MP Niles Foster was aide to."

She returned to the desk, no longer eager to leave the department. "Sir Elliot was supposed to be our guest speaker last night at the WEA meeting. He canceled at the last minute."

Jasper frowned. "That's interesting." And by interesting, he meant odd. Leo could hear it in his tone. "I'll speak to him about it."

There it was—the small twinge of jealousy that she'd felt time and again ever since January, when she and Jasper had come together to solve the deaths of four people after a locket was stolen from a body in her uncle's morgue. Leo had enjoyed hunting down the killer with him, even though she and Jasper had been held at gunpoint and come close to becoming victims themselves. Then again, in March, when she had witnessed a woman die by acute arsenic poisoning, Leo had joined Jasper in unraveling a revenge plot. It had been dangerous, yes. But also riveting. And now, she found herself wishing there was some reason for her to speak to Sir Elliot too. Or to go along with Jasper for his interview.

But there wasn't a reason. And she shouldn't want to be near Jasper at all.

If only her mind and heart could stop being so conflicted, it would make things so much simpler.

Leo started away again, and again, she turned back.

If she didn't acknowledge his help in freeing her from the upstairs holding room, she'd only look and feel churlish. "Thank you," she said, trying to meet his eye with difficulty. "For your help."

She left before he could say anything in response.

Chapter Nine

"Wipe your feet." A hatchet-faced maid stood in front of Jasper, preventing him from taking another step into Sir Elliot Payne's kitchen until he abided her command.

He'd first gone to the front door of the enormous townhouse, but one look from the footman and he'd been ordered to the service entrance used by tradesmen before having the door shut in his face. *Bloody aristocracy.* Even the servants were snobs.

"Better still, you can remove your shoes," the maid said after Jasper had made perfunctory swipes of his soles on the bristled floor mat. "The floors have just been swept, and I won't have you dropping dirt all over the place."

He stood tall and met her haughty stare. "I am not removing my shoes, madam. Take me to your employer. I've questions for him regarding one of his aides."

She sniffed and, though standing a full head shorter than Jasper, managed to look down her nose at him. He could only imagine the reception she would have given him had he not gone home first to bathe, shave, and put on a change of clothes. There, he'd given his ruined coat to Mrs. Zhao and asked her to buy him another with the pound note that had been left in his pocket. She had not been pleased to see that a perfectly good suit coat had been treated so poorly.

"Wait here," the maid said.

He remained where he stood for several minutes while she whispered to a footman, who then disappeared into the main house to announce the detective inspector to Sir Elliot. Jasper would have rather gone to Niles Foster's bachelor's rooms near Parliament to search through his belongings than come to this fine home on Park Lane. Questioning a knighted member of Parliament, however, was a task for a lead inspector. And considering Elliot Payne had been set to give a speech to the WEA on the same night his aide drowned, Jasper was curious as to why Sir Elliot had canceled on short notice.

After receiving Jasper's update that morning, Detective Chief Inspector Dermot Coughlan had agreed that an inquest was warranted on the drowning case, and while they awaited word on the postmortem findings, they were to begin their investigation.

The footman returned to the kitchen, his white-gloved hands clasped behind his back. "This way," he directed solemnly.

Jasper followed him through the home's corridors, noting similar features to his own home on Charles Street. Ornate crown molding, thick Aubusson carpets, intricate woodwork and paneling. This home, however, had a fresher appearance, with touches of elegance and wealth that Gregory Reid had not been able to lavish upon his own home. A copper's income, even that of a Chief Superintendent, would not have allowed for it. How the bloody hell a detective inspector's wages were supposed to maintain a house and servant often kept Jasper awake at night. But that tight spot was something to think about some other time.

The footman entered a small study, and Jasper followed on his heels.

"Ah. Detective Inspector Reid from Scotland Yard," an older gentleman said as he stood from behind his desk. He was somewhere in his fifties, agile and distinguished in appearance, with a head of thick, silver hair, free of the pomade many men used.

"Sir Elliot," Jasper replied. "Thank you for seeing me."

The knight dismissed the footman and gestured toward a pair of leather club chairs in front of a hearth. He came out from behind his desk to take one. Jasper didn't like to sit but relented, perching on the edge of the seat cushion.

"What are your questions about, Inspector?"

"Your aide, Niles Foster."

Sir Elliot settled his elbows on the arms of the chair and laced his fingers. "I do hope he hasn't gotten into any trouble with the police."

"Would it come as a surprise to you if he had?"

He would inform the man of Foster's death momentarily, but here was a small window of opportunity for him to glean something about the aide before the revelation was made.

"It would, yes," the MP replied thoughtfully. "Oh, I know he is young, and young men are prone to trouble, but Niles has been professional and dependable. Of course, what he gets up to when he isn't at work…" He opened his hands, palms raised, as if to say, *who is to know?*

"When was the last time you saw Mr. Foster?" Jasper asked.

He laced his fingers again and frowned in thought. "Yesterday. Early afternoon. Inspector, how has my aide come to your attention?"

There was no reason to delay the news any longer.

"Niles Foster was found dead this morning. I'm investigating his death."

The knight dropped his hands to the armrests, his expression opening with genuine astonishment. "My God. Are you certain it is him?"

"He's been identified."

Sir Elliot stood. Paused, as if not quite knowing what to do next. Then, he retook his seat. "The poor man. How did he die?"

"I'm still waiting on the postmortem results, but at the moment, it appears he drowned."

The knight repeated that last—*drowned*—as if the word did not make sense.

"Where was this?" he then asked. But Jasper knew better than to allow the person he was questioning to seize the reins.

"Sir Elliot, I'm looking into Mr. Foster's final hours and what might have led to his death. You say you last saw him yesterday, early in the afternoon. Can you provide a specific time?"

He blinked and nodded. "Yes, yes. Of course. Let me see. Niles informed me that he had an appointment and that he would not be present when I emerged from chambers. I went in at one o'clock, so that was the last time I saw him."

"Did he say anything about the appointment? Where it was, or with whom?"

He shook his head. "I don't become personal with my aides. What they do in their off-hours is their business."

It was understandable. A man as important as Sir Elliot Payne wasn't likely to care about Niles Foster's private life.

"How did he seem before he left? In good spirits?"

He shrugged, and his expression was one of ignorance. "I suppose. I noticed nothing amiss."

Jasper thought of Foster's appearance. "Did he have any bruising on his face?"

This seemed to interest Sir Elliot. "Bruising? None at all. I thought you said he drowned?"

"It appears he met with some violence beforehand." The bruising had looked fresh, and now Jasper knew for certain Foster had received the beating after one o'clock in the afternoon. What he wanted to know was if the man had been alive or dead when he went into the duck pond. The ormolu clock in the knight's study read a quarter past noon. Claude might have performed the postmortem exam by now.

"Did Foster associate with other parliamentary aides? Clerks?"

"Not that I am aware of, but as I said, I was not on familiar terms with him," Sir Elliot answered. "He never caused any fuss."

"Didn't he? I've been told his argument with Viscount Hayes outside chambers last week was loud and very public."

The MP hitched his chin. "I heard of their dispute, though I didn't witness it myself. I should think you would wish to speak to Lord Hayes about it."

That Niles Foster had been found in the viscount's duck pond wasn't something Jasper wanted to share. It didn't look good for Oliver. Of course, Sir Elliot would eventually learn of it anyhow.

"Thank you, I will." He stood. "One more thing, Sir Elliot. A woman has been arrested in connection with the bombings at Scotland Yard two days ago. Mrs. Geraldine Stewart, with whom, I am told, you are acquainted."

He furrowed his brow. "Mrs. Stewart? I cannot believe it."

"You were to attend the Women's Equality Alliance meeting last night but canceled shortly before," Jasper said, disinclined to reveal where he'd gotten this information. "Can you tell me where you were instead?"

The MP didn't seem to have any motive for harming his aide, but it would be good to have his alibi, nonetheless.

"Yes, it was unfortunate to have to cancel so late in the day, but another meeting came up that I could not miss. I had a message delivered to Mrs. Stewart, giving her my apologies."

"With whom did you meet?"

Sir Elliot seemed perturbed by the pointed question but gave an answer just the same. "Sir Charles Ralston. A fellow member of the House of Commons."

Jasper made a note of the name. He would, of course, need to run the name down and verify Sir Elliot had been with him last evening.

"From what I hear, you were to speak in support of the women's suffrage movement," Jasper said.

Sir Elliot, still seated in the leather club chair with his legs crossed, rotated his left foot in slow circles. "It is only a matter of time before women can vote. I am a progressive, after all. Labor usually is," he added. "It's the Tories who are perpetually stuck a decade in the past."

"Do you think her a violent sort?"

He kept his foot swirling as if in deep thought. "I never saw it. But she is quite passionate about women's equality, and when passions run high… Well, one never knows, does one?" He sighed. "Mr. Stewart won't come out well in any of this. Surely, it will reflect poorly on him."

Jasper hadn't yet thought of the husband. "What is his business?"

"Banking." Sir Elliot seemed to come to attention. "These two cases aren't connected, I presume?"

He answered no, but there was at least a singular thread linking them: Sir Elliot. To what end wasn't clear. Maybe it was truly nothing at all. A coincidence. Though Jasper hated that word.

Thanking the knight for his time, he left the study and exited through the front door onto Park Lane. Several cabs, already hired out, passed by before one stopped at his signal. He directed the driver to Spring Street.

It was a warm, bright day, with hardly a cloud in the sky. However, a chill settled under his skin when he entered the morgue. Even the lobby was cool, and in the postmortem room, the old vestry's natural temperature reminded him of a raw February morning. It was desirable in a morgue, of course. In the height of summer, ice blocks would be brought in to help maintain the chill. But in the end, even ice could not ward off the stink of dead bodies during July and August.

"Inspector, I thought I might be seeing you soon," Claude said as he covered a body with a sheet. Several corpses were lined up on autopsy tables. *The springtime influx,* the older man had called it before. People would begin to emerge from winter solitude, and the unlucky would meet with dire circumstances, ending up here.

Jasper listened for the sounds of a typewriter from the back office, but all was silent.

"Is the postmortem on Niles Foster complete?"

"I saw to it straightaway," Claude replied, moving as swiftly as his shuffling gait would allow toward a draped corpse. He folded back the sheet, exposing Foster's face and neck.

"Did he drown?"

"I suspect you know that he did not," Claude replied, glancing mischievously over the rims of his thick spectacles. "A drowning would cause the lungs to fill with water, and there wasn't a drop in either of his. There was, however, evidence of hemopneumothorax in the left pleural cavity—a lethal amount of blood and air eventually leading to cardiovascular collapse." He pulled the sheet lower, revealing a freshly closed incision down the center of the body's pale chest—and two smaller additional slits.

"He was stabbed," Jasper said, feeling like a fool. Had he been fully sober that morning, he might have seen evidence of it when the man was pulled from the water.

"This one pierced the left lung." Claude pointed to one wound, his hand shaking slightly. "The other, the right ventricle of the heart. This is your cause of death, Inspector. Not drowning."

Niles Foster had been put into the pond posthumously then, carried by at least two other men, if the boot prints were an accurate indication. However, more men could have been present, standing away from the edge of the pond.

"What do you make of the ligature marks?" Jasper asked. "The bruising?"

Claude raised up the sheet from the side this time, revealing Niles Foster's arm. It appeared stiff and unnaturally rigid at the joints. "Yes, my niece was quite put out with you for not mentioning these to her this morning. By the way," he looked up again over the rims of his spectacles. "Thank you for getting her out of that spot of trouble. When I found her bed hadn't been slept in, I admit to feeling somewhat panicked."

Claude cared for Leo like he would his own daughter, had he and Flora ever had children. While Flora Feldman suffered a shortage of warm feelings for her niece, her husband clearly adored her. Respected her, too, considering the trust he placed in Leo and her abilities here at the morgue.

"My pleasure," Jasper said, feeling somewhat bashful. He'd nearly lost his temper when he learned she'd been kept at the Yard all night, while Tomlin had gone home to his warm bed, likely with a smirk on his face. Had Tomlin been present that morning and tried to stop her release, Jasper wasn't at all certain he wouldn't have thrown a fist at him.

"I take it Leo noticed the similarities to the marks on John Lloyd?" he remarked.

"She did. Right down to the gash on the cheek." Claude indicated the mark on Niles Foster's left cheek. "It is a perfect match, according to my niece. Look here." He touched the top of the gash. "It is wider here and then narrows considerably as it descends." He let his finger travel down the gash to the tapered endpoint. The shape of the whole thing looked much like a comma.

"The gashes were made with the same signet ring, perhaps," Jasper said, musing over the possibilities. He did not want to connect the two deaths. One a murder, the other a suicide bombing—or at least that was what it appeared to be on the surface.

The ligature marks on Foster's wrists were thin, like Constable Lloyd's. "Tied with some sort of rope?"

"I believe so. The gauge is a match," Claude replied.

Jasper pinched the bridge of his nose. "I have a witness who last saw Foster at one in the afternoon. How long had he been dead when I found him at five o'clock this morning?"

Claude tipped his head back and forth. "Well, it is difficult to say, considering he was found in water, which would alter his body temperature, but considering the state of rigor when I received him this morning, his death occurred somewhere between midnight and four o'clock this morning."

By midnight, most of Oliver's guests had been dropping into oblivion. Jasper had been too. With a twist of guilt in the pit of his stomach, he thought of Azure and the time he'd spent in his cups with her. Quickly, he pushed her from his mind and focused on a question he wanted answered: Why had someone traveled out to Kensington to dump Niles Foster's body in Oliver's duck pond? There was a purpose behind it. If Jasper could but grasp the answer, he was certain more answers would emerge.

He'd been silent for a few moments, during which the quiet of the morgue began to rub against him like a friction. He looked to the door of the back office. "Where is Leo?"

"It was the strangest thing, really," Claude said while pulling up the sheet to cover Foster's face. "I was finishing the examination when she said she needed to see Miss Brooks."

The sutures closing the postmortem incision looked precise and neat. Jasper wondered if they'd been done by Leo's steady hand. Claude's own hands shook often, though he tried to conceal it by clasping them behind his back.

"Why did she wish to see Miss Brooks?"

Claude's bushy white brows rose in half-moons over his eyes. "She didn't say, but I know my niece, Inspector. When she first saw this man's face…" He nodded toward Niles Foster. "She recognized him."

Chapter Ten

When Leo finally arrived at the morgue after being sprung from Scotland Yard, grating thoughts of Inspector Tomlin and the humiliation of being held overnight so preoccupied her mind that she'd paid little attention to the body her uncle was standing over in the postmortem room: the dead man Jasper had discovered floating in Lord Hayes's duck pond.

After assuring Claude she was perfectly well after her ordeal, he'd turned back to the task of removing the corpse's clothing. It was then that Leo saw the dead man's face. Immediately, her memory brought forth another image—one of this same man, identified as Niles Foster, though in her memory, he'd been very much alive. Leo had seen him before inside Eddie Bloom's club, Striker's Wharf.

She'd held her tongue, but after noting the gash on the man's cheek, his bruised left eye and ligature marks on his wrists for the coroner's report, Leo had made a hasty exit from the morgue. She'd cited hunger and a longing for clean, fresh clothes as her reasons to return to Duke Street. And she had indeed gone there for those things. But she had swiftly departed again, this time heading for Dita's home.

Dita and her father, Sergeant Byron Brooks, resided on a working-class street in Covent Garden in a terrace house that had always seemed warm and cozy. Several years before, when Leo had been on her way to visit Gregory Reid at Scotland Yard, she'd witnessed a constable outside the carriages department stepping into the path of a young, brown-skinned woman. She hadn't known Dita back then, and later, Leo learned that Dita had been attempting to deliver her father's forgotten flask of tea when the constable had started to harass her. Without hesitation, Dita had opened the flask and splashed it onto the hems of his blue woolen trousers. He'd shouted, calling her a *lunatic coolie*, but Dita whisked past him and into the building without batting an eyelash. Leo had waited for her to reemerge from the building, and when she did, she'd approached her.

"Was that tea you splashed onto that horrible constable's trousers?"

Dita had grinned impishly. "Yes, though I wish it had been whisky so that his superior might smell liquor on him and give him the sack."

Ever since then, they'd remained close friends. Most mornings, Dita would collect Leo on her walk toward Whitehall Place and Scotland Yard, and whenever she could, she convinced Leo to go out to a music hall or assembly room. Striker's Wharf was their favorite haunt, and she, Dita, and John Lloyd had gone there often together.

Now, what Leo wanted to know was if Dita recalled Niles Foster from the club and if he'd somehow been acquainted with her beau.

Nearly a full minute passed after Leo knocked on the Brooks' front door. Finally, it opened, and her friend let her inside. Dark smudges under Dita's eyes and the red tip of her nose underscored her grief, as did her sluggish movement as she closed the door behind Leo. It was as though all the lively fire that always filled Dita to the brim had drained away entirely.

She returned to what looked to be a well-worn spot in the corner of the sofa. The sitting room was draped in shadows, the curtains drawn to block out the sunlight.

"I should have come before now," Leo said, realizing her misstep in staying away to allow her friend privacy to mourn.

But Dita shook her head, her fingers already grasping a linen handkerchief and pressing it to her nose. "I didn't wish to see anyone. Not even you. I hope that doesn't offend you."

It didn't. Leo understood the desire for solitude with grief. After the Inspector died, she'd craved the time to be alone, if only so that she would not have to speak of her feelings of loss. Mere words could not do it justice. And after learning that Jasper had been the boy in the attic who'd hidden her and that he'd kept the truth from her all these years, she'd closed herself off wholly. Not just to him, but to anyone who might have noticed their strained distance. That had been a different type of loss. Jasper was still alive, of course, but he would never be quite the same again. Not in her eyes, at least.

"Perhaps we could take a walk along the Strand?" she

suggested. Fresh air and sun might help lift her friend from some of the fog of heartache, although Dita would have to exchange her paisley dressing gown for proper clothing.

Dita shook her head. "I can barely get out of bed in the morning. Father forced me to at least make it to this room before he left for his shift today."

Leo stood. "Then I'll make us tea."

She went to the kitchen, a room she was familiar with by now, and put the kettle on the hob. Normally, Dita would not have allowed her to do any such thing. But several minutes later, when Leo reappeared with two beakers of strong black tea, her friend was still curled up in the corner of the sofa, her expression slack, her eyes distant.

She placed the cup in Dita's hand and sat beside her again. "There is something I need to ask you."

Holding the cup to her lips, letting the steam drift in front of her face, Dita's attention sharpened for the first time since Leo had arrived. "The answer is no. I still refuse to believe John would have carried that bomb toward Scotland Yard. I don't care what the evidence shows; I know him." She took a shaky breath and turned her face into the steam. "*Knew* him."

"That wasn't what I was going to ask," Leo said.

Dita's smooth brow crinkled. "It wasn't? Forgive me. My father has been relentless. Though not half as relentless as Inspector Tomlin."

Sergeant Brooks must have been acutely mortified that his daughter's beau stood accused of being a traitor. And Tomlin was a tactless brute.

"No, I wanted to ask if you recognize the name Niles Foster."

Dita blinked and tucked her chin. Before she could answer, a heavy rapping on the front door interrupted them. Leo set down her tea. "I'll see who it is."

She had every intention of turning away the caller, but then she opened the door. Jasper loomed over her on the front step, his expression stern.

"How do you know Niles Foster?" he asked, forgoing a greeting altogether.

It appeared he'd been to the morgue and that her uncle had observed her reaction to the body and mentioned it to Jasper.

Leo stepped aside, allowing him in. "How did you find this address?"

He'd never been there before.

"I am a detective inspector, Leo," he grumbled, whisking off his hat. "I have resources. Now, tell me, how are you acquainted with my dead body?"

She peered at him, taken aback by the odd wording. He sighed. "You know what I mean."

Closing the door, she gestured toward the sitting room and led the way. Jasper slowed upon entering and nodded to Dita. "Miss Brooks. Forgive me for intruding, but I have a few questions for Miss Spencer."

"And they are related, I believe, to my question for you, Dita," Leo said, retaking her seat.

Dita sat forward, placing her slippered feet on the carpet. "About this Niles Foster fellow?"

Jasper stepped around the sofa but remained standing, his hat clutched in his hand. "You know him?"

"No. Leo just spoke his name now."

It was time for her to explain.

"I did not know him personally, but I did recognize his face when I saw him in the morgue."

Dita gasped. "Do you mean to say he is dead?"

"Yes," Leo replied. Then cautiously added, "Murdered."

The stab wounds to his chest had been the cause of death, and the dumping of the body in the viscount's pond, an attempt at a ruse.

"Where did you see Mr. Foster before today, Leo?" Jasper asked, returning to his line of inquiry. He never was easily put off a topic.

"Striker's Wharf," she answered, expecting the souring of his gaze. He disliked the club because it was operated by a criminal named Eddie Bloom. And he especially disliked that she and Dita went there often.

"Of course it would be there," he grumbled. "How is it that you recall him?"

"Not the man who approached our table last time? The handsome one who asked you to dance?" Dita said, her alarm increasing.

Jasper peered between them. "You danced with my murder victim?"

Leo held up her hands. "Not him, Dita. This was the man we saw being tossed out of the back room." Reluctantly, she explained to Jasper, "It's where Mr. Bloom operates a casino."

His chest inflated as he drew a deep breath. "Please tell me you do not visit that part of the club."

"I'm not a fool, Inspector Reid. And what would I gamble with anyhow? My vast riches?"

He only deepened his glare. Swiftly, she translated the

silence: There were more treasures to gamble with than just money. Especially for a woman.

"I do remember him," Dita said, her melancholy seeming to clear. "This was just last week, wasn't it? He crashed into a server, upending a tray of drinks."

"John was with us at the time," Leo added. "He laughed and called the man a fool for trying to cheat in Bloom's casino."

After finding the heron and fox token in John's pocket and then hearing his brother speak of his new, expensive purchases, she'd presumed his vice had been gambling. Now, she wondered if John Lloyd and Niles Foster had one more thing in common besides having been bound and beaten just hours before their deaths, with matching gashes on their cheeks.

"Dita, did John ever gamble in the back room at Striker's Wharf?" she inquired.

Leo had never seen him enter the casino, but she also had not always accompanied the couple to the club on the Lambeth wharves.

Her friend twisted the handkerchief between her fingers and cast her eyes down to her lap. "Yes."

Jasper straightened. "So, PC Lloyd and Niles Foster both frequented Eddie Bloom's casino. Were they acquainted?"

"I don't know. John never mentioned his name. And really, he said he'd only gambled there a handful of times." Dita tried to flatten the hankie, her fingers trembling. "I didn't like his habit. We had cross words about it, but… He did win often, and you know how meager a constable's wages are. John just wanted to put aside enough for when we..." Her voice cut off, and Leo reached out to cover her hand with her own.

Inspector Tomlin had already questioned Dita extensively, and she didn't want to inflict any more strain on her friend. But the connection between the two men needed to be resolved.

"John's brother said he'd been associating with men of low character," Leo began. "Did you ever see him with people like that? Men you were concerned about?"

Dita shook her head firmly. "No. Never. You can't believe anything Charlie says. He simply hates that John chose to join the Met."

It was what Leo had sensed too.

"Odds are that PC Lloyd and Niles Foster met while gambling at Striker's Wharf," Jasper said.

As the daughter of a police sergeant, and a matron at Scotland Yard, Dita was attuned to the workings of an investigation. She was also naturally clever. "You believe their deaths are somehow related."

Jasper sighed and nodded.

She sat forward. "Why?"

"Miss Brooks, when was the last time you saw PC Lloyd before he died?"

He was clearly avoiding having to explain about the matching marks on the bodies, which might further upset her. Leo appreciated the care Jasper was taking with her friend.

"The previous afternoon, I think." She furrowed her brow in thought. "Yes. He met me for tea."

"What did he do that evening?" Leo asked.

Dita's brow smoothed. Her dark brown irises met

Leo's gaze, her pupils narrowing to pinpricks. "He mentioned he might go out. To Striker's Wharf."

A current of possibility straightened Leo's spine. She and Jasper exchanged a meaningful glance.

"I don't know if he truly did go, though," Dita said.

"Thank you, Miss Brooks," Jasper said, moving toward the front hall. "I'll take my leave."

Leo got to her feet and followed him out of the room. Softly, she said, "Mr. Bloom would know if John was there that night."

Jasper opened the door. "I am aware of that."

"And he might know more about why Niles Foster was thrown out of the back room."

He slapped his hat onto his head. "Astoundingly, I'd already considered that too."

As usual, she ignored his bit of sarcasm. "Are you going there now?"

He stayed on the threshold of the door. "You are not coming with me, Leo."

A knot kinked her stomach. She'd expected that response, and the impulse to argue was on the tip of her tongue. But then, she remembered that she shouldn't want to be near Jasper. Not even for a curious twist in an investigation.

She hitched her chin. "I have no wish to accompany you, Inspector." Oh, how it galled her to fib. "I was merely going to inform you that the man who threw Mr. Foster from the gambling room was tall, fair-haired, and had a drooping left eyelid. He may work for Mr. Bloom. Best of luck."

She made to shut the door, but Jasper put out a hand to block it. She relented and waited for him to speak.

"Lewis said you didn't want him to fetch me this morning when he discovered you were being held at the Yard. Why?"

She kept her hand on the knob, eager for him to be gone. If only so she wouldn't change her mind and beg him to take her with him to Bloom's club. He was so desperate for her to speak to him that he might even allow it. But it would be too unscrupulous of a ploy, and she refused to truly consider it.

"It wasn't necessary," she said with a nonchalant shrug. "I was perfectly fine."

"No, you were not. You were being held without cause."

"I'm sure Inspector Tomlin would disagree."

"Admit it, Leo. You were being stubborn," he said.

Her patience snapped, and Leo pinned him with a glare. "I did not need to be rescued. Not by you."

Guilt instantly doused her temper, which had kindled far too quickly. Jasper moved from the threshold onto the front step, his expression flattening. She nearly parted her lips to apologize when he tipped the brim of his bowler hat and replied, "That's not what it looked like this morning."

He turned on his heel and walked away, and Leo slammed the door.

Chapter Eleven

Detective Sergeant Lewis had already returned from Niles Foster's bachelor's rooms when Jasper arrived at the CID. The laborers rebuilding the wall in the department had stopped their work for tea, giving the cramped space, still dusted by rubble and debris, a respite from all the noise.

"What did you find?" Jasper asked as he tossed his bowler onto the shared desk. His nerves were still bundled tight from his visit with Leo and Miss Brooks. Not only was there now a strong link between John Lloyd and Niles Foster, one that centered around gambling at Striker's Wharf, but Leo's waspish irritation with him was truly starting to get under his skin.

Yes, he deserved her anger. He'd concealed a vital piece of the truth surrounding the most significant event of her life from her. A moment in time that had haunted her as well as him. Jasper knew there was a good chance she would never forgive him.

But *hell*. He was not ready to give up.

"Learned some interesting things at Foster's rooms," Lewis answered.

He was seated at the desk, a half-eaten cheese sandwich in newsprint open before him. His wife sent him with a bite to eat with tea every day, but Jasper had yet to meet her or their two little boys. A part of him wondered if it was because Lewis did not truly like him and was only cordial since they worked together. It was also possible the detective sergeant simply wanted to keep his family shielded from his work. That would be understandable; he dealt with criminals and murderers every day, the real bottom-feeders of London.

"His landlady had warned him last week she'd give him the toss if he couldn't pay his yearly lease," Lewis said.

The man's bachelor's rooms weren't far from the Thames and Houses of Parliament. In that busy part of the city, there were plenty of men looking for lodging. A landlady couldn't be faulted for evicting a lodger who couldn't pay.

"How much was the lease?"

"Fifty pounds," Lewis answered.

Jasper nodded, the row between Oliver and Foster now becoming clear. "He asked Lord Hayes for that amount last week, which the viscount refused."

"It isn't cheap lodgings, but a single man with a good paying job shouldn't have been so hard up," Lewis commented as he picked up his sandwich and looked at it with lackluster interest.

"According to Hayes, Foster was an inveterate gambler." Jasper hesitated to share what Leo had imparted, but his sergeant needed every bit of information if he was to be truly effective. "Miss Spencer recognized his body. She'd seen him at Striker's Wharf previously. It appears he was tossed out of Bloom's back room, which is reserved for gambling."

Lewis chewed his sandwich, his forehead creasing. Once he swallowed, he said, "Miss Spencer witnessed this?"

Jasper nodded, and before anything more could be said about Leo and her frequenting a criminal's nightclub, he asked, "What more did you learn from the landlady?"

Lewis dropped his sandwich to the newsprint and brushed his hands together, dislodging crumbs. "It was her daughter who had something more interesting to impart. She caught me on my way out. It seems she and Foster had a...beneficial arrangement." He tucked his chin and winked to indicate this arrangement was of an intimate nature.

"And?"

"Foster appealed to her when her mum told him to pack his things. Claimed that he'd come by some information that was going to make him a small fortune."

Jasper braced his hands against the desk's edge. "What information?"

"She didn't know. He never said. But if it was information he had, he probably planned to use it to blackmail someone."

Jasper agreed. "What did you find among his belongings?"

"Nothing much. Clothes, a few photographs, some folios and papers that looked to be from his work. I've sent Price and Drake–to collect the boxes containing Foster's possessions."

He anticipated the tedious work of poring through

those boxes later, perhaps well into the evening. Jasper had no other plans, though. It was curiously freeing not to have to worry about whether he'd given enough time to Constance. Odd, how only now could he clearly feel the weight of that struggle no longer resting on his shoulders.

Lewis finished his lunch and drained his beaker of tea. "What's next?"

"I suppose I should tell you that I've found a connection between John Lloyd and Niles Foster."

It had the expected effect—Lewis went still in his chair, staring. The leftover crumb clinging to his mustache accentuated the sergeant's dumbfounded expression.

Quickly, Jasper explained about the matching wrist ligature marks, indicating they'd both been bound in the hours before their deaths; the similar gashes on their left cheeks; their swollen, blackened left eyes; and their shared connection to Bloom's backroom casino.

Lewis drummed his fingers on the pitted desktop. "You really don't want to get involved in Tomlin's bombing case, guv."

"You don't need to convince me of that. But it might have some bearing on *our* case and cannot go ignored."

The detective sergeant exhaled. "Tomlin won't like it."

Jasper thought of the surly detective inspector and found he quite enjoyed the idea of being a thorn in his side. "All the more reason to press forward."

The laborers began to reconvene at the hole in the exterior wall of headquarters, and Jasper and Lewis gathered their coats and hats to leave. Their natural next step was to pay a call on Eddie Bloom's club across the river on the Lambeth wharves.

The long, rambling structure built upon a pier had a distinct air of neglect during daylight hours, while at night, gasoliers and brackets throwing off golden light disguised it as a posh place. Though it wasn't yet early evening, Bloom already had muscle guarding the entrance. Jasper and Lewis opened their warrant cards for the man to see. He barely looked at them.

"Mr. Bloom is busy."

Jasper didn't have the patience for stonewalling today.

"I'm sure he can find a minute to speak to us," Jasper said. "Unless it is more convenient for him to be escorted to Scotland Yard for an interview."

The sentry held firm his unimpressed glower for a moment longer, then went inside. A minute later, he returned and gestured for them to follow him.

They found Bloom at a table with three liveried wait-staff, white gloves on as they handled a variety of glassware.

"Back again, Inspector?" he said jovially. "I'd say it's a pleasure, but I've been told not to lie to the police."

Bloom might have been in his mid- to late forties, but he exuded a youthful vigor that most men his age tended to have already lost. He dressed well, slicked back his full head of jet hair with pomade, and wore a consistently bemused expression. It made him appear affable to those who were less aware of his true nature. Although his syndicate was not as far-reaching as some of the others in London, it was still strong. Eddie Bloom was not a man to be crossed.

"We have questions about two of your regular patrons," Jasper said. "John Lloyd and Niles Foster."

Bloom set a wine glass down and stripped the white

gloves from his hands. "I have many patrons. Am I supposed to know all their names?"

The last time Jasper had been here, questioning Bloom after one of his patrons had been poisoned, he'd certainly seemed to know a lot about Leonora Spencer. Her family's brutal murders sixteen years earlier. Her closeness to Jasper's father, Gregory Reid, and of course, to Jasper himself.

"John Lloyd was often here with Miss Spencer and her friend, Miss Brooks," he provided.

Bloom's expression lightened. "Ah, Miss Spencer, is it? I remember now. Lloyd was that PC that got himself blown up a couple days back."

He'd known the constable's name all along. Eddie Bloom didn't miss much.

"What can I possibly tell you about him, Inspector?"

Jasper reached into his waistcoat pocket and retrieved the gaming token Leo had given him the other night. He hadn't delivered it to Tomlin as he'd intended.

"Is this one of your markers?" He showed him the face of the marker stamped with the heron and the fox. Most establishments kept their gaming markers consistent, with some even customizing the cast.

Bloom gave it a look. Deliberated. Then nodded once. "It is."

To deny it would have been folly; they could easily prove otherwise with a look at his casino room.

"Was John Lloyd here three nights ago?" Lewis asked.

"I couldn't say for certain. This here is a busy establishment. I don't keep tabs on all my patrons' comings and goings."

Jasper knew Bloom wasn't going to like his next question, but he didn't have time or patience for finesse.

"I think you'd remember a police constable at your gaming tables. Especially if that constable was turning a blind eye to anything he wasn't meant to see."

Bloom's amused façade vanished. "Are you accusing me of paying your bobby to look the other way?"

"Was he receptive?" Jasper replied, feeling a touch of hedonistic pleasure at being able to rile Bloom.

"I'm offended. I don't have a thing to cover up around here." He came forward a step. "It's your bobbies who might have an indiscretion or two to hide."

Jasper took the dangled bait. "Lloyd specifically?"

Bloom shrugged. "Tell me about this other bloke," he said, avoiding the question. "What was his name?"

"Niles Foster," Lewis said. "A parliamentary aide."

Bloom crowed a laugh. His serving staff, still looking on, did the same. However, Jasper couldn't tell if they were genuinely amused or if they only knew it was wise to follow their boss's lead.

"My place attracts all sorts these days," he said. "How would I have known him?"

"Mr. Foster was ejected from your back room about a week ago," Jasper answered. "He was forcibly thrown out by another man, described as being tall and fair-haired, his left eyelid drooping lower than the right."

In his peripheral vision, he saw Lewis shoot him a startled look at the precise description.

"Is the man I described employed by you?" Jasper asked.

Bloom started for the bar along the wall, where his bartender was polishing the top with a rag. "He's not one of mine. You're talking about Olaf," Bloom said, tapping the glossy walnut to order a drink. The bartender produced a shot of whisky in a blink.

"A German?" Lewis asked.

"A Swede," Bloom answered, tossing back his drink. "A heavy for Barry Reubens."

The name lit an unexpected spark in Jasper. Barry Reubens was the head of a motley gang out of Spitalfields, known as the Angels.

"You associate with the Angels?" Jasper asked.

Bloom shrugged. "I've got nothing against them or any other outfit, so long as they don't do business or cause trouble at my place. These are established rules, Inspector."

Two months ago, when Andrew Carter's new wife was poisoned at Striker's Wharf, tension between Bloom and the Carters had ensued. But the truth—that her murder had been planned by someone wholly unassociated with any crime syndicate—seemed to have alleviated that tension.

"What complaint did Olaf have with Niles Foster that night?" Jasper asked.

"No idea. Whatever this Foster bloke did to get on Olaf's bad side, it's nothing to do with me. You'll have to ask Olaf."

Approaching Barry Reubens, however, wouldn't be simple. Spitalfields was a den of thieves and criminals. Police officers patrolled there in pairs, sometimes as trios, for their safety. While the Carters had worked to elevate themselves in society, the Angels had stayed true to their cutthroat roots. By Bloom's smirk, he knew as much.

"I'd like to speak with your dealers to see if they can

recall PC Lloyd at their tables three nights ago," Jasper said. He'd inquire about Niles Foster as well, but it would be a waste of time. If Bloom instructed them to stay quiet, they wouldn't go against him.

"They'll be here tonight, Inspector. Do come back and enjoy yourself," he replied with a falsely bright grin.

Thanking Bloom for his time, they left, emerging onto the wharf in quickly warming sunshine. The briny scent of the Thames held a note of rot and waste.

It illustrated Jasper's thoughts on Eddie Bloom perfectly.

Chapter Twelve

Carlisle Street was part of an upscale neighborhood near Soho Square, just south of Oxford Street. As Leo approached the front door to the Stewart household, she felt as out of her depth as she had the previous evening. This time, however, the house was serene, bathed in afternoon sunlight, without the busy murmuring of voices emanating from within.

After Geraldine's dramatic arrest and the horrific charges levied against her, Leo wondered how many of the women who were present last night would continue in their support of her and the WEA. As much as some ladies believed in the vote for women, they believed more devoutly in decency and decorum. For many, having their leader carted away in a police wagon would be insupportable.

Not for Dita, however. Before Leo had left her, she'd written a brief note to Geraldine. In it, she reassured her that she did not believe the WEA leader was involved in any way with the bombing that had taken John's life and that she would support her publicly whenever the time called for it. "It isn't much," Dita had said tearfully. "But I want her to know she still has friends."

It had given Leo a good reason to stop by the Stewarts' home. If she could ask about the valise that had been stored in the attic, all the better.

Leo brought the brass knocker down onto its plate and only then considered that she, too, had been carted away in a police wagon. Perhaps Mr. Stewart would not wish to admit her. The door opened, and the maid, whom Leo had seen whenever she came to WEA meetings, gave her a questioning once-over. She waited for Leo to speak.

"I have a note for Mrs. Stewart—"

"The lady of the house isn't in," the maid said sharply.

"Yes, I am aware. I was here last evening."

She lifted her nose, as if scenting something. "I know. You were the other one they took away."

Leo wasn't sure what expression to form. Not a smile, for she wasn't proud of having been arrested. Yet, she also wasn't ashamed, so she would not look remorseful either.

"That's correct. I have a note from a mutual friend who wanted to get word to Mrs. Stewart—"

"As I said, she isn't in," she said, interrupting again, this time with a tone of finality.

"If I could leave the note for her?" Leo said, taking the small card from her pocket.

The maid flared her nostrils as if she were about to be handed a dead mouse.

"Betty, who is it?" Another voice sounded from behind the maid. One which Leo recognized.

Mrs. Emma Bates, Geraldine's sister-in-law, appeared over the maid's shoulder. Her forehead wrinkled with surprise. “Oh, Miss Spencer. Why, hello. I didn’t expect a call from you today. Do step aside, Betty. Miss Spencer is to be invited in.” Mrs. Bates shooed the stern maid out of her sentry post.

“Thank you,” Leo said as she entered the foyer.

The tasteful décor spoke of refined affluence and understated elegance. It was the kind of wealth where one felt welcomed rather than towered over. However, her attention tripped as she noticed a few changes to the foyer since the previous evening. A Wedgwood vase had been moved from a credenza to another table next to the stairs; an urn that was used to hold umbrellas and walking sticks was gone entirely; and the placement of two paintings on the walls had been swapped. Leo’s memory held a clear image of the arrangements as they’d been, and she puzzled over the changes as the maid assisted her with removing her capelet. Mrs. Bates then led her to a sitting room.

A small fire leapt in the grate, and a tea service was already laid out on a table. An embroidery hoop with a nearly completed floral design had been set down on the seat of a chair. Mrs. Bates picked it up and put it aside before retaking her seat, while calling for Betty to bring more tea. Leo lowered herself onto the adjacent sofa.

“I must say, I did not know what to expect after last night’s episode,” Mrs. Bates began. “Those awful police officers, taking you and Geraldine away as if you were both criminals. It was utterly demeaning.” She drew in a shaky breath as if to calm her temper. “I am happy to see you were released from custody. Pray, what did they ask of you?”

“Nothing, in the end. I believe Inspector Tomlin

simply does not like me." Leo didn't want to go too in depth about her night spent at Scotland Yard, so she said, "I've heard that Mrs. Stewart has been taken to Holloway Prison. Has there been any word on how she is faring there?"

Mrs. Bates shook her head, her frustration evident in the hardening of her jaw. "No. And Porter is in such a state. The poor man doesn't know which way is up. He at least had the cognizance to ask me to stay and mind the children."

Leo considered the statement odd. The Stewarts were a wealthy family. Surely, they employed a nanny.

"That is kind of you," she replied rather than ask such a prying question.

"Oh, I adore them. Zachary is the very image of his father, and little Jessamin reminds me so much of my late husband, Hubert, Geraldine's brother," she explained. "I do lament not having any children of my own."

It was a rather intimate topic, and Leo wasn't certain how to respond. She and Mrs. Bates were hardly acquainted. To comment on or ask the circumstances of her childlessness would be offensive. So, she said nothing. However, her lack of a response was apparently also gauche.

"I know what you must be thinking," Mrs. Bates said with light laughter. "To be childless at my age. A sorry state, indeed."

"Not at all," Leo was quick to say. "And you are still quite young, Mrs. Bates."

The woman was in her thirties, pretty, and quite refined. There was every reason to believe she could marry again and bear children, if that was what she desired.

"You are too kind, Miss Spencer. I admit to holding a flame of hope." She leaned forward conspiratorially. "After all, what are we without children?"

Leo stiffened, again feeling trapped by a statement and uncertain how to respond. Her reflexive reaction was to disagree with Mrs. Bates. It wasn't a very feminist point of view. Women were not only here on this earth to bear children. She couldn't help but think that Mrs. Stewart would speak up and say as much, rather than hold her tongue as Leo chose to do.

Thankfully, the maid arrived just then with a fresh pot of tea. Mrs. Bates poured for them and then settled back into her chair. "Now, Miss Spencer, what was it I heard you say about a note for Geraldine?"

Leo set down her cup and retrieved the note she'd returned to her pocket. "Yes. You see, I spoke to her while we were being transported to Scotland Yard. My friend, a matron at the Yard, wrote to her. Her intended was the young police constable—"

A great stomping of feet and giggles converged on the sitting room suddenly, and two children burst in through the open door. A young girl of about five and a boy of seven or eight years of age. The boy held something aloft, out of the little girl's reach.

"Give it back, Zachary!" she complained.

Leo's chest squeezed as she thought of her own older brother, Jacob. The last memory she had of him was nearly identical to this scene. He'd taken her doll, Miss Cynthia, and wouldn't give her back to Leo.

"Jessamin, stop that at once," Mrs. Bates said. "A young lady does not shout or run about the house."

"But Auntie Emma, he's taken my paper doll!"

"I do not care what he has taken; you must mind your manners."

Leo rather thought Zachary should be scolded and made to return the paper doll, but Mrs. Bates didn't say as much.

A young woman in maid's attire hurried in, her face flushed. "My apologies, Mrs. Bates," she said. "Come, children. Your aunt isn't to be disturbed."

She tried to shepherd the children from the room under Mrs. Bates's disapproving gaze, but Jessamin threw back her head and released a wail. Zachary groaned. "Oh, here, take it then." He shoved the paper doll at her and stalked out, but she only continued to cry.

The nanny, Leo presumed, grew even more flustered and all but dragged the little girl from the room.

"Geraldine really was not strict enough with that one," Mrs. Bates said with a heavy sigh as she lifted her teacup. "She was always so busy with her club."

Leo gripped Dita's note a bit tighter as more tension rippled through her. Calling the WEA a *club* was condescending, as was intimating that Geraldine had fallen short somehow in her mothering of Jessamin. Mrs. Bates, Leo began to suspect, was not a true ally.

The front door to the home opened, and from where they sat in the front room, Mr. Stewart was visible as he swept inside.

"I'm home," he called, doffing his hat and coat and handing them to Betty as she rushed to meet him.

Mr. Stewart caught sight of his sister-in-law and Leo

and turned to join them in the sitting room. Mrs. Bates rose to her feet. Leo quickly did as well.

"Good afternoon." Mr. Stewart's eyes filled with recognition. "You are the young woman from last night."

"Miss Spencer," Mrs. Bates provided. "Do sit, Porter. You could do with a spot of tea, I'm sure."

He shook his head and waved a hand. "No, no, Em, I'm fine. Miss Spencer, I'm glad to see you were released from Scotland Yard."

"I am sorry to hear your wife is still being held," she replied.

He rubbed his forehead as if it pained him. "At a prison. I cannot fathom it. I've heard from our solicitor that they are charging her with conspiracy to commit treason."

Mrs. Bates took his arm and forced him to sit upon the sofa. "I won't hear any objection. You'll have tea."

He nodded absentmindedly, strain painting his expression. Leo sat as well.

"Mr. Stewart, has Detective Inspector Tomlin been here, or anyone else from the Metropolitan Police, to inquire about the valise they say was used in the bombing?"

He blinked, as if coming out of a stupor. "Yes. I spoke to him, as unpleasant as it was. I showed him to the attic, where the maid stored Geraldine's luggage. It had been there for years and years, but…it was gone." He paused. "You are acquainted with this inspector?"

Leo wanted to tread carefully. As gentlemanly and welcoming as he had been so far, she doubted Mr. Stewart would continue to be once he knew where she worked and her ties to Scotland Yard.

"I have friends within the police force, yes, but Inspector Tomlin is not one of them," she replied. "Mrs. Stewart also told me that the valise should have been in the attic. Do you know of any way someone could have taken it without your knowledge?"

Mrs. Bates handed him his teacup. "We know exactly how it was done. Porter told the inspector too."

His hand shook somewhat as he brought the cup to his lips. "A housebreaking. About a month ago."

Leo's interest piqued. "Did you report it to the police?"

"At the time? No." He frowned into his tea. "However, now I realize it would have been prudent."

"How were you to know?" Mrs. Bates asked as if to appease him. She remained standing near his side, ready to assist.

"Nothing was taken, or so we thought," he went on. "Geraldine and I had brought the children to the park for the afternoon. When we returned, we found the back door to the mews lane open. A pane of glass in the door had been smashed."

It was something a maid or cook would have noticed. "Was Betty present? Or any other servants?"

But Mr. Stewart shook his head and explained that it had been a Sunday, when their small staff all had the afternoon off.

"We searched the house but found no sign we'd been burgled. The safe in my study had not been touched, and none of Geraldine's jewelry was missing."

That was very odd indeed. Why would anyone break into their home but take nothing except the valise?

"Inspector Tomlin did not believe you, I presume," she said.

"He did not," Mr. Stewart said. He then seemed to startle. "I'm sorry, Miss Spencer. I didn't ask why you've come."

She extended Dita's note to him. "From one of your wife's supporters. I thought you might be able to pass it along to her…if you see her?"

He took the small envelope and gave a sad nod. "Of course. Thank you."

As the crackling fire in the grate became the loudest sound in the room, Leo had the distinct feeling she had overstayed her tenuous welcome.

She placed her cup and saucer onto the table. "I'll be going. Thank you for the tea, Mrs. Bates."

"I insist you call me Emma," she said. Leo welcomed her to call her Leonora in return, as it was the polite thing to do.

As any gentleman would, Mr. Stewart shot to his feet to see her out. Standing so tall over her, Leo was struck by his handsome looks and graceful figure. A harmonious balance of polished masculinity. It was clear Mrs. Bates doted on him, and Leo thought she could see why.

"Thank you for your visit, Miss Spencer," he said as he and Mrs. Bates walked her to the front door. "It's heartening to know my wife still has friends."

Leo nodded, understanding that no matter how things turned out with Geraldine, it would be difficult for them to regain any social standing in London now.

Betty took her plain black capelet from where it had been hung next to a decadent, wine-red, velvet cloak—surely belonging to Emma Bates—and as the maid helped her don it, Leo again peered at the rearranged items in the front hall. This time, she wondered if Mrs. Bates had directed the changes. There was no proof of it, but it was her first thought.

Once on the front step, she turned back as the maid closed the door behind her. Through the prismatic glass of the sidelight window, she made out Emma Bates putting her arm across her brother-in-law's back as she walked him further into the foyer. He truly did seem unmoored with the upheaval surrounding his wife. Mrs. Bates, however, did not. She was entirely in her element, practically relishing the opportunity to run the household and play mother. A dark and wicked thought crept through Leo's mind as she started back along Carlisle Street: Perhaps Mrs. Bates wouldn't mind playing wife to Porter Stewart as well.

Chapter Thirteen

Jasper checked his watch. He'd been waiting underneath the small portico at the front entrance to the morgue for several minutes past the appointed hour. A steady pour of rain emptied over the arched roof, spraying inward whenever the wind gusted.

He'd woken up that morning to the sound of rain pinging off the window glass in his room, and though the day was now closing in on the noon hour, the blustery weather and low-lying mist still made things look and feel like early morning. He could have waited inside after arranging with Claude for Oliver Hayes to view Niles Foster's body. However, he wasn't in the mood to endure more of Leo's icy reception. As soon as Jasper had arrived, she'd turned into the back office and hadn't reemerged.

He would have Oliver formally identify the body, and then Jasper would return to headquarters and the cramped desk where he and Lewis had spent the morning poring through Foster's possessions.

The boxes had been delivered by PC Price and PC

Drake the previous afternoon, and Jasper had taken aside Drake before he could dash off again.

"The time I saw you at Striker's Wharf, you were with PC Lloyd," Jasper reminded the constable. The two had been at the club with Miss Brooks and Leo in January; Drake had been there as Leo's escort.

The constable nodded, nervously shifting his feet.

"Did you go there often with him?"

"No, sir," the PC answered. "Not after that."

"Why not?"

Drake had licked his lips, hesitating. Then checked around the department before lowering his voice. "I didn't want any part of what he was doing. Who he was talking to."

Nodding, Jasper thought he understood. "Bloom? Or someone else?"

"Not Bloom." Looking acutely uncomfortable, he said, "Some tall bloke. A Swede."

Olaf, the man who'd tossed Niles Foster from the casino. So, Lloyd was connected to the Spitalfields Angels too.

"How were Lloyd and this Swede associated?" he asked.

Drake swallowed hard, then with his voice lowered to a rasp, said, "The one time I went with John to the casino room, the Swede fronted him a few bob. He won it back and all, but I had the impression it was a regular thing between them."

If Lloyd had been borrowing gambling money from the Angel, there was a high probability he might have become indebted to him.

"Is there anything else you know about Lloyd's...activities?" Jasper asked. "Anything you've heard?"

Warnock had walked by then, eyeing Jasper and Constable Drake's hushed conversation.

"No. Nothing," Drake was quick to reply. Jasper took pity on him and then, with a jerk of his chin, dismissed him.

That evening, he and Lewis returned to Striker's Wharf in the hope of finding Olaf. They spent nearly three hours at the bar, and Jasper had even entered the casino room, receiving scathing glares from all present. But no one matching the description of Barry Reubens' hired muscle had been at the club.

"Bloom probably tipped him off not to come," Lewis said as they were returning to the north bank of the Thames.

Jasper had known it was a possibility, but they'd needed to take the chance.

After a few moments of quiet in the cab, Lewis had said, "Do you remember the bombing in the cloakroom at Victoria Station last year?"

At Jasper's nod, he'd continued, "An Angel was arrested. He had connections to Clan na Gael. And LaChance has mentioned more than once that they're watching some Angels rumored to be assisting the IRB."

"Are you suggesting the Angels might have been involved with Clan na Gael's strike against the Yard?" Jasper asked.

The detective sergeant had shrugged. "It's something to consider. We have a connection confirmed between Lloyd and a member of the Angels," Lewis said. "If the Angels were helping the Irish, maybe they used Lloyd as a delivery boy."

Jasper had considered the suggestion but ultimately shook his head. "The bomb Lloyd carried was a different make than the ones that detonated later that night," he reminded Lewis. "I don't see how Clan na Gael can be connected."

And yet, for the rest of the evening, he'd tried to think of some proof that would verify Lewis's theory.

Now, rain speckled Jasper's right side as the wind blew in under the portico. With some relief, Oliver Hayes's carriage came into sight and drew alongside the curb. Jasper opened the door to the morgue as Oliver approached, and they entered the lobby.

"Forgive the delay, Reid. I went past Gillman's to arrange for the collection of the body for burial," Oliver explained.

"That's good of you."

It seemed that, with no other family, the funeral arrangements had fallen to Oliver. The bell over the front door had signaled their presence, and now, the viewing room door opened. Claude gestured for them to enter.

"I've already confirmed it is Niles. Is this really necessary?" Oliver asked, again looking pallid.

"It's police protocol," Jasper explained. "It won't take long."

He and Oliver entered the small room, lit by weak daylight coming through a window of milk glass. Claude folded back the top of the sheet covering the body.

Oliver grimaced. "Yes, it is still Niles." Then he asked, "So then, did he drown?"

Claude waited for Jasper to give a nod. The coroner then adjusted his spectacles, something he tended to do before delivering bad news. "He did not drown, my lord. He was stabbed—twice."

The viscount swore softly and looked as though he might be ill. "He was *murdered*?"

Jasper opened the door to the lobby and, with the brief task of the formal identification concluded, ushered his friend from the room.

Leo was waiting for them in the lobby, a paper in her hand. She appeared guarded and serious as she approached Oliver.

"The morgue requires a signature to release the deceased to the appointed funeral service," she explained.

Oliver took the pen and jotted down his signature, but he was still reeling from the news Claude had shared.

"Are you investigating his murder, Reid? Tell me something is being done."

"I'm already following some leads," he assured the viscount. "And I have a few questions for you before you go."

Leo took the signed paper and, with a curious glance between him and Oliver, left the lobby without a parting word. Once the postmortem room door closed softly behind her, Jasper spoke.

"You said your row with Foster was about money." Oliver nodded, and Jasper continued, "It seems the amount he requested was the amount his landlady required for the yearly lease of his rooms."

Oliver swore under his breath. "I didn't know."

"Did Niles let slip anything having to do with his gambling? Maybe a name like Olaf or Reubens? Or John Lloyd?"

The viscount took a moment to consider the names,

turning his bowler around by the brim between his hands. "No, I'm sorry."

Jasper shook his head. "It's all right. What about the Spitalfields Angels?"

This grabbed Oliver's interest. "The criminal syndicate? You think he was involved with them?"

Jasper wanted to be careful with what information he provided, even to Oliver. "I have reason to believe Foster had an altercation with a man associated with the Angels the week before his murder. It occurred at a gambling casino."

Disappointment clouded Oliver's face, and he shook his head. At the same time, a soft brushing sound against the postmortem room door turned Jasper's ear.

"He really did know how to mess up, didn't he?" Oliver said with a sigh. "No, he never mentioned anything to do with the Angels or any other criminal gang. But I keep thinking..."

Jasper pushed aside the notion that someone—namely, Leo—had been listening at the door and focused on Oliver. "Tell me."

"Why my duck pond? I can see if Niles was inebriated and came stumbling onto my property only to fall into the water and drown, but now, knowing that he was killed—stabbed—well, that means whoever did it knew of my connection to him."

It was the same conclusion Jasper had been pondering. "The question is whether the killer is a mutual acquaintance or if Niles, before his death, told the killer of your connection," Jasper said.

There was, of course, no easy way to determine the answer.

"If I can think of anything to help, I won't hesitate to contact you." Oliver paused a moment longer, then said, "Niles was troublesome and a weight on my shoulders. But he didn't deserve this. Whatever you need for your investigation into his death, you have only to ask, Reid." Oliver clapped him on the shoulder, then left.

Jasper tucked his chin before pushing open the post-mortem room door. The dreary weather had left the stained glass windows dull and muted, but the gasoliers were turned up to provide enough light for Claude to work by. However, the coroner was alone.

"Where is Leo?"

"I hope you will join my niece, Inspector. I don't think she should go to that prison alone," the old man said as he was making an incision along the back of a corpse's skull. "You might want to look away."

Jasper did, but not before Claude began to peel back the dead man's scalp. With a sick twist of his stomach, Jasper started for the back office.

"What prison?" he asked as he entered, his thundering voice bouncing off the high ceiling.

Leo was buttoning her coat. "I'm visiting Mrs. Stewart at Holloway."

A prickle of anger surprised him.

"You are not going to a prison," he heard himself say. Instantly, he knew it had been stupidity to do so.

"I am free to try to visit her." She finished with her buttons and pulled on a pair of gloves. "And I am more than capable of *going alone*." Leo raised her voice just enough so that her uncle might hear.

"Women visitors aren't permitted inside prisons," Jasper said. She wasn't family, and the warden was under no obligation to allow Mrs. Stewart a visitor at all.

"There was a burglary about four weeks ago at the Stewart home. Did you know that?" Leo asked, circumventing his comment, as she so often did. "Mr. Stewart said he didn't report it because nothing appeared to have been taken. However, something had—a monogrammed valise from the attic. The one used to house the bomb that John Lloyd was carrying."

Jasper rubbed his temple. "You don't know that for certain."

"But it makes perfect sense. Why would the Stewarts go to check their attic for missing items? It would be so easily overlooked. And not only that, but the person who took it knew that it would be there. They knew it would implicate Mrs. Stewart. This person was known to her."

The temptation to follow this line of inquiry nipped at Jasper's heels. If it had been his case, he would certainly question the Stewarts' staff. But he had no role with the bombing investigation, and it left him feeling utterly thwarted. Especially since Leo was so keen to plow onward, with or without him.

"You were listening at the door when I spoke to Lord Hayes," he said.

She bit her bottom lip and turned to take her handbag from where she'd hung it on a stand.

"I might have been," she said. "Niles Foster's murder is connected to John Lloyd's. You know that as well as I. If Niles had an altercation with a Spitalfields Angel at Bloom's club, it's entirely possible John Lloyd did as well. John was forced to bring that bomb to the Yard; I am certain of it. Shouldn't we ask if Mrs. Stewart has any connection to the Spitalfields Angels or why they might wish to target her?"

Disbelief surged just beneath his skin. "Tell me that isn't your plan. You aren't going to a prison to ask about the Angels?"

She frowned at him as she went to the back door, which emptied out into a dirt lane behind the former church vestry. "You make it sound like it's a bad idea."

He threw out his arms. "It is a *wretched* idea, Leo. You cannot simply go into a prison asking about members of a gang. My God, have some sense."

At her peeved glower, he reined in his temper. Taking a steadying breath, he added, "There are members of that gang in every one of Her Majesty's prisons. If anyone were to overhear you and then send word to someone on the outside, what do you think would happen?"

She held still, visibly mulling over the question. The slightest bit of awareness and understanding shifted across her defiant expression.

"All right," she said, with a firm nod. "I'll whisper." She opened the door and stepped outside.

A knot tangled inside him. *Bloody woman.* He joined her on the narrow dirt lane, closing the back door behind him.

"You're not going alone," he grumbled. It wasn't as if he didn't already have plenty to do back at the Yard. Lewis was still going through Foster's papers, and Jasper needed to find a way to speak to the Olaf fellow. But Leo was going to Holloway Prison, whether he accompanied her or not.

She walked ahead of him. "Maybe I don't want your company."

"Maybe I'm not giving you a choice," he replied, catching up swiftly. "You remind me of my father. He'd get his teeth into something and refuse to give it up—like a stubborn mongrel."

Leo glanced up at him, a ghost of a smile on her lips. "I'll take that as a compliment."

He held his tongue. It was a compliment, he supposed, even if she infuriated him.

At Trafalgar Square, they hired a cab to take them the five or so miles north of Camden Town. Holloway Prison housed men primarily, but there were two smaller wings, one for juvenile offenders and one for women. Female warders were tasked with looking after both of these smaller groups of inmates. He'd been to Holloway a handful of times, transporting prisoners when he'd been a constable and once, to question a suspect.

"Have you ever been to a city prison?" he asked as they rode along.

"I've never had reason to," Leo answered pointedly.

"They aren't civilized places. You should prepare yourself."

Leo only cast him an annoyed glance before turning toward the window again. With no conversation for the first many minutes, Jasper sat back and contemplated the connection between Foster and Lloyd. He didn't want to approach Tomlin until he had more than similar bruising patterns and a habit for gambling at Striker's Wharf to link the two deaths. What he needed to do was find out what had happened inside that casino and how Foster had incurred Olaf's ire.

Leo's voice broke the quiet. "It is kind of Lord Hayes to see to Mr. Foster's burial. They must have been close."

"Their fathers were close. As such, Oliver felt a responsibility toward him."

"I see." Leo laced her fingers together in her lap. She wanted to say something more, though it took her a moment to get it out. "And was Miss Hayes also acquainted with Niles Foster?"

Shifting in his seat, Jasper tugged awkwardly on the panels of his coat. "Not that I am aware."

"You haven't inquired?"

He supposed there was no need to be secretive about what had happened between him and Oliver's cousin. Now was as good a time as any to confess. "I've ended things with Constance."

Leo blinked. "Oh." Her lips parted, as if truly stunned. Jasper noted the full curve of her bottom lip, then dragged his attention away.

"I'm sorry," she offered.

He arched a brow. "You didn't like her."

She had the good grace to look contrite. "Nevertheless, I am sorry."

He was only sorry for how long he'd strung Constance along. Maybe it was because deep down, Jasper had known she was courting him out of defiance of her parents, her role in society and the life she'd been born into. She'd been pushing against others' expectations for her and perhaps the unpolished detective inspector from Scotland Yard had been an exciting addition to her rebellion. It might not be generous toward her, but in his gut, Jasper suspected it to be true.

He was also now willing to admit that Constance's own suspicion had possessed some legitimacy. *Your precious Leo.* The echo of her bitter comment would not quit his mind…much like his thoughts of the woman seated across from him in the cab.

He thanked Leo for her sympathy with a nod and hoped the topic would be dropped. The silence lasted until they arrived in rural Holloway in North London, outside the imposing castle-like prison. The driver let them off at the wrought iron gate, and Jasper paid him to wait. The visit would be brief, if it was permitted at all.

"Gracious, it truly is a fortress," Leo said, her eyes turned upward at the Gothic castellated stone towers and ramparts. A high brick wall surrounded the entire premises.

The rain had tapered to a drizzle, wetting their shoulders as they walked between the Governor's House and Chaplain's House toward the solid, iron-bolted gate centering the porter's lodge. Jasper brought his fist down upon the gate, and a pair of prison guards in uniform greeted them with expectant, wary once-overs. As he'd hoped, his warrant card gained them access inside the walls of the prison, but they were made to wait inside a small room in the lodge while the chief warder was summoned.

When he arrived, dressed in a uniform distinct from the other warders, he did not welcome them warmly. He inspected the warrant card closely before asking their business with his prisoner.

"I'm investigating a murder. The victim may have been connected to that of the Scotland Yard bombing, for which Mrs. Stewart stands accused," Jasper replied. "I have questions for her."

The chief warder, Mr. Vines, pursed his lips, his walrus mustache wriggling. He peered at Leo. "And what does this woman here have to do with your investigation?"

Before Jasper could answer, Leo spoke for herself, her annoyance with the chief warder evident. "My name is Miss Spencer. I am known to your prisoner and may help ease the questioning process."

Mr. Vines sniffed his disapproval but granted them both access. He led them into the graveled courtyard, where the three-story ragstone exterior of the juvenile wing stretched to the left and the female prisoners' wing loomed to the right. The spring flowers and greening shrubs that bordered the wall drooped morosely in the rainfall.

An inner warder greeted Mr. Vines at the wicket gate and showed them into the reception hall of the main prison. A large staircase led to the central halls of the prison cells for the juveniles and women in this first building. The men's cells were in another building, separated by an exterior courtyard. The reception warder, Mr. Smythe, joined them and, after a hushed conversation with Mr. Vines, took over and guided them forward into the long reception hall. At the far end were the women's receiving cells.

"As Mrs. Stewart has not yet been tried or sentenced, she is currently being held here rather than in general detention," Mr. Smythe explained.

He approached a woman warder, standing guard outside a line of steel doors. The woman wasn't tall, but she was broad and muscular. Jasper would have placed a steep wager that she could easily hold her own should any ruckus erupt. "Visitors for Mrs. Stewart," Mr. Smythe said to her.

The warder kept an impassive expression and knocked upon one of the doors before promptly unlocking it.

"Miss Hartley will stand guard with the door open while you visit," the reception warder said. "Ten minutes."

He stepped aside, allowing Jasper and Leo entry. The whitewashed cell walls were unadorned, except for a list of the prison's rules and regulations for the occupant to read if they were capable. A dark-haired woman stood timidly near the back of the cell, her hands clasped in front of her as she waited to see who had come.

"Oh, Miss Spencer." The barest tremor of disappointment crossed her face. She realized it and shook her head. "Forgive me, I mean no insult. I was hoping to see my husband. He hasn't been to visit since yesterday morning."

"It is perfectly understandable why you'd wish to see him," Leo replied.

Mrs. Stewart's attention turned to Jasper, and he felt her scrutiny. "You are a police officer," she presumed. He knew he had the look of one.

"Detective Inspector Jasper Reid."

Like any well-trained hostess would, she invited them to sit at the fold-down table attached to the sidewall. There were just two chairs, so Jasper stood while she and Leo settled themselves. Above them, a gas jet went unlit, draping the cell in gray shadow. The single window, near the ceiling, was barred and permitted little of the bleak, outside light to filter in.

"Thank you for coming to see me," Mrs. Stewart said. She sounded exhausted, and by the untidy state of her hair and the dark smudges beneath her eyes, it looked as if she had not slept well. The narrow cot, without so much as a pillow, was likely one reason why.

"I see you were released from Scotland Yard," she said to Leo. With a shaky grin, she added, "I'm glad."

"Mrs. Stewart—"

"Please, call me Geraldine. I consider you a great friend for braving these prison walls to visit."

"Then you must call me Leo," she said and, at the other woman's surprise, explained, "It is short for Leonora. I was named after my father, Leonard."

"Leo," Mrs. Stewart said, trying out the name. "Latin for lion, I believe. It has strength."

Jasper hadn't thought of that before, but it was true. The moniker suited her perfectly.

Leo smiled at the compliment, then got back to the point of their visit. "Inspector Reid and I have come because we have reason to believe another murder victim might be connected to the death of the constable killed in the Scotland Yard bombing."

The woman sat straight, her attention jumping toward Jasper. "How do you mean?"

Briefly, Jasper outlined Niles Foster's and John Lloyd's matching wrist ligature marks; the gashes on their cheeks, possibly made by the same signet ring; their deaths within 24 hours of each other; and their gambling addictions that had led them to the same backroom casino in Lambeth.

"However, the natures of their deaths are not at all the same," he continued. "Constable Lloyd apparently was the cause of his own death, while Mr. Foster was stabbed twice by an unknown assailant. My job is to find out who killed him. I might be able to do that if I can determine why Constable Lloyd was carrying that bomb in the first place."

Mrs. Stewart spread her palms open. "I cannot tell

you. I know no one believes me, but I had nothing to do with that poor constable's death. If my valise was used to conceal the bomb, I have no idea how it came to be in his possession."

Visibly overwrought, her eyes welled with tears. Leo covered her hand with her own, still gloved. It was cold in the cell, and the spring storm had reached through the thick walls to dampen the air.

"I believe you, Geraldine. And I believe your luggage was taken during the break-in at your home last month. I saw your husband and sister-in-law, Mrs. Bates, just yesterday. They believe the same and have told Inspector Tomlin."

Mrs. Stewart hardened at the mention of the inspector. "He doesn't believe them, does he?"

Leo shook her head. "But we do," she said, speaking for Jasper, even though he'd rather she wouldn't. He kept his lips pursed in a thin line. "And furthermore, we believe that whoever took that luggage broke into your home at a time when they knew it would be vacant. They bypassed expensive items, their only design being to steal the valise, which they knew exactly where to find."

Mrs. Stewart sniffled and touched a crinkled handkerchief to her nose. "You believe this has been done by someone I know?" The appalling thought drained the rest of the color from her already wan cheeks.

"Someone who wished to implicate you once the bombing was carried out," Jasper said. Laid out so starkly, he found he did believe it. The woman seated before him was no criminal mastermind.

She was a pampered, upper-class woman who had likely received a top-notch education from either private tutors or a women's university, and who had the time and intellect to know that women were not treated as equal citizens to men. Using her influence, her money, and her social standing, she'd become a voice for the women's equality movement. But she wasn't violent.

"Do either you or your husband have any enemies?" he asked. "Political enemies, maybe?"

"I'm sure plenty of politicians dislike me," she said with a humorless laugh. "Lord Babbage comes quickly to mind as one who loudly disagrees with the WEA's tenets. Not Porter, however. My husband isn't political at all."

Leo folded her hands upon the small table. "Mr. Foster had a run-in with a man who has ties to a criminal gang known as the Spitalfields Angels."

Jasper tensed, checking the open door. The warder, Miss Hartley, was still standing there, but she had her back turned. Leo must have recalled her earlier promise to him because she lowered her voice to a near whisper.

"Do you know of this gang?" she asked.

Mrs. Stewart screwed her expression into a grimace. "A criminal gang? Of course not."

"You have servants," Jasper said. "Might they be connected?"

She shook her head vigorously. "No, that's impossible. We have a small staff, and all their references were fully vetted when my housekeeper hired them. It's been nearly a decade. I can guarantee you; my servants are not in league with criminals."

Jasper still wanted to question them, but he'd have to approach Mr. Stewart for permission. And were he to do that, word would get back to Tomlin. He rubbed his thumb along his chin, not wanting to make more work for himself.

"Who are these Spitalfields Angels anyhow?" Mrs. Stewart asked, her voice not nearly as soft as he would have liked. "Do you think they have something to do with the bombing I'm accused of?"

"Certain members of the Angels have been connected to Clan na Gael activity in the past. The gang is operated by a man named Barry Reubens," Jasper said, hoping the name might spark something in her. But she only frowned. "Some other names associated with the Angels are Tricky Mills, Clive Paget, Harry Golding...do you recognize any of them?"

She continued to frown. "I'm sorry, but no. None of those names are familiar."

Miss Hartley knocked on the frame of the door. "Time," she said.

Leo pushed back her chair and stood. But Mrs. Stewart had frozen in her seat, her eyes blinking rapidly.

"Wait a moment," she said softly. "Paget, did you say?"

"Yes." Jasper's pulse caught. "Clive Paget."

"Odd," she said, looking between him and Leo. "My late brother's wife, Emma Bates...if I'm not mistaken, Paget is her maiden name."

Leo spun toward him. The elation in her eyes reflected what he felt right then: the singing strike of gold.

Chapter Fourteen

Seated inside the cab that had been waiting for them, Leo's thoughts buzzed as she and Jasper started away from the prison. While she'd hated to leave Mrs. Stewart in that desolate place, at least she was leaving her with a sliver of hope. The connecting factor that had been eluding them had finally surfaced.

"When I visited the Stewart home yesterday, Mrs. Bates admitted that she wasn't truly a suffragist," Leo told Jasper. "She claimed to attend meetings to support her sister-in-law's *club,* as she referred to it, but I can't ignore the way she has regarded Mr. Stewart the few times I've been in her presence."

Rain lashed the cab's glass windows. Gray afternoon light and pockets of fog lowered visibility inside the carriage. Jasper removed his bowler and set it on his thigh.

"How do you mean?"

Leo had tried to disregard her intuition earlier but

now gave in to it. “I think Mrs. Bates is fascinated by him. Perhaps even in love with him.”

He drummed his fingers on the crown of his hat. “She wanted his wife out of the way?”

“That could be.” It would be beyond despicable. However, Mrs. Bates had openly, almost gratuitously, fawned over Porter Stewart, lauding him as an exemplary male, even sighing when she mentioned how fortunate Geraldine was to have married him. And during Leo’s visit yesterday, Mrs. Bates had been so snug in that sitting room, her satisfaction with settling into Geraldine’s role of mother complete. Not to mention the rearranged appearance of the foyer. As if she was already claiming the space as her own.

“Did you get the impression Mr. Stewart might also want to be rid of his wife?” Jasper asked.

“I didn’t,” she answered. “On the contrary, he seemed lost without her. However, Emma Bates isn’t some wizened widow. She’s shapely and pretty, and she and Mr. Stewart aren’t far apart in age.”

“All to say, any comfort she might offer could very well tempt him.” Jasper exhaled as he sat back in his seat.

“And then there is the valise,” Leo said. “Mrs. Bates is likely to have known about it and had easy access to it.”

She would have also known when the home would be empty.

Jasper and Leo rocked side to side as the carriage wheels left the dirt road and mounted a cobble-paved street.

“Even if Mrs. Bates is, in fact, related to Clive Paget, why would he agree to a bombing scheme just to help her end the Stewarts’ marriage?” he asked.

Put that way, it did seem unlikely. Unless Mrs. Bates hadn't asked for his help and had constructed a bomb on her own. It wasn't out of the realm of possibility. When Leo and Jasper were working to solve the death of Gabriela Carter two months ago, they'd met a woman whose two toddlers were poisoned by gumming arsenic-laced wallpaper in their nursery. Driven mad with grief after their children's deaths, Mr. and Mrs. Nelson had wanted to exact revenge on the company that had manufactured the deadly papers, which had already sickened and killed many others. While Mr. Nelson had wanted to kill the innocent children of the wallpaper company owner as eye-for-an-eye vengeance, Mrs. Nelson had planned to bomb the factory in protest. She'd constructed the device herself. Who was to say Emma Bates could not have done the same?

But how would Mrs. Bates have convinced John Lloyd to plant it? And Leo remembered the scowling man in the cap, watching the constable approach the Yard. Who was he in all of this?

Jasper pulled at his collar, stretching his neck as if uncomfortable.

"I know what you're thinking," Leo preempted. "The valise bombing isn't your case."

He looked at her, his dark green eyes sooty in the muted light. "Despite what Mrs. Stewart just revealed to us, I need to concentrate on finding Niles Foster's murderer."

"You already know that he and John Lloyd were bound and beaten by the same man," she argued, her pulse beginning to pump harder. "And that man may be connected to the Spitalfields Angels, who are connected to Mrs. Bates."

"We don't yet know that for certain," he said. "And if I bring any of it to Tomlin, my head will roll for undermining his investigation."

"You would allow an innocent woman to languish in prison, or even hang, to avoid a *reprimand*?"

Instantly, Leo felt regret for the cutting remark, which only angered her more. As did the heat of shame as Jasper leveled her with an incredulous glare.

"Allow an innocent woman to hang," he echoed her words with a mirthless huff of laughter. "You think so little of me?"

"I don't know what to think," she said, her throat cinching. "I thought I knew you. Now, I'm not sure of anything."

She didn't want to talk about this. It was easier to focus on the two perplexing cases and how they aligned. It was easier not to remember that Jasper had lied to her —for years. That she'd promised herself never to speak to him again. Now, here they were, sharing a cab and an investigation. Several seconds of tense quiet ticked by.

"I'm the same person you've always known," he said softly.

"You cannot be serious." Leo crossed her arms over her middle. "I've *known* you as Jasper Reid, and that isn't even your real name. You're James Carter."

She hated the sound of it. Hated saying it aloud. She couldn't even think of him as *James*. He'd hidden so much from her. Another life. A whole different identity.

"I'm not James. Not anymore." He sounded calm and looked it too. His body swayed in rhythm with the carriage. "Yes, I concealed the truth about that night from you and from the Inspector. I lied to you about where I came from. About the *people* I came from."

"To protect yourself," she said, her voice cracking.

He set his jaw. "Yes. I didn't want to go back to them. I couldn't—" He shook his head, his throat working as he tensed. "I couldn't go back."

The way he said it, not returning to his family wasn't just a desire. It sounded like an impossibility. Maybe even a fear. Leo licked her lips, considering why that would be.

"Because you didn't kill me like you were supposed to?"

Jasper cut his eyes from hers, gazing toward the window. They were starting to enter the urban streets of London, but she thought he might be seeing a long-lost past instead.

"Saying my uncle was disappointed is an understatement," he replied. "With the news the next morning that you were found alive, hiding in the attic, he was ashamed. Humiliated. And that made him angry."

Leo recalled the bruises distorting Jasper's face when she'd first met him at Scotland Yard four days later. "He beat you."

He turned from the window and met her eyes. "That isn't why I couldn't go back. I wasn't afraid of him or his fists. I was afraid that the next time, I wouldn't be able to hide the person they wanted me to kill."

Leo's stomach dropped. It wasn't something she'd considered before.

He held her stare. "I'm not a murderer. If I'd stayed James Carter, I would have become one."

Words failed her. She'd been so angry, grasping for reasons why he would have kept such a secret from her and from the Inspector, that she hadn't tried to think about that night from his perspective. Or what a life as James Carter would have held in store for him.

Without warning, Leo's anger dissipated. In its place came an equally unexpected rush of gratitude. She didn't know if she could forgive him completely, but she was at least glad he wasn't what he would've become had he gone back to the Carters. He wasn't lawless or corrupt. He was principled and determined, and he devoted himself to hunting down and arresting criminals, when he would have been one himself if not for the choice he made in the attic of her old home all those years ago.

"I've thought about that night countless times," she said, her breathing slightly off-kilter. Her heart thumped hard in her chest for some reason she couldn't understand. "About the boy I stabbed and how, instead of hurting me back, he helped me."

Jasper shifted, straightening his posture as he searched her face for any hint of what she might be feeling. He was wary, she presumed.

"I wondered if he'd regretted helping me," she said. "I wondered if he ever thought of me afterward."

They'd closed in on Westminster, entering traffic and the bustling streets of the city. But as Jasper held her stare, his own unwavering, Leo felt as if the rest of the world was barely there at all. The tip of her nose began to prickle, as did her eyes.

"I've never regretted it. Not once." His brow tensed, then softened as his gaze drifted to her mouth. It lingered there a half second, if that, before lifting to meeting her eyes again. "And I have thought of you. Every day."

She held her breath, the functioning of her lungs pausing. Under his heated stare, her pulse skipped unevenly. She didn't know what to say or what he'd meant by those words. He'd thought of her every day? Even now? With a start, she suddenly realized how often she'd thought of *him*. And how much she didn't wish for him to know it. Not yet, anyway.

Speechless, she drew in a long breath at last and lowered her attention to her hands, her fingers knitted together in her lap. For several more minutes, they rode in silence, allowing the noises of the city streets to carry them along. When Admiral Nelson's statue in the center of Trafalgar Square appeared, Jasper banged a fist against the top of the cab. The driver pulled alongside the pavement and stopped.

"I imagine you need to go to the morgue," Jasper said. She nodded.

Jasper descended, extending his hand to her. More than ever, Leo didn't want to take it. But this time, it wasn't out of anger or spite. It was because when she touched his hand, she expected to feel a strange coiling in the center of her chest. One that had everything to do with the way his heated gaze had just briefly touched on her lips.

She braced herself, took his hand, and stepped down. Then swiftly retracted her palm. "I'm going to see what more I can learn about Emma Bates."

"Leo—"

"I'm not going to speak to her directly. Trust me, Jasper, I know better than to approach a murder suspect."

He sealed his lips, biting back a certain retort. Maybe he only refrained because she'd addressed him as *Jasper* rather than Inspector, as she had before. Jasper was who he was. Leo knew that now, even if the rest of it was still muddled and confusing.

"I'd worry less if you stayed out of it," he said.

"I have to go," she said, moving off. She'd been away from the morgue long enough. "Uncle Claude needs me."

He grumbled under his breath, then climbed back into the cab, telling the driver to go to the Yard. She hurried through the rain to the front door of the morgue, pretending that parting company with him wasn't a bit of a comedown.

She was grateful the lobby was empty, but as she shook the rain from her coat, a low murmur of voices could be heard in the postmortem room. Listening at the door, she recognized two voices: one belonged to her uncle. The other, to the deputy assistant coroner, Mr. Pritchard.

Grimacing, Leo entered the postmortem room. She was met with not two men, but three.

"Ah, Miss Spencer," the deputy assistant coroner said, failing to mask his disappointment in seeing her, despite the smile he pushed onto his lips. A mustache and long beard obscured most of his mouth and weak chin.

"Good afternoon, Mr. Pritchard." She joined them around the corpse of a woman whose rib cage and abdomen were open for examination.

The second, unfamiliar man moved quickly to pull the sheet over the corpse's head. He was younger than Mr. Pritchard, under thirty years old, with a neatly trimmed mustache and black hair that curled at his nape.

"That isn't necessary, Mr....?" Leo waited for someone to introduce them.

"Quinn, miss," the young man said for himself. "Connor Quinn."

"May I introduce my niece, Miss Leonora Spencer," Claude said, his hands clasped behind his back as he rocked forward, heel to toe, and back again—something he only ever did when nervous.

Mr. Quinn bowed his head in greeting.

"Miss Spencer is not affected by morbid sights as most ladies are," Mr. Pritchard explained, though by his tone, he ought to have said, "…as most *normal* ladies *should be*."

"Ah, yes, my grandfather mentioned a woman helps here on occasion," Mr. Quinn said.

"Grandfather?" Leo echoed.

"Chief Coroner Giles," Claude explained. His mild grin appeared to be a warning for her not to visibly react. The chief coroner directed every morgue in London as well as all the coroners and clerks employed within them. And this was his grandson.

"Mr. Quinn has recently graduated from London Hospital Medical College with top marks in surgery," Mr. Pritchard explained, laying a hand on the young man's shoulder. "He's shown an interest in the work of a coroner."

Connor Quinn smiled tightly, rolling his shoulder ever so slightly so that Mr. Pritchard would remove his hand. The deputy assistant coroner did and cleared his throat.

"As I was saying before your arrival, Miss Spencer," Mr. Pritchard went on, "the influx of ordered inquests these last few months have quite outpaced one man's capabilities here. And not to put too fine a point on it, you're not getting any younger, Claude."

Mr. Pritchard laughed good-naturedly, as though he

was teasing. Leo held her breath, suddenly wary. In March, an apprentice from the medical college, Mr. Higgins, had spent a handful of weeks working with Claude. The young man had been placed at Spring Street Morgue by his professor, who also happened to be a friend of Chief Coroner Giles. Mr. Higgins had been morose and lazy, and he'd soon moved on, but both Leo and her uncle suspected he'd witnessed the palsy affecting the steadiness of Claude's hands. It was entirely possible Mr. Higgins had informed his professor and that the rumors had spread to the chief coroner's ears.

"I'm placing Mr. Quinn at Spring Street for the foreseeable future under your training, Claude," Mr. Pritchard now said. "I think it will be a good transition for everyone."

Transition. The word spoke volumes. This young surgeon, fresh out of medical college, would be working here now. And in short order, he would replace her uncle. Leo had known to expect something like this, but it still managed to take her breath away.

"As for you, Miss Spencer," Mr. Pritchard continued, forcing more artificial gaiety, "surely you desire to move along in the natural direction of a young woman's life. I'll be turning next to finding a more suitable clerk for the morgue."

Leo held her tongue, though it felt as if the floor had started to tremble beneath her feet. So now that Claude was being pushed out, she would be as well. Of course, the only reason she'd been allowed there to begin with was because Chief Superintendent Gregory Reid had put in a good word for her with the police commissioner and the chief coroner. But during the years she'd been there, she'd worked hard and done well. Postmortem reports were detailed and thorough, the morgue was organized, as was all the paperwork. Mr. Pritchard, however, wasn't the sort of man who would acknowledge the advantages her presence had provided.

"Now, I must be off," he said. "Connor, I'll leave you to receive a tour of the premises. I'm sure you've questions for Mr. Feldman."

Mr. Quinn stood in place as the deputy assistant coroner left, and then the three of them were alone. No one seemed quite sure what to say until Claude finally pierced the quiet.

"I'll find you some garments." He went to the supply closet, where chemicals and tools were stored, along with extra tall rubber boots, vulcanized rubber gloves, leather aprons, and dark brown laboratory coats.

"You are a typist here, Miss Spencer, is that correct?" Mr. Quinn asked.

Leo bristled. "Typing is one of my duties. I also log personal possessions in the register, transcribe notes during examinations, and attend the families and funeral workers when they arrive for identification or collection."

That she would make incisions on corpses from time to time and then close them afterward was not something the incoming surgeon would ever need to know.

"Forgive me, but when my grandfather said a woman was helping at the morgue, I could not quite imagine what it was she'd be doing. It seems a queer thing for a lady to involve herself in the business of death."

This sentiment was no new thing. It didn't bother Leo. What did cause her to bristle was knowing that this man would be the one to push her uncle from his much-needed job.

"But it makes perfect sense now," Mr. Quinn continued. "It is commendable that you help your uncle when the work must be so very disagreeable for you."

In the supply closet, Claude was whistling a made-up tune, as he did so often while working.

"Actually, Mr. Quinn, I enjoy the work," she said. "And I plan to continue with it."

He frowned. "But as Mr. Pritchard has said—"

"Mr. Pritchard stated that he wanted a suitable clerk for this morgue's increasing number of cases," Leo cut in. "As he has had no complaint with my work for nearly five years, I believe I am quite suitable."

Her anger was driving her to be purposefully obtuse. This wasn't about wanting better work or more competence. Mr. Pritchard simply wanted a suitable *male* clerk.

Amusement crossed Mr. Quinn's face. It was smug and condescending, and his eyes, which were the light brown color of weak tea, conveyed disbelief.

"Are you paid for your work here, Miss Spencer?"

She pressed her shoulders lower at the unexpected question. "That is none of your concern."

"I'll take that to mean you are not. So may I ask why you would wish to continue working for no pay?"

In the closet, her uncle's whistling stopped. Leo's cheeks warmed. The truth was, as soon as her uncle was let go from his position, she would no longer be able to afford to work for free. She would need to support him, Aunt Flora, and herself.

She was grateful for Claude's timely return, carrying a lab coat, apron, and appropriate boots for his new assistant. Overwhelmed by the feeling of being thwarted, Leo would not be able to stomach showing Mr. Quinn around the morgue with her uncle.

"I'm going to start going through those boxes you mentioned were stored in the crypt," she told Claude. She'd not yet had a chance to search for her family's few possessions that he'd stored there, and now seemed to be the perfect time to begin.

"Ah yes, let me show you where they are," he said, latching onto the excuse to step away from their unwanted guest.

As Mr. Quinn donned his garments, they stepped into the back office, out of sight.

"What now?" Leo whispered. "There is no chance Mr. Quinn isn't going to notice your hands shaking. And he won't hesitate to tell his grandfather, I would guess."

Claude rubbed his palms together, looking down at them as if they had betrayed him. With a sad shake of his head, he sighed. "I'm sorry, my dear." He gripped her arm and gave it a light, reassuring squeeze. "I fear my time has come. And I don't think there is anything we can do except to let it."

Chapter Fifteen

After leaving Leo at Trafalgar Square and returning to Scotland Yard, Jasper tried—and failed—to forget the return carriage ride from Holloway Prison. The boxes of items collected from Niles Foster's rooms provided a good attempt at a distraction, but as he joined Lewis, who'd been sorting through the clothing, legal texts, ledgers, and folios that Foster had presumably brought from Parliament to his rooms, Jasper's thoughts continually crept back toward his conversation with Leo.

He didn't know if they'd made any strides toward a truce or if he'd only pushed her further away. She hadn't missed the way his attention slipped to her lips. And he hadn't missed the blush staining her cheeks. What they'd learned from Mrs. Stewart about her sister-in-law should have been of more consequence than those few beguiling moments in which Jasper had suppressed a crushing desire to move across the carriage and seat himself next to Leo. She would have been appalled, he supposed. So, he tried to pretend the urge had not tempted him at all and instead kept the disconnected threads between his own case and Inspector Tomlin's foremost in his mind.

"His handwriting is something awful," Lewis complained, paging through papers in one of Foster's folios. He slapped them onto the desk and shoved them aside. "I can't understand half of what he writes, can you?"

Jasper had put away a stack of papers and started to go through a box of clothing. The hemlines of Foster's trousers pointed to them having been purchased second-hand. The cuffs and collars he'd attached to shirts were frayed from overuse, and his stockings had been darned several times over.

"No, but I was hoping for a financial ledger of some sort. You've seen nothing?" Jasper asked. Lewis shook his head.

The laborers had left a short while ago, the rain having slowed their progress on rebuilding the corner wall, and other officers in the CID had also started home for the evening. Lewis was likely eager to return to his family too.

"Foster must have kept a desk outside Sir Elliot's office at Parliament," Jasper said. "Go there tomorrow and have a look. I'll work on hunting down Olaf to inquire about the altercation at Bloom's club."

That would mean approaching Barry Reubens. It wasn't an enviable task, and the crinkling of the detective sergeant's forehead spoke to it. "I should come with you for that. Me and a few constables."

He wasn't wrong. "I'll take Drake and Price with me. Go on home, now. I'll finish with this box." Jasper lifted out a black frock coat showing signs of wear in the threading around the shoulders.

Lewis stood and stretched his back as Jasper turned out the pockets. A scrap of crumpled paper fluttered to the floor. Retrieving it, then flattening it out, he read an address: *7 Lisle Street, Leicester Square.*

The writing resembled Foster's own from what he'd seen among the man's belongings. Jasper turned the scrap of paper over, but there was nothing else written upon it. Leicester Square wasn't far; it was likely nothing, but to disregard it would be madness, especially when they had so few other leads. He decided to go by the address before heading home for the evening.

Jasper rummaged through the boxes until he found the framed photograph he'd seen earlier. In it, Foster was standing behind a man and a woman, presumably his parents. He took the back off the frame and slipped the photograph into his coat pocket.

Jasper went north on foot from Whitehall Place. The tapering rain didn't bother him; Mrs. Zhao might complain that he was damp through and through, but her scolding would bring some normalcy back to the day.

The visit to Holloway Prison had only further muddled the connection between Niles Foster and Constable Lloyd. Inspector Tomlin hadn't been in when Jasper returned to the Yard that afternoon, but he would be there tomorrow. He couldn't avoid bringing up the possibility their cases were linked for much longer, but at least his temper had cooled somewhat regarding Leo being held overnight without cause.

At Leicester Square, carriage traffic moved in spasms. Gas jets within the lamps surrounding the park square reflected off wet pavement and glistening cab roofs. Once residential, the square was now populated with shops, hotels, and entertainment, including a few museums and theatres. When Jasper came upon Number 7 Lisle Street, north off the square, he felt an itch of interest. The etched windows read Seale and Company Bank. Jasper tried the door, but it was after hours. The place was closed for the night.

He stared at the exterior a few more moments, considering why Niles Foster had the address for this bank in his pocket. How long ago had he stuffed it there? If it had been his own bank, why write down the address as if he might forget it? He might have been running an errand for Sir Elliot…but the MP had been clear that they did not associate outside chambers. A banking errand seemed personal.

The spitting rain regained some of its strength, and Jasper turned back toward St. James's Square. There was nothing more he could do with the bank lead that night. Exhaustion pulled him forward, as did the promise of warm, dry clothes, a liberal pour of whisky, and whatever Mrs. Zhao had created in the kitchen for his supper. He felt spoiled at times. She cared for him as if he was family, and he did not believe that was merely because she was paid to do so.

The first wrong thing he noticed as he approached the house on Charles Street was the darkened upstairs windows. At this time of night, the brackets and lamps in the study should have been lit. He'd never arrived home to find that room, or his own bedroom, unprepared. Jasper held still on the pavement an extra moment, then went to the front door. He used his key to enter, but as he did, he felt a chilly absence. The gasolier overhead was lit, but there were no sounds of approaching footfalls. Mrs. Zhao's ears could detect the click of the front door lock from the kitchen. She should have been here by now to greet him, as was her custom.

He pocketed his key, his concern mounting. She was an older woman but not in ill health. That wasn't to say she was invincible.

"Mrs. Zhao?" he called into the quiet. No answer came.

He started for the kitchen but pulled up short of reaching for the knob. Light reached under the base of the door, fanning out over the wooden boards and the tips of his boots. A prickle of premonition lifted the small hairs along his arms and the back of his neck. Jasper reached for his Webley revolver, smoothly drawing it from the leather holster. Pushing open the door, he entered in a swift lunge, his revolver raised.

In a chair directly in front of him, Mrs. Zhao sat bound and gagged. Her muffled cry of warning came in tandem with the shove of a body slamming into his back, taking him to the floor. Jasper landed hard on his side. A foot connected with his wrist, dislodging the Webley from his grip. A sharp kick to his temple, and pain exploded in his head, wiping out his vision. The blows continued against his ribs as more boots assailed him from all sides. The unrelenting scream coming through Mrs. Zhao's gag paired with the grunts of the men standing over him, as they repeatedly kicked his prone body.

And then, the attack ceased. He heaved for breath, his ribs searing as a man's grating hiss burrowed into his ear: "Quit asking about the Angels."

It was all he heard before another strike to the face brought an impenetrable cloak of darkness.

The dabbing of a cloth against his cheek stung. It pulled him from an endless, spinning abyss of nausea and pain. Fragments of a fever dream lingered in his head. Mrs. Zhao's whimpering cries. A cold stretch of darkness. Leo's strained voice, fraught with worry, as she called to him through ever-shifting shadows.

Jasper opened his eyes. Or rather, *eye*. The right one refused to budge.

"Leo." Her name clawed along his dry throat. When he tried to move, every muscle, every joint and rib seized in pain.

"No, don't move, Jasper. Please."

Through his foggy vision, he saw her, perched over him. He might have thought he was dreaming if not for the bloodstained cloth in her hand. *His* blood. *Christ.*

The men in his kitchen. The attack.

"Mrs. Zhao." He grimaced as he tried to lift himself up from… a sofa? He was on a sofa. In the front sitting room of his house on Charles Street, a room that usually collected dust.

"She's perfectly fine, I promise." Leo gently pressed her hands against his shoulders to try and keep him down. At the news, Jasper released his tightened muscles. He fell backward against the cushions, and a deep throb pulsed through his body. It was somehow both agonizing and pleasant.

"They didn't harm her?" Jasper asked, his swollen bottom lip tugging painfully. It seemed to have its own heartbeat.

"No, they only frightened her," Leo answered. She was

backlit by the dim gas jet of a wall bracket. "They cut the rope from her wrists before leaving, so she came to Spring Street for my uncle. He'd already left, but I was still there. I've sent for him. He should be here any moment."

Jasper closed his eye, grateful Mrs. Zhao hadn't been hurt. They could have killed her. The Spitalfields Angels. *Damn it.* He took shallow breaths, his ribs complaining with each one.

"Who did this to you?" Leo asked, her damp cloth dabbing at his lip again. He winced and lifted his arm to stop her. Miraculously, his arm wasn't broken. He recalled a kick that had felt as if it should have splintered the bone below his shoulder in two. Jasper stilled her hand.

"That hurts," he said.

"Because you've been badly beaten," she replied. "Mrs. Zhao said there were four men. They caught you by surprise and piled on."

Only four? "It felt like a dozen."

A swift knocking came, and Leo jumped from the edge of the sofa.

"Is he awake?" Claude appeared, a leather bag in hand as he came to stand over him.

"Were you at Duke Street?" Jasper asked. If the Angels had come here so soon after his and Leo's visit to Holloway, they may have also gone to Leo's house.

"Yes," Claude answered.

"Everything was fine there?"

Bending at the hip, the old man took an incisive look at Jasper. "Why wouldn't they be? I think you're concussed. Quite badly, by the look of you."

Jasper tried to prop himself up on his elbow but gave

up when his brain felt as if it were flipping over inside his skull.

"Mister Jasper." Mrs. Zhao appeared beside Claude. "My poor boy. I thought they would kill you." Her throat squeezed over the last few words, and her hand covered her mouth. She was on the verge of tears, her eyes swollen from prior sobbing.

"I'm all right," he tried to assure her, even though he currently felt as if he'd been run over by an omnibus. "I think I am, at least."

Leo guided the distraught housekeeper from the room, suggesting they go to the kitchen to prepare tea and some poultices. Claude continued to inspect him, murmuring to himself under his breath. "You've some gashes to your face that will need sutures, and that blackened eye is impressive, but I'm more concerned about your head and ribs. I'll need to have a look at your torso, Inspector."

Jasper nodded and, with a hand from Claude, sat up slowly. He paused, waiting for the wicked throbbing throughout his skull and the surge of nausea that came with it to subside. He and Claude were attempting to slip the sleeves of his coat off when Leo returned to the room.

"Mrs. Zhao said the intruders mentioned angels." Her eyes rounded. "The Spitalfields Angels?"

"Yes," he answered, dispensing with his coat at last. He started with the buttons of his waistcoat. "It seems our visit to Holloway and what we discussed with Mrs. Stewart was noted after all."

Leo stared at him, horror and guilt slashing her expression. "I didn't believe you when you warned me... I'm so sorry, Jasper. This is my fault."

His lingering nausea weakened for a moment. "It isn't your doing. The warder..."

"Miss Hartley," she said, biting the name off.

"You can discuss that later," Claude said. "We need to get you into bed, Inspector. I'll be better able to assess your torso there."

Claude gave him his arm, but the old man was too frail, and Jasper too unsteady. His head became an eddy of pain as he rose to his feet. He was about to go down when Leo braced him at the waist and draped his arm over her shoulder.

"I'm fine." It wasn't true, and he felt pathetic for it.

"Don't be so proud," she said as she and Claude led him from the sitting room, up the stairs slowly, then toward his room. By the time they settled him onto the edge of his bed, his ribs were on fire. He refused to allow Claude to undress him and began to open his waistcoat buttons on his own.

"I'm sure it's just some broken ribs," Jasper said, wincing.

"What if he's bleeding internally?" Leo asked her uncle with an edge of panic. It was at least nice to know she didn't want him to die. He huffed a laugh at his own thought, and she glared at him. "It is entirely possible, you know."

With an impatient sigh, she came forward and batted his fumbling fingers away from the small abalone buttons on his shirt. Leo bent at the hip and began to pop them free.

"I've seen corpses at Spring Street that expired from ruptured spleens or livers, or lacerated intestines. They are all serious conditions. I think we should take you to hospital. The closest one is St. Thomas's," she said as she deftly undid his buttons, leaning close enough for him to breathe in the faint scent of honeysuckle. Her soap, perhaps, or perfume.

All swirls of nausea subsided, pushed out by the shock of Leo next tugging the bottom of his shirt from his trousers so she could continue with her task.

"I don't need to go to St. Thomas's." Glancing toward Claude, who looked on with a raised brow, Jasper lifted his heavy arms and stilled Leo's wrists with his hands. "And I can take it from here."

He heard a small intake of air. As she froze, he knew Leo had realized what she'd been doing.

"Oh. Yes, of course." She backed away, taking the sweet, floral scent with her. "I'll see to helping Mrs. Zhao."

As soon as she left, with his buttons taken care of, Jasper tried to shrug out of his shirtsleeves.

And then, without realizing how, he was on his back, opening his eyes to see the ceiling above. Time had passed. How long, he didn't know. But his boots were off, his bare chest was wrapped snugly in linen, he was tucked under a sheet, and Claude was seated beside him, measuring his pulse.

"I have assured my niece that you are not bleeding internally," he said conversationally. "However, your concussion is quite severe. Rest. But I'll need to wake you every hour."

He felt ill with fury. The Angels had broken into his home, terrified Mrs. Zhao, and bested him. *Damn it.* He felt like a weakling just lying there. It wasn't the pain that bothered him the most. It was the powerlessness; it wasn't anything he was accustomed to.

"Who is with Mrs. Feldman?" Jasper asked. A thready panic remained that the Angels might still pay Leo's home a visit.

"She is here. I brought her with me. Now rest. All is well," Claude answered.

Jasper closed his eyes. A minute later, or what felt like a minute, he opened them to find Leo perched on the edge of his bed.

"My uncle fell asleep," she whispered.

"You need rest too. I'll be fine." Shifting in bed, his ribs screamed that it was a lie. He groaned and shut his eyes. The soft brush of cool fingertips drifted over his brow. Somehow, the touch loosened the stiffness in his chest and abdomen, and a languid sleep claimed him.

Chapter Sixteen

The lumps in the armchair kept Leo awake most of the night. So did worry. Though Claude had been certain Jasper didn't have internal injuries, he'd expressed concern for the state of his head.

"He is in and out of consciousness," Claude informed her, when she'd reentered Jasper's bedroom several minutes after leaving hastily. She wasn't sure what had come over her, openly undoing his shirt buttons like that. Even in his deplorable condition, Jasper had known to stop her from undressing him further.

"I don't believe his skull is fractured, but it is possible his brain might swell if it was injured badly enough in the beating," Claude explained.

She'd approached the bed, her stomach cramping at the sight of the fresh sutures closing his gashed brow, the purpling bruises on his stomach, and those peeking out from his cotton linen-wrapped chest. The helpless panic was unlike anything she'd ever felt before.

"How will we know if that happens?" she'd asked, and the answer—seizures—had only exacerbated her worry.

Claude said he'd check on Jasper hourly throughout the night, but Leo had stayed awake too. When she'd found her uncle sleeping on the guest bedroom's slipper sofa, with Flora snoring softly in the bed, she'd decided to keep watch over Jasper herself. Each time she eased him awake, he'd murmur nonsense, still half asleep even though his eyes were open. She'd felt his forehead countless times, checking for fever. Her eyes had grown hot and dry, her mind muddled as she forced herself to stay awake, watching for any sign of a seizure.

At some point before dawn, she must have drifted to sleep anyway. She now shook herself awake at the sound of her name.

"Leo?"

She winced at a crick in her neck and a tightness in her legs as she straightened them. She'd tucked them underneath her as she slept, slumped against the broad wing of the armchair.

Jasper was sitting up in bed, the sheet and blanket around his waist. It was reminiscent of how she'd found him when she'd entered this room a few months ago at dawn, the same muted morning light coming through the gaps in the curtains. She'd been too single-minded in that moment to allow his undressed state to affect her. Now, however, the impropriety of it came at her from all directions.

"Did you sleep in that lumpy chair?" he asked, his voice cracking. Mrs. Zhao had left some water in a glass by his bed. He reached for it, groaning as he did.

"I didn't intend to." She got to her feet, blinking

rapidly and trying not to stare at his bare skin. Especially not at the scar on his upper left pectoral. She'd inflicted it long ago with the jagged shard from her china doll.

He lowered the glass and sat back against the headboard, breathing heavily as though already fatigued. His left eye was swollen and discolored, his split lower lip starting to scab.

"How is your head?" she asked, averting her attention from his chest and the welts and contusions on the well-defined planes of his abdomen.

"Ask again tomorrow. I might have a more favorable answer."

"I'll fetch my uncle," she said, eager to leave the room.

"Wait." Jasper shoved off the blanket and tried to stand.

"What are you doing? Sit back down at once." She charged toward him as the blanket dropped. At least he was wearing trousers this time.

"I can stand just fine." He did, though with some assistance; he gripped the edge of his bedside table. "You need to stop looking into anything having to do with the Yard bombing."

His concern was understandable. His attack last night was a result of their visit to Mrs. Stewart. "But we don't know if the Angels don't want you asking questions about Niles Foster, or if they don't want you asking questions about Mrs. Bates's connection to them."

"It doesn't matter," Jasper replied. "I don't want them paying you a visit the way they did me."

"I was with you yesterday," she reasoned. "If they'd wanted to threaten me, they would have by now."

He gritted his teeth. "Leo. Just…stop. This is serious."

"I'm aware of that. I did find you unconscious on the

kitchen floor, if you recall. And I stayed up all night, fearful that your brain would swell!"

A knock landed on the open door. Claude stood there, peering between them. "I'm quite sure the Inspector's head could do without you raising your voice, my dear." He came inside the bedroom. "I'm glad to see you're up. Leonora, you should have woken me during the night."

She gathered her temper, sorry that she'd shouted at Jasper. A little, anyway. "I didn't want to bother Aunt Flora."

Her aunt had been confused about where they were last evening, even though she'd been to the Charles Street house several times over the years. It wasn't their regular routine, though. Mrs. Zhao had helped to calm her, and after adding a little brandy to her tea, Flora had fallen asleep easily.

Claude checked Jasper's head, including both pupils, and pressed lightly on his injuries, eliciting a muffled curse in response.

"You look worse than you are," her uncle announced. "Your head should feel better in a few days, but with a concussion like that, you'll need to be cautious not to overdo things. Just go slowly."

The advice was sound, but Leo knew Jasper wouldn't heed it. Going slowly and not overdoing things simply weren't in his blood.

Jasper thanked him, and Claude announced that he would be taking Flora back to Duke Street before going to the morgue. He eyed Leo over the rim of his spectacles. "We'll wait for you downstairs, my dear."

She would go with them, of course, as she was still in her dress from the day before.

"You'll stay at home today?" she asked Jasper after her uncle was gone.

He started toward the tall bureau. "No. I need to get to the Yard and let Chief Coughlan know what happened."

Leo imagined the whole of Scotland Yard would wish to know why the detective inspector looked like he'd lost a boxing match to an opponent twice his size, which Jasper would loathe explaining.

"You heard my uncle," she said. "You must take things easy today." But it wouldn't change his mind. He was too stubborn.

"I have a murder investigation," he said, moving stiffly to the wardrobe.

"Your only lead is a man named Olaf, who works for the Angels," she pointed out. "You truly mean to press forward with contacting them? Jasper, you were nearly killed last night."

He pulled a pressed and starched white shirt from a hanger. With slow movements, mindful of his injuries, he slid his arms into the sleeves. The sight of him dressing slammed into her with fresh impropriety.

"If they'd wanted me dead, they would have either gutted me or put a bullet in my head. Besides, I have another lead."

The blithe description of how they might have killed him made her feel ill. But the mention of another lead lit her interest. "What lead?"

Jasper began to do up the shirt buttons. Warmth gathered under her skin. She really ought not to have been watching him dress.

"A bank," he said.

"Which bank?"

"Despite my being concussed, I'm not addled enough to tell you." He sent a wry glance in her direction. "But it's possible Foster visited it shortly before he died, and I'd like to know why."

Leo wasn't sure it would lead to anything. The man had been penniless. He'd likely wanted to borrow money. But she kept the pessimistic thought to herself.

"Claude is waiting for me," she said, moving to leave. "He doesn't want to be late to the morgue today. He has a new assistant. Mr. Quinn."

Jasper pulled at his collar. "That can't be good."

He knew of Claude's infirmity and that any assistant would be watching him closely.

"It isn't. Mr. Quinn is fresh out of medical school and just so happens to be the chief coroner's grandson." The man had been infuriating the evening before, pointing out that she wasn't being paid and assuming she would wish to work for a wage. He wasn't entirely wrong. She did want paid work—*at the morgue.*

She'd avoided Mr. Quinn for the last few hours of the day, searching the vast crypt for the boxes containing her family's belongings. The trouble was that Claude couldn't quite recall where he'd stashed them. Leo had gone through piles and piles of detritus before hearing Mrs. Zhao's voice upstairs, shouting for help.

"Please be careful today," she told Jasper as she stepped into the corridor. He nodded.

"And Leo?" She glanced back into his room. "Thank you." He hooked a thumb at the armchair. "For keeping vigil and putting up with that lumpy relic."

She smothered a grin and went to meet her aunt and uncle in the foyer.

Mr. Quinn attended Claude during three postmortem examinations before noon. Leo did as well, much to the young man's discomfort. During the first, in which she stood unflinching as Claude removed the dead man's clothing, Mr. Quinn blushed furiously. He even asked her if she might be more at ease stepping out until the deed was done.

"Mr. Quinn, do you suppose I have never seen a naked dead body in all the years I've worked here?" she'd asked, slightly pleased by the additional splotches of red appearing on his cheeks. Mr. Higgins, Claude's past apprentice, had not been embarrassed by her presence—just irritated.

Mr. Quinn had spluttered, turning a deeper shade of tomato red. "Surely, this poor fellow would not wish for a young woman to look upon him in this state."

Claude had not been able to interject before Leo replied, "As he is deceased, I'm not convinced he would care who looks at him now, man or woman."

He'd frowned for the rest of the morning, throwing wary and incredulous glances at her as Claude proceeded with the examinations. His hands shook here and there, but whenever the tremors grew serious, Leo distracted Mr. Quinn with a comment or question, the most outlandish being, "What is that cologne you are wearing? Or is that ammonia that I smell? Forgive me, they're so similar." And with each postmortem closing, Claude stepped back to allow Mr. Quinn to do the suturing, claiming the more he did, the better he'd become at it.

By noon, with three examinations complete, they paused for tea.

Leo had been taking notes all morning, jotting postmortem findings down, as had Mr. Quinn. She'd presumed he was taking notes on the examination procedure itself, perhaps recording pieces of insightful information Claude provided. However, when Mr. Quinn took the chair behind Leo's desk and fed paper into the typewriter, she put her hands on her hips.

"What do you think you are doing?" she asked, perhaps a bit more sharply than necessary.

"Typing a postmortem report," he replied. "It is part of my duties here."

She fought the desire to stomp her foot and order him out of her chair. But it was only a matter of time before she was ejected from this morgue and the duties she had grown accustomed to—and was quite good at. Though it pained her, she held her tongue as she slapped her notes down upon the desk. Instead, she went to the possessions register to record the personal items that had come in with the three corpses that morning.

The first man had expired of heart failure, the second of untreated pneumonia, and the third corpse, an older woman, had been a vagrant who'd been attacked by a dog. The animal's sharp teeth had torn at a bundle of varicose veins in her left leg, which had then hemorrhaged profusely. Without immediate medical care, and in her weakened state, she'd died. The woman's possessions had been limited to her clothing and tatty shoes, though the two men had quite a lot in their pockets. The first man had come in with a leather case stuffed with documents and random bits, easily identifying him.

"Don't you require your notes for that?" Mr. Quinn asked after pausing his typing for a few moments. He was tediously slow, his pointer fingers hunting arduously for each letter.

"No, I do not," she replied, filling in the lines for the pneumonia victim.

"Are you logging the possessions for all three bodies?"

"Yes." Leo sighed, realizing that he was unaware of her unusual memory. What a bother to have to explain.

She lowered the register and faced him. "I have an impeccable memory, Mr. Quinn. Photographic, some call it. Very useful for tasks like this."

He rested an elbow on the desk and turned toward her. "A photographic memory? Truly?"

Oddly, he looked intrigued rather than doubtful—the latter of which most people were whenever they learned of her preternatural ability. She nodded and turned back to the possessions register.

"Can you remember everything then? Say, what I was wearing yesterday, when we first met?"

She closed her eyes and groaned. "That is hardly a difficult question. You were wearing the same ugly brown suit that you're wearing today. Besides, I am not going to prove my memory to you by performing like some circus monkey. Take my word for it, or don't. It makes no difference to me."

She finished with the possessions log while Mr. Quinn went back to his stilted typing. With him still occupying her desk, and nothing more to do in the postmortem room, Leo decided on another search of the crypt for her family's boxed-up belongings.

Without windows or natural light, the darkened crypt

required her to bring a paraffin lamp. A series of arches constructed of block stone divided the vast crypt, which ran not just beneath the old vestry but also reached under the adjacent St. Matthew's Church. Everything from broken pews, crates of moldering hymnals, a discarded confessional, and rolled-up tapestries to a series of older autopsy tables, chairs, and, of course, boxes upon boxes of unclaimed personal items belonging to past corpses packed the arched spaces. Somewhere among it all—Claude had given her a general idea of their location—were her family's things.

When Jasper revealed her father had been working for the East Rips, she hadn't wanted to believe him. But the truth was, she could hardly remember her father. Leonard Spencer was a mystery to her. And now, Flora's comment about his *bloody, bloody business* had become more ominous knowing that her father had, at some point, formed ties to a criminal gang. If she could find his papers, or even Flora's letters to her mother, she might better understand what he'd done to make his family a target for revenge.

Leo went past the section she'd finished off the previous evening, before Mrs. Zhao's panicked arrival, and set her lantern on a rusted metal surgical table. The boxes and crates here were coated in at least an inch of dust. Even the spider webs were aged and dusty, drifting loosely like old lace. She reached for a box made of once-stiff corrugated board, now soft and limp.

"What is all this?"

Leo hadn't heard Mr. Quinn descending the wooden steps and now felt encroached upon.

"Storage." She wasn't inclined to fully explain.

"There's quite a bit of it," he commented, running a hand over some of the boxes she'd searched yesterday. "Storage for the church or the morgue?"

"Both. Is there something I can help you with?" Leo asked, eager for him to leave so she could get on with her search.

He exhaled and came to a stop within the circle of lantern light. "I wanted to apologize."

It wasn't what she'd expected.

"It was rude of me yesterday to ask if you were paid a wage. It's none of my business."

The apology at least sounded sincere.

"No, it isn't," she agreed.

"And I shouldn't have quizzed you on your memory," he added. "Though, it really is quite impressive."

She fiddled with a softened corner of the box that she wanted to go through, suddenly discomfited by his changed bearing. It would be easier if she could simply dislike him. He was, after all, going to be replacing her uncle here. And *her*.

"Well… Thank you, Mr. Quinn."

He stepped back. "I should finish my report."

She should have been typing that report. The reminder was enough for her to harden again. Once he'd left the crypt, Leo exhaled forcefully, scattering the top layer of dust on the wilted box. She went through it quickly, finding yellowed sheet music for the church organist. Moving on, she reached for an old carpetbag that sat upon a crate on the floor. Then froze.

Next to the crate, the side of a large trunk jutted out. It was made of dark, oiled wood and straps of iron, and the lid was rounded into a camelback dome. The plated corners of the trunk were tarnished and dull. For several moments, she stared at the ornate fanned design of the bolted overlays. Stooping, Leo grabbed hold of the metal ring set into the side of the trunk and pulled. Heavy as it was, laden with possessions inside, it didn't move far along the rough stone floor. She pulled again, employing more force, and slowly, the trunk came out of its hiding place into full view.

Dropping the handle, she staggered back. A wave of dizziness whirled through her. Leo stared at the steamer trunk, her breaths coming short, and her eyes stinging. She had no doubt that when she opened the latch and threw back the lid, she'd find cushioned walls in bright green velvet and an uncomfortably hard, spring floral-papered bottom. She had seen the interior of this trunk countless times in her memory.

She'd found her family's steamer trunk. The one in which Jasper had hidden her to save her life.

Chapter Seventeen

The clock in the front sitting room chimed the nine o'clock hour. Impatience crawled along Jasper's skin.

"Mrs. Zhao, are you ready?" he called, raising his voice for the housekeeper to hear from her rooms off the kitchen, where she had disappeared earlier in a fine temper.

She wasn't pleased with his decision, but he wasn't going to change his mind. Not even when she came around the corner in the back hall, her mouth fixed in a scowl.

"I'm made of tough stuff, Mister Jasper. I won't be chased out of my home," she said, even as she carried a large carpetbag and wore her hat and long coat.

He took the bag from her. "The Angels are dangerous people. Since I'm not going to be deterred from my duty at the Yard, I won't have you here alone if they come back to see their threat through."

Speaking pained his swollen bottom lip as well as the

tender bruise that encompassed most of his jaw. His ribs, though wrapped in cotton linen, smarted something fierce if he drew breath too deeply. He'd consented to tea and porridge when Mrs. Zhao insisted it would help the ache in his head. It hadn't—much.

"I don't like to leave you," she said as he ushered them outside.

"You'll be safer at your sister's home for now," he replied. "And I'll feel easier knowing you're there."

He'd never forgive himself if something having to do with his work brought harm to Mrs. Zhao. Last night had been too close.

"Very well," she said as they walked toward a cabstand near St. James's Square. "But make sure you eat. And use the salve on the kitchen table for your cuts and bruises."

He assured her he would. "Don't worry about me. As soon as the danger has passed, I'll send for you."

A cabbie near the stand noticed his signal and urged his horses forward. The housekeeper patted Jasper's cheek. "If you're anything like Mr. Reid, I have reason to worry. He was relentless too."

He made no reply as he gave her the money for the fare, handed her into the cab, and saw her off. Perhaps he was like his father, even if they weren't of the same blood. Gregory Reid wouldn't have allowed a vicious beating to keep him down. If anything, it would have spurred him on more persuasively. After Leo left that morning, he'd allowed himself just five minutes of frustration and feelings of impotence before shaking them off. He had a lead to follow up on and a murder to solve.

Signaling another cab, he directed it to Leicester Square. When he entered the lobby inside Seale and

Company Bank, the alarmed looks he received seemed to only make his bruised face throb more intensely. He waited in line for one of the clerks to summon him forward to the tall, granite counter. An arched opening allowed an unobstructed conversation. The man eyed him with a touch of skepticism until Jasper introduced himself and showed his warrant card; his skepticism then increased.

"What is it you require, Inspector?" the clerk asked.

"I'd like to know if a man named Niles Foster kept an account with your institution."

"That would be private information, I'm sure you understand. I cannot divulge—"

"Mr. Foster is dead. I'm investigating his murder, and I need to know why he would have come to this bank, as I have evidence that he did."

The clerk looked apprehensively over Jasper's shoulder to the line forming behind him. "Please lower your voice, Inspector. I do not wish to alarm our patrons."

"And I do not wish to have to return with constables and a police search warrant, which would be a much more chaotic scene," he replied.

The clerk lifted his chin with understanding. He stepped away, moving to a long desk behind him with shelves and thick, leather-bound ledgers. He plucked down one and began to thumb through the pages. A minute later, he returned.

"There is no Niles Foster listed among our clientele," he reported with a smug arch of his brow.

It wasn't surprising, considering the aide had been in reduced circumstances. Jasper took the photograph he'd pocketed from the boxes of Foster's things, a bit creased after the attack last night, and placed it on the marble counter. He tapped it. "This man, standing behind the chairs. Do you recognize him?"

The clerk sighed and leaned forward for a look. There was a second clerk assisting another line of patrons; Jasper would ask him next. But the first clerk straightened and made a small sound of interest. "I believe I do recall this man."

Jasper pocketed the photograph. "When did you last see him?"

"Last week," the clerk answered. "Thursday, it was."

Oliver had last seen Niles Foster either Monday or Tuesday. So, he'd come here after his request for money had been rejected by the viscount.

"Why do you recall him with such specificity?" Jasper asked the clerk.

Behind him, a man in line coughed loudly to indicate his growing impatience. The clerk looked around Jasper's shoulder and politely told the gentleman he'd be right with him.

Less politely, he returned his attention to Jasper and said, "It was his manner that was quite memorable. The man in your photograph asked to speak to our manager. When he was told that the manager was in a meeting with members of the board of governors, he insisted upon waiting." The clerk pointed to a row of chairs against the wall behind Jasper. "He sat there for nearly half an hour before the meeting let out. Fidgeting and coughing and tapping his foot incessantly. Rather a nuisance, as it does echo in here. High ceilings and marble, you see."

"He then spoke to the bank manager?" Jasper queried.

"Yes. However, he spent no more than five minutes

with Mr. Stewart before coming out again. In quite a fit of pique too."

Comprehension stole down Jasper's spine. He stared at the clerk. "Stewart?"

"Mr. Porter Stewart, yes," he replied. "He is our manager."

Banking. Sir Elliot had informed him that was Mr. Stewart's business. Niles Foster had come here to speak to Geraldine Stewart's husband? His mind tumbled over the revelation for a prolonged moment, though the lingering throb from his concussion slowed him considerably.

"I'd like to speak to Mr. Stewart," he said. The clerk shook his head.

"He isn't in today."

Without a doubt, the clerk knew of Mr. Stewart's predicament with his wife. The story had been in numerous newspapers, and surely, the bank's board of governors were scrambling to protect its reputation. They would likely sack Porter Stewart to cleanse themselves and their institution of any connection to her purported crime.

Jasper took down the clerk's name and thanked him for his time. As he left, the lingering nausea from his head injury cleared. With a witness now who could place Niles Foster with Mr. Stewart, there was no longer any doubt—the connection between his murder case and Inspector Tomlin's case against Mrs. Stewart was solid.

He went on foot to Whitehall Place rather than hire a cab or catch an omnibus. Though his ribs regretted the choice as he approached the Yard, the extra time gave him the opportunity to clear his head and prepare for Tomlin's certain displeasure. Ignoring the startled looks and questions lobbed at him as he entered the building, he made his way to the detective department. The bricklayers had made good progress on the reconstruction of the wall, but the clamor of their work hammered at his brain.

"Hell's bells, guv," Lewis said, standing up. "What in the blazes happened to you?"

Jasper removed his coat and tossed it onto his chair, longing for his office and some privacy. "I'll explain later."

A shrill whistle pierced the department. "Look at you, Reid," Tomlin called from the collection of desks in the corner of the room dedicated to the Special Irish Branch detectives. He had his boots on the blotter, hands laced behind his head. "Did you lose to one of the toffs at your fancy boxing club?"

Tomlin and a few other detectives around him snickered, including Constable Wiley. He looked to be socializing with them rather than doing his own job. Jasper's membership at Oliver Hayes's boxing club had become common knowledge, and some men, like Tomlin, mentioned it at every opportunity, if only to draw a line in the sand between them. Jasper was, in their opinion, reaching beyond his station.

He braced himself and walked toward them. Passing over Tomlin's goading remark, he got to what needed saying.

"I'm investigating the murder of a man named Niles Foster. His postmortem showed the same bruising patterns on his wrists as were on Constable Lloyd's and matching gashes on their cheeks, most likely inflicted by the same ring. Both men were bound and beaten in the hours before their deaths, and it appears their assailant was one and the same."

Rapidly, Tomlin's smug grin fell. Jasper pressed onward.

"I have a witness who says my victim approached Geraldine Stewart's husband last week, before his death and before Constable Lloyd's. I have another witness who can place Foster in some sort of tussle with a Spitalfields Angel, and yet another witness who says PC Lloyd had some interaction with the Angels, too."

Tomlin took his feet from his desk and stood up. "What is all this you're spouting, Reid? I've closed the Lloyd bombing case. We're now centering our attentions on Clan na Gael for the other three explosions."

They didn't look especially industrious at the moment, but Jasper kept that observation to himself.

"Other than a monogrammed suitcase, you have no evidence Geraldine Stewart was behind the Lloyd bombing. No motive, either," he said. The gloves were coming off, and he was ready for it.

"She's a radical suffragist, and Lord Babbage was due to be here that day—an appointment Miss Spencer, with her many contacts here, could have easily gleaned and shared with her fellow political shrew. Not to mention that the suitcase belonged to the woman. She admitted to it," Tomlin said. "I don't need anything else."

Jasper disregarded the absurd insinuation against Leo. The man was reaching.

"The Stewarts say they had a break-in a month ago. You didn't consider that the suitcase could have been taken then to set Geraldine Stewart up as the culprit?"

Tomlin's flat stare hardened. "The Stewarts never made a report because it didn't happen. They're lying." He then cocked his head. "What is it you're doing, Reid? Are you falling short with your own investigation, so you've decided you need to desperately leap into mine?"

"The two cases are linked," Jasper replied, aware they were drawing attention from around the department room. "It warrants a deeper look. Both Foster and Lloyd were connected to the Angels; Foster was connected to Porter Stewart; and Mrs. Stewart informed me that her sister-in-law, Emma Bates, may be related to Clive Paget of the Spitalfields Angels."

Tomlin crossed his arms and came forward. "When did you question my suspect?"

"Yesterday." He rubbed his jaw. "And then the Angels paid my home a visit last night to warn me off their scent."

The other inspector's pasty coloring reddened. "I'm going to bet Miss Spencer's had a hand in your meddling."

Jasper kept his mouth shut. He wouldn't confirm or deny it. Though it bothered him that Tomlin had so easily suspected as much.

"You'd be better off putting that harridan in her place instead of indulging her," Tomlin said.

Behind him, Constable Wiley grunted his agreement. "The previous Inspector Reid made a fuss over her too. Now she thinks she belongs here."

"She got a taste of reality the other night, didn't she?" Tomlin said, forming a malevolent grin. "A holding room upstairs is the only place inside this building that woman belongs. A few hours locked up will have put her right, I expect."

Jasper inhaled evenly, careful not to overstretch his broken ribs. He clenched both hands into fists, then relaxed them again. He would not rise to Tomlin's bait, or

Wiley's, no matter how profound his desire to knock them both flat.

"Did you find any other connection between PC Lloyd and Geraldine Stewart?" he asked instead. "How did she get him to transport the bomb?"

"That isn't your concern, Detective Inspector," Tomlin barked.

"So, you haven't found another connection besides the valise."

Tomlin came toe-to-toe with Jasper, using his beefy frame and height to bear down on him. The intimidation tactic might have worked on others, but Jasper wasn't afraid of this man. He was a geyser of hot air and speculation and showed a complete deficiency of comprehensive investigative police work. He wasn't resting on his laurels; he was floating through the air on them.

"Lloyd's lady friend, Miss Brooks, is one of Mrs. Stewart's radical followers," the Special Irish Branch inspector said, chewing off each word. "As is Leonora Spencer. *There* is my connection, Reid. Now, stay out of my case. And I don't care how pretty she is or how much you want to get up those skirts of hers; you keep that snooping woman out of it too. I won't tell you again."

A vision of cracking his knuckles into the bridge of Tomlin's nose was so vivid, for a half second, Jasper thought he'd done it. His pulse slammed hard in his neck, his blood rising at the lewd suggestion. The whole department watched, waiting for a fight. Even the clanging of the bricklayers had fallen off as they looked on with interest. Just barely holding his temper in check, he allowed reason to win out over temptation. He was already a battered mess; one strike from the Special Irish Branch inspector would likely leave Jasper unconscious on the floor.

"My investigation is crossing with yours, Tomlin. There is no doubt about it, and I'll follow wherever it leads." He started back for his desk, where Lewis was pulling on his coat. He tossed Jasper his. It seemed the detective sergeant understood that they needed to pay a call on Porter Stewart right away.

"And as for Miss Spencer," Jasper said, taking stock of the seething inspector over his shoulder. "Speak of her in that manner again, and I promise this department will get the bloody fight they want to see."

Chapter Eighteen

No new bodies arrived at the morgue for the remainder of the afternoon, and for that, Leo was grateful. Had she needed to, she would have emerged from the crypt to distract Mr. Quinn while her uncle worked. However, the postmortem room remained quiet above her, allowing her the time to gather her courage and open the old steamer trunk. As she'd expected, the padded interior walls were covered in green crushed velvet, although they were mostly obscured by the mountain of items Claude had decided to keep from the rooms of her family's home.

Leo's hands shook as she went through it all, pulling out ledgers, papers, books, trinkets, hoops of half-finished embroidery, a moth-eaten wedding gown, delicate lacework, and, heartbreakingly, baby swaddling and clothing. Even little leather booties, mildewed from storage.

A box of photographs distracted her from her search for a short while. Claude and Flora kept a few framed photographs of her lost family in the front sitting room, and Leo had one of the five of them together in her bedroom. She knew her parents' faces because of those images. Jacob's and Agnes's too. They were all frozen in time, their expressions always the same. Finding more photographs, with her family in different clothing, in different poses felt…otherworldly. Like an unexpected gift, and yet, one that pained her.

Leo had been given the feminine form of her father's name, and she did resemble him. More so than she did her mother, Andromeda. She'd inherited his sable brown hair, rather than her mother's lighter blonde; his straight and serious nose, rather than her mother's sweet button nose; and his intense eyes, instead of Andromeda's warm, inviting gaze. It was no wonder Aunt Flora looked upon Leo with such wariness; in her addled state of mind, she likely saw Leonard Spencer instead of her niece.

Inside a large, cherrywood jewelry box, Leo found what she'd been looking for. Among some modest brooches, paste rings, and necklaces, a stack of letters had been bound with yellow ribbon. They were in their original envelopes, and a cursory look showed they were from Flora.

At last.

Though it was only one side of the conversation, Leo eagerly read them by the light of the paraffin lamp, while she sat on the crate. Most of the letters were mundane, asking after the children, the weather, any news from London, and relaying events happening where she and Claude were living. Their location changed over the course of the letters, from Turkey to Cyprus to Greece, and finally, to the small island of Crete. Only in these later letters did Flora broach anything interesting regarding Leo's father.

Your concerns about Leonard are valid, dear sister. I fear for you and the children if he does not stop taking these risks, Flora wrote in one letter. In another: *You and the children should leave at once. Come to us in Crete. We haven't much space, but we will make room. Claude will purchase tickets and send them to you, if you'll agree, and you must.*

Leo tried to decipher what her aunt was replying to in some letters, such as when she wrote: *No, I do not believe that to abide by your marital vow is of the utmost importance. Your safety is, and that of little Jacob, Leonora, and Agnes.* And then, in the final letter Leo's mother had received from her sister, Flora wrote another chilling sentiment: *What use is integrity or justness if he is caught? If he is dead? It will all mean nothing in the end.*

It was clear that Flora had known the nature of her brother-in-law's business and that whatever he was doing was putting his family in danger. Leo's mother had shared whatever concerns she had about it with her older sister in her letters. And yet, none of Flora's replies gave even a sliver of a detail that could help Leo discover what, exactly, her father's transgression had been. Jasper said he'd betrayed the East Rips. But how?

She turned to the ledgers and papers she'd first retrieved from the trunk and began to page through those. Shipping invoices for coffee and tea, cargo lists for ships sailing from Canada and Boston, correspondence with clients, though none of them bore the name Carter. The reading grew tedious, her father's handwriting poor. He at least marked numbers clearly in his account books. One appeared to be a banking ledger for his own account, and his record-keeping was meticulous. For an accountant, it should have been.

Leo turned to the back of the ledger after a while, looking for dates closer to the time of the murders, and she picked up on a pattern. Beginning in the early autumn of 1866, Leonard Spencer began to receive monthly payments of five pounds. The only markings next to the deposits were initials: *BR*. Though she looked through the ledger again from front to back, she found no one mentioned with those initials.

Leo's eyes ached. The poor light and lack of sleep from the night before had caught up with her. Finally, she called it a day. She emerged from the crypt to find Mr. Quinn had gone. It was four in the afternoon, and Claude was preparing tea on the cottage cast-iron range in the corner of the back office.

"I presume you found the trunk," he said, lifting the kettle from the hob.

Leo wiped dust from her skirt and cuffs. "Uncle Claude..." She hesitated, uncertain if it was important to ask. But she wanted to know. "Did you know that I hid in that trunk?"

Claude held still. Then the blackened bottom of the kettle met the hob again with a clatter. He turned to her. "That trunk?"

She nodded.

"Oh, my dear." He forgot the kettle as he came forward. "I didn't know. I knew you hid, of course, but I didn't realize... I'm sorry if it has upset you."

Leo shook her head. Oddly enough, after the initial

shock of seeing it again in person rather than just in her memory, she found she wasn't upset at all.

"It hasn't." She took over at the range to finish preparing their tea. "I just wonder how I could have ever been small enough to fit in there."

Again, the darkened outline of the boy came charging forward in her mind. Jasper had been taller than her, his voice coming from above her head. From his whispers, she hadn't been able to tell how old he was. But somehow in the dim moonlight, he'd found the steamer trunk and flung back the lid, urging her inside. Her palm had been bleeding, hot and painful, and she'd been sobbing, her breaths rattling. *You can't let them hear you. Not a sound.* When he'd closed and latched the trunk's domed lid, Leo had nearly screamed. But even in her nine-year-old brain, she'd known that he'd had to latch it. The men downstairs, who'd come up into the attic no more than a minute later, would never think to check a latched trunk, for how could she have hidden inside and latched it afterward?

It wasn't until hours later, when she'd heard voices again downstairs, with one man in particular addressing another as 'constable' that Leo had started shouting at the top of her lungs. She'd pounded on the lid of the trunk, kicked against its side panels, and screamed until the Inspector found her.

"I found some letters to my mother from Aunt Flora. Ledgers belonging to my father too. Do you ever recall him mentioning anyone with the initials BR?"

At that question, Claude's brow crinkled. "I'm afraid Leonard and I weren't close. I hadn't seen him in years before… Well. Why do you ask?"

She sighed and sipped her tea as she stood next to the range. Her backside ached from sitting for so long. "It doesn't matter. I'm exhausted. I'm sure I'll think more clearly tomorrow."

He nodded. "I'm locking up early tonight and going to check on Jasper before I return home to your aunt. Do you wish to accompany me to Charles Street?"

Leo was curious to know how Jasper was faring and had thought of him several times that day. With any hope, his concussion hadn't stopped him from following the lead at the bank—whatever it had been. While she did wish to see him and discuss any gains he'd made in the case, she had also been turning over another idea. One neither Jasper nor Claude would approve of.

"I think I'll stay a little longer. You go. I'll lock up before leaving," she assured him. Claude finished his tea and prepared to leave, and although a part of her felt guilty for the deception, it didn't change her mind.

Shortly after her uncle departed, she extinguished the gasoliers and brackets and locked up for the evening. She then started on foot for the omnibus stand at Trafalgar Square. The bus she required didn't arrive for ten more minutes, and a cold drizzle had started falling. When it arrived a few minutes early, she boarded the crowded omnibus, glad for the shelter and warmth inside. The bus slowly made its way across the river toward Lambeth, and though its route didn't turn down past the wharves, Leo disembarked at the closest stop, walking the rest of the way to Eddie Bloom's club.

It wasn't a safe part of London, and Jasper would have had a fit if he knew where she was going, but she arrived at the entrance to the club just past five o'clock, no worse for wear. It was still too early for revelry, but there were some people inside when Leo paid the entry fee.

Still wearing her muted green cotton dress and her plain black coat and hat, she was hardly presentable for a night out. Attention drifted in her direction as she approached the long, glossy bar. Mr. Bloom's regular bartender had met her a handful of times, and yet, he peered at her with the blank look he might give a stranger.

"Is Mr. Bloom available?" she asked as he was running a rag around the inside of a glass. His eyes lifted to a spot over her shoulder, and when she turned to follow the direction of his gaze, she saw that Eddie Bloom had already noticed her and was approaching.

"Miss Spencer," he said, a flirtatious grin spreading over his lips. He was handsome in a slick, untrustworthy sort of way, though Leo could see why he was so successful with his club. Even though she knew he was a criminal, he didn't come across as such. He seemed more like a host you knew better than to cross. However, he'd never been anything but courteous to her.

As he looked Leo over, his happy expression turned to one of amused confusion. "Forgive me, but you appear a bit more somber than usual."

"I suppose I am," she said. "I've just come from the morgue." Mr. Bloom arched a brow. "Forgive me. You see, I work at a morgue."

"I know. Read those articles on you a few months back. Nice illustrations, but the real thing's much better." He snapped his fingers, and in the next moment, the bartender had placed a glass of claret at her elbow.

"Oh, that isn't necessary," she said, but Mr. Bloom

indicated she should sit upon one of the tall chairs at the bar.

"It's on the house," he said with a devilish wink.

She thanked him and, though uncomfortable, did as he suggested. He took the seat next to her.

"Are you meeting your friend tonight?" Mr. Bloom asked as Leo took a shallow sip of the claret. "Miss Brooks, correct?"

"No," she said, setting her glass down. "I've come to speak to you, if you have a few minutes to spare."

Intrigue lightened his countenance, making him appear almost boyish. Propping an elbow on the bar and turning fully toward her, he said, "Take as many minutes as you'd like."

Leo took another sip of wine to steady her nerves.

"Does this have anything to do with what the detective inspector came here asking about? That police officer your Miss Brooks would often dance with?" Mr. Bloom asked.

"No." Leo swallowed the claret, the smooth wine warming the center of her chest. "I wanted to ask you if you knew my father. His name was Leonard Spencer."

The club owner laced his fingers together. A few gaudy gold rings caught the light and glittered. The barest tick of a muscle above his left brow was the only indication that he was taken aback by her question.

"I won't be coy with you, Miss Spencer. I know your history. But what makes you think I would have known him?"

Leo observed him carefully. That he knew her story wasn't so surprising. Eddie Bloom was a man who made it his business to know things. However, what did surprise her was how his suave, easy flair suddenly tempered.

"I'm trying to discover why my family was murdered. I know they were targeted by a criminal organization." Leo wouldn't mention that she knew which one.

The Inspector had theorized it could be the Carters, but he'd never found any proof. She considered the papers stored in the steamer trunk. Claude mentioned the Inspector had gone through them. Had they given him any leads? Leo would need to look at the Inspector's own file on the murders to find the answer, and she wasn't sure she was ready for that yet.

"I've come across some of my father's papers that have been stored away these many years, and I think it's possible that—"

"I need you to listen to me now, Miss Spencer." Mr. Bloom unlaced his hands and took the glass from her, even though she'd still been holding the stem. He then settled his palm atop of her hand, tensing his fingers into a cage. "I like you. I think you're a good sort, so I'm going to tell you something."

Deftly, he glanced over his shoulder toward where the bartender stood, filling a few snifters with whisky. He didn't want his bartender listening, Leo deduced. She took a breath and held it, anticipating that the club owner knew something of value and was about to share it.

But then, as he spoke, a chill spooled from the base of her skull, down her spine, straight to the tips of her toes.

"The people you're referring to haven't forgotten about the little girl they overlooked that night. There are some who see you as a loose end. Right now, in their eyes, you were young. Just a little kid who hid in a trunk and probably couldn't remember a thing. No real threat at all." He spoke conversationally and softly, pausing to lean closer. Leo sat rigid in her chair, the mistake she'd made dawning on her.

"But if you start poking around, asking questions like the one you came here to ask me, well then, it might begin to sound like you remember more than they're comfortable with."

Mr. Bloom lifted his coarse palm from her hand, but instead of drawing back, he brushed his knuckles down her cheek. The intimacy of it shocked her. He gripped her chin lightly between his thumb and forefinger.

"This here, this meeting you're having with me, is being observed," he said even more softly. She tried to pull away from his grip and look out toward the rest of the club, but he held on more firmly.

"Eyes on me, Miss Spencer." He leaned forward, close enough for her to smell his cologne and to see the brown streaks radiating through his light blue irises. "If anyone asks, this here is me requesting a dance with you. Now, tell me no. Turn me down flat, and say it loudly."

Her tongue wouldn't function for a moment. He arched a brow, waiting. Self-preservation kicking in, Leo cleared her throat. "No."

He frowned. "You can do better than that."

"*No*," she repeated loudly.

He released her chin and held up his hands as if in surrender. "If you say so," he said, no longer whispering. Behind the bar, his bartender smirked at what he thought was his boss's advance being rejected.

"You're welcome to finish your drink, of course," he said, his glib charm falling back into place. A mask, slipped on with proficient ease. "Though, I don't think Inspector Reid would like you being here."

Leo couldn't stomach another sip of wine. She felt ill and shaky as she rose from her chair, ready to flee the club. "The inspector doesn't tell me what to do, Mr. Bloom."

"Much to his discontent, I'm sure," he replied with a laugh. "Have a pleasant evening, Miss Spencer."

Chapter Nineteen

Clear sunlight cut sharply into Jasper's eyes on his way to Scotland Yard the next morning. He'd have preferred the rainy spring weather that had drenched London the last few weeks, if only to help ease the aching of his head. Claude had come by the previous evening, arriving just after Jasper had admitted defeat and returned home. The city coroner had taken one look at him and then shaken his head disapprovingly.

"I said not to overdo it, Inspector."

The thing was, Jasper hadn't thought he had been. At least, not until he was stricken with a bout of severe nausea and vomited into the Carlisle Street gutter. He and Lewis had been leaving the Stewarts' residence, where the maid had informed them that Mr. Stewart was not in. Nor did she know when to expect him, especially since the children were no longer at home. Mrs. Bates had taken them, a boy and a girl, to their grandparents in Kent for the time being.

"They can't step a foot outside without a reporter

shouting at them," the maid had explained with indignance.

He'd gotten the address in Kent from the maid, albeit with difficulty, and left his name and an order for Mr. Stewart to contact him.

"Have a telegram sent to the Canterbury Borough station," Jasper instructed Lewis as they left. "I want an officer to check in and make sure Mrs. Bates is where she claimed to be going."

Leo had expressed concern that the woman seemed eager to settle into Mrs. Stewart's role now that she was in prison, facing charges of conspiracy and murder. Taking the children from London might have been benign, or something more ominous.

It was then that Jasper had stopped along the street, suddenly overwhelmed with dizziness and nausea. Grimacing, Lewis had told him to go home. As there was nothing more for them to do that evening, he followed his sergeant's suggestion.

At home, Claude had rechecked his pupils, given him headache powder, and pressed on his sore ribs.

"Where is Leo?" he'd asked, grunting at the renewed tenderness of his ribs.

"Closing up the morgue," Claude replied, before taking a glance over his thick spectacles. "She found some of her family's belongings in the crypt today. I think she is going through them."

Jasper hadn't known anything from the house on Red Lion Street had been stored there. He'd waited for Claude to say more, but he hadn't elaborated.

Now, after a night of poor, sporadic sleep, Jasper arrived

at the Yard earlier than usual. Constable Woodhouse greeted him in the lobby, but Constable Wiley wasn't yet at his desk in the detective department. Which was likely why Leo was seated in Lewis's chair, the contents of the boxes from Niles Foster's rooms taken out and stacked into piles.

"Isn't it a bit early in the day to be interfering with evidence?" Jasper asked. Thankfully, neither Chief Coughlan, nor Inspector Tomlin or any of the other Special Irish Branch detectives were in yet. The laborers hadn't even arrived to work on the wall, so all was peaceful.

Leo stayed seated. "I'm not interfering. I'm reading." Her eyes skipped from the slim book open before her to his face. "My uncle said you overdid it yesterday."

Jasper suppressed the pleasure he felt that she might have come to the Yard to check in on him. "I'm fine."

She appeared skeptical but didn't comment. Instead, she set aside the book she'd been flipping through to reveal a thick prisoner album underneath. "I found him."

Jasper groaned as he took off his hat and coat while she flipped the album open to a marked page. "How on earth did you get that?"

"Sergeant Richards lent it out to me. All I had to do was ask kindly," she said with a sly quirk of her mouth. "And bring him a Chelsea bun."

He sighed, though he wasn't surprised the records room officer had been so soft with her. He gave in. "Who did you find then?"

She turned the album out for him to see and tapped a photograph.

"The man I saw scowling at Constable Lloyd just

before the explosion. He was wearing a brown cap at the time, but this is most certainly him."

The man was scowling at the camera too. Lester Rice, arrested for assault and thievery. Sentenced to eighteen months at Coldbath Fields. Released less than a year ago.

"Look." Leo pointed to a smaller photograph on the page, alongside Rice's portrait. It was of his hands. On his left middle finger was a large signet ring. The police would often photograph hands or any distinct features, like tattoos, moles, or scars, to make identifying criminals easier.

"That signet ring could be what made the matching gashes on John Lloyd's and Niles Foster's cheeks," Leo said.

Though Jasper hadn't received any gashes like the ones on the constable and parliamentary aide during his own attack, it was possible Rice had been one of the thugs in his kitchen the other night.

"If he is muscle for the Angels, then yes, maybe," Jasper agreed. But he continued to frown as he read further into Rice's file. Lester, a known associate of the Angels, was also a brother to Peter Rice, who had been hanged for the murder of Police Sergeant Charles Brett nearly seventeen years ago.

"Peter Rice was a member of the Irish Republican Brotherhood," Leo supplied, already knowing what had captured Jasper's attention.

The notorious murder of Sergeant Brett was still well known, even among the youngest Met constables. In the autumn of 1867, five IRB members had intercepted a police transport of two Fenian leaders to Belle Vue Gaol in Manchester. One of the police officers, Sergeant Brett, had been shot and killed in the failed attempt to free the prisoners. Peter Rice and two others were hanged for his murder.

"I would wager Lester Rice is tied to the Irish cause, just as his brother was," Leo said. "Lester might have known about the planned bombings on the evening of the thirtieth. If the Angels did too, then… Well, I wonder if John's bomb was meant to go off at the same time as the others. When the remains of Geraldine's valise were found in the wreckage, she would then be implicated."

"You're suggesting the Angels used Clan na Gael's campaign to cover their own tracks?"

"It's possible," she said, shrugging. "Will you bring Rice in for questioning?"

"I'll put a few men on it. But we have to be careful. I don't want Rice finding out you're the one who saw him."

The Angels would certainly be compelled to pay her Duke Street home a visit if he did. Jasper's lingering headache sharpened at the thought.

Leo set aside the prisoner album, then held up the other book she'd been looking through. "Did you see this?"

He took the chair across the desk from her, again longing for his office. The bricklayers had started erecting the walls, at least. "Lewis and I went through everything," he said, though he didn't recognize what she held. Lewis must have looked at that one.

"It's a scheduling diary," she said, then turned to a page she'd marked with a fountain pen. "Sir Elliot Payne's excuse for not attending the WEA meeting the night of Mrs. Stewart's arrest was that he had a scheduling conflict and had to meet with Sir Charles Ralston, correct?"

Jasper sat forward. "How do you know that?" He'd interviewed the MP alone.

She reached for a folder and held it up. "I read your report."

He swiped it from her hand. God save him, the woman was a menace.

"But look here." Leo turned the diary for him to see and pointed to an entry. "Sir Elliot's meeting with Sir Charles Ralston didn't take place that night. It was scheduled for the evening before."

He looked, and according to the diary, she was right. But there might still be a reasonable explanation for the discrepancy. "The time and date might have changed, and Foster didn't record it."

"Why bother to strike out the WEA meeting but not write in that the meeting with Sir Charles had changed to take its place?"

Jasper turned the page to the next day's listing. A line had been drawn through the six o'clock appointment for the WEA meeting. As Leo said, nothing had replaced it.

"I had PC Price check with Ralston's office to be sure Sir Elliot's alibi was solid. He said the aide confirmed it."

Leo leaned her elbows on the desk. "What if Ralston's aide made a mistake? Or lied?"

"So, Sir Elliot might not have an alibi, after all," Jasper said. "But what would his possible motive be to harm his own aide?"

"Perhaps Mr. Foster learned something about him that he shouldn't have," she suggested.

Jasper didn't need this, not today. He needed to speak to Mr. Stewart about why Niles Foster had gone to the bank to see him a few days before the bombings. Clarification of Emma Bates's possible relation to Clive Paget was also imperative. But now, it seemed he needed to have another interview with Sir Elliot. It would likely come to nothing, but Jasper didn't like being lied to. Anyone connected to his murder victim who was being untruthful—about anything—required a second look.

"Very well, I'll pay him a call." He massaged the back of his head. Claude assured him he'd begin to feel better with each passing day. He sure as hell hoped so.

Leo began to gather the items she'd taken from the box to store them away again.

"Your uncle said you found something in the crypt. Family belongings."

She stilled. Then reached for another paper pile. "He kept the steamer trunk," she said, her voice subdued. "Filled it with some of their things."

Jasper swallowed. He'd thought of that trunk often and how lucky he'd been to spot it in the diffused moonlight coming through the attic window. Even with bright pain hammering through his chest after the little girl had gored him with something sharp, his thirteen-year-old self had focused on directing her toward it.

"Are you all right?" Immediately, he regretted asking Leo that. She'd spent hours locked inside that trunk because of him. It had likely become part of her nightmare too. A nightmare that he'd played a role in creating.

"The trunk didn't bother me. Not after the first minute or two, at least." She finished refilling the box and gripped the edges, her fingers cinching tightly. "But something else happened last night."

He stood from his chair slowly. "What happened? What is wrong?"

Roy Lewis chose that moment to arrive. "Morning, guv," the sergeant called as he entered the department. "I stopped by the telegraph room. They have something interesting from Kent." He slowed as Leo moved out from behind his desk. "Oh. Miss Spencer." He crossed a look between them and seemed to realize he'd interrupted something.

"Kent?" she inquired, then shook her head subtly at Jasper to indicate that she would tell him what happened later. Impatient and irrationally annoyed that Lewis had interrupted them, he asked the detective sergeant, "Is Mrs. Bates there?"

Lewis held up a telegram from Canterbury Station. "The Stewart children are there, but she's already gone."

"Gone where?" Jasper asked.

"She told Mr. Stewart's parents she was taking the train back to London." Lewis set the telegram onto their shared desk.

"Do we know where Mrs. Bates lives?" Jasper asked.

"Rupert Street," Leo offered. At his and Lewis's looks of surprise, she shrugged. "She hosted a WEA meeting once. Are you going to see her?"

Jasper was more interested in calling on Mr. Stewart. And if Leo's theory about Mrs. Bates wanting to come to roost in Geraldine's nest was correct, he thought she was more likely to be found there.

He turned to his sergeant. "I'll join you in the lobby in a moment."

Understanding, Lewis tipped his hat to Leo and went on ahead. A few constables had trickled into the department, including Wiley, who shot Leo a scowl.

"What happened last night?" Jasper asked. Whatever it

was, it had unsettled her. Perhaps it was why she'd been here so early.

"It will hold," she said. "I'm missing something. What happened yesterday?"

Picking up his hat and coat, he considered telling her that it was related to the case and thus, something he couldn't discuss with her. However, she would only take umbrage with being fobbed off. She'd then likely retaliate by not telling him what had happened to her the previous night.

So, as they left the detective department, he quietly and quickly explained that the address in Foster's pocket was for the bank managed by Porter Stewart, that Foster had gone there a few days before his death to meet with him specifically, and that the meeting had lasted less than five minutes before Foster left in an ill humor.

"Mr. Stewart said something to make him angry?" Leo guessed.

"Or Niles Foster upset Mr. Stewart and was then told to leave." They walked slowly toward the lobby, Jasper's eyes peeled for Inspector Tomlin. If they crossed paths with him and he said even one word to Leo, Jasper wasn't sure he would be able to keep his temper as he had yesterday. "Mr. Stewart wasn't at home when Lewis and I called on him yesterday. We're going to try again today."

"We know Niles Foster was desperate for money. He'd had an altercation with a Spitalfields Angel while gambling at Striker's Wharf, and he'd also argued with Lord Hayes," Leo said. "Now, we have him in a bad interaction with Mr. Stewart shortly before Sir Elliot decided against speaking at the WEA meeting. Don't you think it all a bit odd?"

It was certainly questionable. "Not only that, but a young lady whom Foster was…having relations with," he said, selecting his words more carefully than he might have with Lewis, "said he'd claimed to have come into some information that was going to make him a small fortune."

Leo stopped walking. "Do you think he might have tried to blackmail Mr. Stewart with this information?"

"It's possible. I plan to find out."

"May I come with you? I've met Mr. Stewart and—"

"Have you forgotten that I was attacked in my home after our visit with his wife?" he interrupted. "Leo, you cannot be involved in this any longer. I've sent Mrs. Zhao to stay with her sister, and if I could, I'd send you too."

She balked, but he wasn't about to back down. Not even when she set her jaw and started to walk past him. He caught her elbow. Then lowered his voice.

"I know you want to help, and I know you're sharper than half the men here," he said, the admission as surprising to him as it was to her. She gazed at him in awe. "But this is dangerous work, and I cannot do it properly if I am constantly worried that something bad will happen to you."

He held her stare until she blinked and averted her eyes. Releasing her arm, he took a breath and put some space between them. The narrow corridor where they stood was beginning to fill with officers.

"You should leave before Tomlin arrives. He's not fond of either of us at the moment."

"Why, what did you do?" she asked.

"Nothing I regret," he said, deciding not to tell her about their tense interaction the day before.

Leo tried but couldn't hold back her grin as they passed Constable Woodhouse and stepped out into the yard. "Did you punch him in the nose for me?"

Jasper barked a laugh. "As satisfying as that would have been, I can't afford being reprimanded by Chief Coughlan again."

"I suppose you're right. The man isn't worth that sort of trouble," she said. "Good luck with Mr. Stewart."

He'd expected more of an argument from her but dismissed his skepticism as he spotted Lewis, waiting by the stone arch. Leo started away.

"About what you wanted to tell me before," Jasper called. She tarried a moment, looking back at him. "Come to Charles Street tonight."

The request was met with a hitch of her chin. He'd said it without thinking. Mrs. Zhao wouldn't be there, so inviting an unmarried young woman—even if it was Leo Spencer—to his home wasn't proper. In fact, it was just short of indecent. And yet, he made no move to rescind the offer or apologize. He would be a gentleman, of course.

If she considered the invitation unseemly, she said nothing of it. Leo only nodded and continued along her way.

Anticipating that there would be little for her to do at the morgue that morning, thanks to Connor Quinn's undesirable presence, Leo had bought a copy of *The Times* from the boy hawking them on the corner of Whitehall Place and Charing Cross Road.

There were still plenty of her father's papers for her to go through, and Aunt Flora's letters to her mother were worth another read. But she hadn't slept well after her conversation with Mr. Bloom, and the idea of going into the crypt to search for more clues to their deaths seemed to put lead ballast in her boots. The newspaper would occupy her, and she wouldn't have to think about the murky, dangerous endeavors her father had been undertaking and for whom.

She'd left the house earlier than usual, eager to look through a prisoner album before the detective department filled up and to tell Jasper about Mr. Bloom's warning—even if he would be tempted to throttle her for going to Striker's Wharf alone. That she was unsettled enough to endure one of Jasper's lectures just so that she would be able to share what Mr. Bloom had warned her about was alarming in and of itself.

The Carters hadn't forgotten about her. They were keeping an eye on her even now. If that was so, was Jasper also within their view? Did they suspect who he might truly be? Their long-lost James... A boy who had betrayed them.

Leo clutched the newspaper, a shiver jumping through her limbs despite the bright sunshine shedding warmth over the street. The rain and fog of the last few days had cleared, leaving pale blue sky and a promise of spring. She would tell Jasper tonight. Mrs. Zhao wouldn't be there, but that didn't matter. At least, she didn't think it did. If any other man had invited her to his home, she would never have dreamed of accepting. But there was nothing wrong with her visiting Jasper.

She let herself into the morgue through the back door.

The scent of coffee wafted under her nose. Mr. Quinn stood at the cottage range, pouring himself a cup of the steaming black brew from a beaker. He was wearing a different suit this morning, she noted. Gray rather than brown. She felt slightly guilty for saying the brown one was ugly. It hadn't been, and it had been petty of her to say as much. So was the decision not to apologize, but she could live with it.

"Coffee, Miss Spencer?" he asked.

"No, thank you, I prefer tea." She tossed the paper onto the desk and hoped it signaled her claim to it.

"Would you mind having a look at the reports from yesterday before they're sent to Mr. Pritchard?" he asked. Leo hung her hat on the stand and peered over at him.

"Why? Is there a problem with them?"

"I hope not," he answered with a theatrical grimace, followed by a smile. "No, I was simply reading through past reports yesterday when things were slow and noted how thorough and detailed all of yours have been."

Leo continued to look at him, uncertain if he was being sincere. Mr. Quinn's expression remained expectant as if waiting for a reply.

"You're complimenting me?"

He smiled again. "I suppose I am." He touched a small pile of manila folders on the desk. "They're here. Of course, I understand if you don't have the time."

She picked up the folders and set them on the other side of the typewriter, silently assenting that she would read them. He thanked her and left for the postmortem room, where a corpse had been delivered overnight. Though she would have much rather seen to the corpse, Leo fixed herself some tea and then opened the top folder.

She was reading through the third report when Claude arrived.

He hung his coat and hat on the stand, then rubbed his hands together the way he often did when the tremors were stronger.

"It will be quite noticeable today, I'm afraid," he said. Leo started to stand, intending to join him and distract Mr. Quinn. But he raised a hand to stay her. "It's for the best to just be done with it. Let things take their course."

She knew he was right, even if it made her heartsick. Claude wrinkled his brow in resignation before joining Mr. Quinn in the postmortem room. It was foolhardy to think she might be able to distract the younger surgeon forever during the postmortems. He would see Claude's tremors eventually, and it seemed her uncle wanted to get the moment over with.

Finishing with Mr. Quinn's reports, which she had to admit were sufficiently organized and thorough, though studded with misspellings, Leo drained her tea and eyed the postmortem room door. The urge to go in was nearly all-consuming. But she opened the morning issue of *The Times* instead. On the third page, under the heading Metropolitan News, which was a compilation of events and accomplishments, a printed surname pulled her eye directly to it. Backing up a few lines, she read from the start: *The Conservatives for Political Values met at the Guildhall Tuesday last. Mr. Jos. Banford, MP, presided over the meeting, in which Banford announced several new members and future MP candidates, including Mr. Timothy Rye, Mr. Virgil Andrews, and Mr. Porter Stewart.*

Leo read the notice again, her nerve endings beginning to tingle. Porter Stewart…a member of Conservatives for Political Values? And a future candidate for Parliament? But Geraldine had said her husband wasn't political at all. He supported her endeavors with women's suffrage and the WEA, while the conservatives in the government most certainly did not. Why would he align himself with them? It would be tantamount to turning his back on his wife's work. Unless there was another Porter Stewart in London. Though, she doubted that was the case.

She folded the paper, trying to make sense of this new revelation. There was something to it. A betrayal that Geraldine surely had not known anything about. But now, here it was, printed in ink for all of London to see.

Leo entered the postmortem room, where Claude and Mr. Quinn were peering into a chest cavity. "The scar tissue on the aortic valve is quite severe, as you can see," Claude said, indicating the heart valve with a rubber-clad glove.

"Damage like this is typically caused by rheumatic fever," Mr. Quinn said.

"I agree," her uncle said. Looking up, he spotted Leo. "You've been quiet this morning."

"I've been reading," she replied, then eyed the corpse. "Perhaps she had scarlet fever beforehand, then developed rheumatic fever and later, severe valvular heart disease?"

The corpse belonged to a woman in her thirties. By the state of her hair, skin, and teeth, and the callouses and chilblains on her hands, she'd lived in poverty. There always seemed to be intermittent outbreaks of scarlet fever winding through the poorer parts of the city and boroughs.

"Yes, quite right, Miss Spencer," Mr. Quinn said. His

surprised tone, as if she was rather plucky and clever to have made a correct guess, grated.

"Your reports from yesterday are fine, Mr. Quinn, except for some misspellings. I'd say they are ready for Mr. Pritchard's eyes." He started to thank her, but she abruptly turned to Claude. "I've an errand to run, if you don't need me."

His watery gray eyes skipped to his new assistant, then back to Leo. "We have things handled here, my dear."

She couldn't tell what that meant. Had Mr. Quinn already spotted his trembling hands? There was no way to discuss it now.

"I'll return shortly," she said, then went back to the office to gather her things. Jasper had said his first stop was to be Mr. Stewart's home. Leo hurried from the morgue, hoping to catch him there.

Chapter Twenty

As it turned out, Emma Bates's home on Rupert Street wouldn't take Jasper and Lewis far from their path to the Stewarts' residence, so they agreed to try there first.

"If she took the kiddies to see their grandparents, what reason does she have to go back to her brother-in-law's home?" Lewis asked as they strode toward the intersection of Shaftsbury Avenue and Rupert Street.

Reluctantly, Jasper explained that after their visit to Holloway Prison—which Lewis had muttered was a barmy idea to begin with—Leo had divulged a suspicion that the widowed Emma Bates was smitten with Porter Stewart.

"And with her possible relation to the Spitalfields Angels, you think she had access to a bomb and set up Mrs. Stewart to get her out of the way? Come on, guv," Lewis said with a snorting laugh.

It did seem rather convoluted. If the woman's maiden surname hadn't been Paget, Jasper would've dismissed

Leo's suspicion. But as the Angels were now linked to both Niles Foster and the case against Mrs. Stewart, he couldn't set it aside.

"I don't have the answers yet, but we do know some of the Angels have strong ties to Clan na Gael," Jasper said, then launched into what Leo had theorized earlier, including the bit about Lester Rice and his deceased brother, Peter. "If Clan na Gael planned to carry out three bombings that day, and the Angels knew about it, they might have forced PC Lloyd to plant Mrs. Stewart's suitcase so that it would be found amongst the rest of the wreckage."

He sighed, still wanting more to back up their theory. It was as if the pieces were floating around in his head, out of order, connecting for only a moment before splitting apart again.

Lewis murmured half-hearted support for this possibility, then said, "Tomlin's going to go to the superintendent. You know that, right?"

He exhaled. "Yes."

Chief Superintendent Monroe had replaced Gregory Reid when he'd become ill enough to step down. Monroe was an aloof man, tall and imperial, and he would not like that Jasper had disregarded Inspector Tomlin's findings in the Stewart case. Subversion in any form was more than frowned upon. Jasper would be reprimanded, though how harshly he wasn't sure.

"I'll worry about that later," he said.

At Mrs. Bates's address, a young maid opened the door and told them that her mistress was out.

"Has she returned here after her trip to Kent?" Jasper asked.

The maid bobbed her head in affirmation, but when Lewis asked where they might be able to find her, she became skittish and quiet.

"Does Mrs. Bates have family in London?" Jasper tried when the maid looked ready to close the door on them. "Other than Mr. and Mrs. Stewart," he added.

The maid frowned. "I can't say."

"Can't, or won't?" Lewis asked.

She pursed her lips and looked back over her shoulder into the house. Then whispered, "*Can't*. I don't want to lose my position. I were just brought on last month."

Jasper didn't want to get the girl in trouble, but she knew something, and he wasn't willing to risk letting it go just to be polite. "Does the name Paget sound familiar to you?"

The maid's visible fright was an answer. He pressed onward.

"Has anyone by that name come here, looking for your mistress?"

Still miserable, she slipped onto the front step and closed the door all but an inch behind her. "Mrs. O'Toole says we aren't ever to speak of them. If Mistress has a visitor by that name, they're to be directed to the back door."

The tradesmen's entrance for family? Emma Bates was either ashamed or wished to secret them away for another reason.

"Have any of them come here recently? Within the last few weeks?"

She frowned and shook her head. "Not in the month since I've been here."

Jasper considered asking to speak to this Mrs. O'Toole,

who was likely the housekeeper. But then, the maid's frown pinched even more deeply. "But Mistress did put a letter in the post my first week. I only noticed the name because Mrs. O'Toole had just told me about sending them ones to the back door."

"It was addressed to someone named Paget?" Lewis asked.

At the maid's nod, Jasper said, "Do you recall anything else about whom it was going to? A first name? Street address?"

An indiscernible voice came from within the house, and the maid jumped and hurried back inside.

"Please, miss, anything at all?" Lewis asked as she was closing the door. All that remained was a sliver of her face when she said, "Mr. C. Paget. That's who it were addressed to. That's all I know."

The door shut on them then. It was enough.

"All right," Lewis said as they started back out on the pavement. "So, she's got kin in the Angels."

"Not just kin." Jasper ignored the soreness of his ribs as he walked more swiftly. "Clive Paget is top brass. Old enough to be her father, maybe."

"You really think this lady made a bomb?" Lewis didn't believe it, even now. Jasper wasn't sure he did either.

They turned north toward nearby Carlisle Street, where they ended up having more success. Mr. Stewart was in, though the maid who allowed them to step into the foyer was not nearly as cowed by their warrant cards as Mrs. Bates's maid had been. She glared at them, as if they were personally responsible for dragging her mistress off to prison.

"Wait here while I see if Mr. Stewart is in."

"Betty, I told you not to allow Mrs.—" A tall, handsome man in his middle thirties swept into the foyer from a back hall. His stride stalled, as did his reprimand for the maid, when he saw the two Scotland Yard officers.

"Mr. Porter Stewart, I presume?" Jasper said.

The man blinked and cleared his throat, attempting to recover his poise. "Yes. And you are?"

As he held up his warrant card and introduced himself and Lewis, Jasper took in Porter Stewart's appearance. The knot of his ascot was loose, and a bright red mark colored his left cheek. He had the stunned look of a man who'd just been slapped.

"Who were you telling your maid not to allow inside your home?" Jasper asked.

"What is the reason for your visit, Inspector?"

"We'll get to that in a moment. First, I'd like to know who you instructed your maid to keep out."

Mr. Stewart gaped like a fish. "That is none of your concern."

"That cuff on your cheek looks fresh," Lewis said.

"A couple minutes old, at the most," Jasper agreed. "My guess? You told your maid not to allow in the woman who landed it."

The banker touched his reddened cheek reflexively, then lowered his hand. "It's a personal matter, Inspector. And I find I need a drink."

He turned into a large room, divided into two spaces by a cloister-like arch. The front half of the room was a sitting area, and the back was a dining room with a large marble hearth. Stewart went straight for a cart of decanted spirits and crystal glasses. He poured himself a liberal splash of amber liquid and tossed it back in one gulp.

"Mr. Stewart, we're investigating the murder of Niles Foster," Jasper began. "We have a credible witness who can place Mr. Foster in your office, in your presence, at Seale and Company Bank just days before his murder."

The banker refilled his glass. "The name isn't familiar. I deal with dozens of customers every day. How am I to remember this one man?"

Jasper showed him the photograph he'd kept in his pocket. Mr. Stewart swallowed his drink smoothly, without reaction. "I've no recollection of him."

"He was a parliamentary aide to Sir Elliot Payne. You recall *him*, don't you? An MP, scheduled to speak at the Women's Equality Alliance meeting on the night of your wife's arrest?"

Mr. Stewart squared his shoulders at the mention of his wife. "What does this have to do with Geraldine?"

"That is what we're trying to determine," Jasper replied. He held up the photograph again for the banker to see. "You know him. There is no point in pretending otherwise. So, why don't you tell me why Sir Elliot's aide came to your bank and waited thirty minutes only to speak to you for less than five?"

Porter Stewart touched the corner of his mouth and a spot of blood on his lip. The woman's strike had been fierce. Jasper had a good guess who she was.

"Ah, yes, I remember now," he said without a shred of dexterity. "He wanted a loan. Without any collateral, however, I was forced to turn him down. He became rather hot over it, I'm afraid."

The man was lying, but there was no way to prove it.

Jasper took another tack. "Why did your sister-in-law cuff you across the cheek just now?"

Mr. Stewart's purposefully distant expression came alive. "What... I don't know what you mean."

"Your ascot is mussed, you've been slapped, and Emma Bates came here this morning after getting your children well out of London so she could have you all to herself."

It was pure theory, but Jasper slung it out with confidence, hoping it would stick. He had nothing to lose anyhow.

"You cannot know that," Mr. Stewart protested, but he was more in awe than he was angry.

"I know plenty," Jasper hedged. It worked.

Mr. Stewart turned away and sipped his drink, this time more restrainedly.

"She's a beautiful widow, still in her prime," Jasper went on, drawing from what Leo had told him, as he'd never made the woman's acquaintance. "And she admires you a great deal."

"That is quite enough, Inspector. What you are suggesting is offensive."

"I'm sure it is. How long have the two of you been having an affair?"

Jasper could always tell when a person was holding something back—usually for self-preservation. Mr. Stewart was doing just that. He needed to needle the man until he gave up whatever he was hiding.

"I will ask you to leave this instant," he snapped.

"Your wife's valise was used in one of the Scotland Yard bombings. Would Emma Bates have had access to your attic?" Jasper pressed further. "Or perhaps you fetched the valise yourself and staged the break-in."

The banker slammed his glass onto the drinks cart. "Enough! This is ludicrous. I had nothing to do with that bombing, and it does not matter what Emma feels for me because I most certainly do not feel the same toward her."

He drew a shaky breath. Ran his fingers through his already unkempt hair.

"Where is she?" Lewis asked.

"No longer here. She ran off after she…" Mr. Stewart capitulated. "After she struck me."

"Why did she do that?" Jasper asked. When the banker hesitated, he guessed, "You rejected her?"

With a nod, he swiped up his glass again. "This is a bloody disaster. It was a lapse of character. *One* dalliance," he said, his voice cracking. "I told her that it could not be. That I'd made a mistake. I thought she understood and agreed. But then… I don't know, she got it into her head that I was going to leave Geraldine. Divorce her. Can you imagine?"

Lewis stopped just short of rolling his eyes. "What was she thinking?"

Mr. Stewart didn't note the detective sergeant's sarcasm. "I know. I tried to reason with her, tried to keep her calm."

"But?" Jasper asked.

He rubbed his temple. "She would not be mollified."

"This all happened today?" Jasper asked.

"No, no. It was a month ago. Nearly two. But today, she brought everything up again. And again, I had to tell her it would not happen. It *could* not." Mr. Stewart no longer looked ready to toss them out. If anything, he appeared eager to confess. Jasper imagined he'd been struggling in secret with his *lapse of character*, as he'd called it.

"Em has always been sympathetic. She saw how much of my attention and effort went toward Geraldine and her political group. My wife, well, she is a force. It can be difficult to get a word in edgewise about anything. But Em seemed to recognize that I needed support too. Attention, perhaps. She encouraged me to speak up for myself." He sounded nearly nostalgic and forgiving, and his calling her *Em* was proof of familiarity.

Mr. Stewart lowered his head, sobering. "I am ashamed that I strayed, but it was only once. One mistake," he repeated.

A vigorous slamming of the front door knocker punctuated Mr. Stewart's confession. The maid, Betty, had been lingering close by—listening in, most likely—and hurried to open the door. The murmur of a female voice reached them in the large gathering room, and the small hairs on the back of Jasper's neck stood at attention. His blood stirred. And then, Leo swept inside, her cheeks flushed and eyes bright. Her lips bowed with a rare smile.

"Oh, good. You're all here," she began. "I think I know why Mr. Foster was killed."

Chapter Twenty-One

Leo had kept a brisk pace on the way to the Stewarts' home, her mind flying as swiftly as her feet. Now that she'd arrived, she paused to take several breaths.

"Miss Spencer," Jasper said, his tone stern with warning. The formal address was surely due to Mr. Stewart's presence. "What is this about?"

On the way to Carlisle Street, she'd kept the image of the announcement for the Conservatives for Political Values in the front of her memory. The newsprint was as clear in her mind as the actual article, which she'd folded and stuffed into her coat pocket. It was the name *Mr. Jos. Banford, MP* that her attention had kept sliding toward, again and again. It wasn't until she'd crossed Shaftsbury Avenue that she understood why.

She turned to Geraldine's husband. "Mr. Stewart, were you aware that *The Times* would reveal your political ambitions in today's paper?" Leo pulled the crumpled newsprint from her pocket and held it up. His nostrils flared, and a flicker of panic brightened his eyes. "Perhaps last week's meeting of the Conservatives for Political Values fled your mind, what with everything happening with your wife."

Jasper gestured for her to hand him the paper. "Explain."

She relinquished the paper, not needing it any longer. "Mr. Porter Stewart is listed as a new member of the conservative group and a future candidate for the party in next year's general election."

Sergeant Lewis whistled. "Conservative? They're up in arms against women's rights, aren't they?"

"Most are, yes, but not all," Mr. Stewart said, his cheeks flushing.

"Your wife told me that you weren't political in the least. That you supported her and the WEA entirely," Leo went on.

"Ah, but we've just learned that Mr. Stewart here has thoughts and opinions of his own, which he shared not with his wife, but with Emma Bates," Jasper said, glancing up from the Metropolitan News column. He cocked a brow, and Leo understood perfectly—not only did Mrs. Bates have a romantic interest in Mr. Stewart, but he had welcomed her attentions.

"It is not a crime to hold differing political views from one's wife," the man said.

"Views Emma Bates perhaps encouraged you toward," Jasper said.

"Views your wife was in the dark about," Leo added, her mind readily absorbing this new information. "When did you plan to inform her?"

He shifted uneasily, pulling at his ascot. "In due time, not that it is any of your concern. How are you even involved in this, Miss Spencer? Are you colluding with the police?"

Leo overlooked his questions, unwilling to let her attention be diverted. "I couldn't understand why the name Banford was familiar to me. He's a member of Parliament and the president of Conservatives for Political Values," she said as an aside for Jasper and Sergeant Lewis. "I knew I'd seen his name somewhere recently, but it took me some time to realize where. You see, while reading through Niles Foster's scheduling diary for Sir Elliot, I'd been so focused on the days immediately surrounding the bombing that I put the entries for the weeks before then to the back of my mind."

But the images of the earlier diary entries were still there, waiting for her to draw them up and re-examine them.

Lewis frowned. "You went through Foster's things?"

Jasper held up a hand to silence him, though he would have to make some excuse for her prying later.

"It was written in the diary that *Banford's new member* met with Sir Elliot Payne two Mondays ago, a day before the meeting in which your membership in a Tory party committee was announced," Leo said. "Was it during that meeting with Sir Elliot that you asked him to cancel his speaking engagement with the WEA?"

Mr. Stewart began to splutter just as the maid, Betty, entered the room to ask if she should bring tea. He shot out a hand to send her away.

"Or maybe you bribed him to do so," Jasper suggested.

"Bribed him? This is offensive. You have no proof," he spat.

Leo conceded. "Perhaps not, but I think Niles Foster

did. He was either present or overheard your conversation with Sir Elliot."

Lewis turned to Jasper. "An MP hopeful offering a bribe to a member of the opposite party and having it accepted. That could be the valuable information Foster told his lady friend he'd come into."

Jasper slapped the newspaper into his palm. His stare burrowed into Mr. Stewart. "Foster came to see you at your bank to blackmail you."

"I'm sure you didn't take kindly to that," Lewis tacked on.

Mr. Stewart stalked to the other side of the room as if to get away from the accusations. "You aren't seriously fitting me up for that man's murder?"

"You have motive," Jasper said. "Damn good motive. He tells you he's going to expose you unless you pay him, but of course, you know he'll just keep coming back for more."

"No." The man goggled, looking between the three of them. "No, that isn't true. I had nothing to do with what happened to him."

Unwilling to relent, Jasper followed Mr. Stewart to the other side of the room. "Then tell me what did happen because right now, you are my prime suspect for his murder."

Leo was struck again by the livid bruising of Jasper's eye and the healing gash on his lip. They were evidence of the very real danger these linked cases posed—and yet, he would not give in.

Mr. Stewart raised his hands, palms facing out. "All right. Yes, I met with Sir Elliot. Emma had encouraged me to run for Parliament, to speak up for what I believe in. I did, and soon, I was being courted by Banford. But I knew Geraldine's antics with the WEA would put my acceptance at risk."

Leo's jaw loosened. *Antics?* His wife's passion and purpose were far more serious than a silly lark. And yet, he was ready to reduce the value of her cause without a thought. Any admiration Leo had previously held for Porter Stewart was instantly obliterated.

"It didn't matter if I mostly agreed with her, I couldn't support Geraldine once I went public with my run for MP. If no debate was brought to the floor, and if Payne—her only real support—turned her away, I thought she must surely see reason. There would be no way forward. If I could convince her to put her support behind me, perhaps in time she would gain alliances among other conservatives."

The man's manipulation and selfishness were stunning.

"So, you asked him to cry off. Not only from the WEA speech, but in his support of women's suffrage when the vote was debated in the House," Leo said.

"Asking did no good," Mr. Stewart said bitterly. "He wouldn't drop the debate. Not without incentive."

"How much money did you offer him?" Jasper asked.

Mr. Stewart rubbed his forehead. "Does it matter? He was amenable."

"But when Foster tried to blackmail you, you panicked," Lewis said while jotting some notes down on a pocket notepad.

"Of course, I panicked. But I did not kill the man! I'm no murderer." He appeared panicked now too. Leo found she believed him. He was readily confessing to all his wrongdoings and yet standing firm on this point.

She tried to align all the different moving pieces in her mind as they formed. Whom would he have turned to after Niles Foster's visit to the bank? Surely not Banford, who would cast Porter Stewart out of the committee if he carried with him any potential scandal. Not Sir Elliot either, who might return the bribe he'd accepted, if only to clear himself of any misconduct. That left one person.

"You turned to Mrs. Bates for help," Leo said.

Mr. Stewart's glare slammed into her and filled her with conviction.

"You told her everything. What you stood to lose," she went on, speaking as the words came to her. "She'd already professed her support, her love. You trusted her."

When he remained silent, Jasper nodded. "She wanted to protect you. She turned to her family—"

"No." Mr. Stewart barked the single word. "No. She had cut them off. She promised she had."

"You knew about her criminal relations," Lewis said. "Maybe hinted that she should turn to them."

Mr. Stewart shook his head vigorously.

"So, she is related to Clive Paget?" Leo asked Jasper, who nodded, and it all came clear. "They went after Niles Foster to silence him."

She dragged in a breath as another revelation struck.

"All to protect whatever leverage they might gain when Emma married Mr. Stewart, future member of Parliament. She was the one who encouraged him to run in the first place."

Having a family member in the House would certainly

have been beneficial for a criminal organization looking for favorable connections.

"Marry Emma?" Mr. Stewart scoffed. "Absurd. She knew I would not divorce Geraldine. For God's sake, once my wife was arrested for that bombing, my sole focus was to clear her name. To clear my own name. I am ruined if she is convicted."

Leo bit her tongue against calling him a selfish bastard. He was worried for his own reputation and political aspirations when his wife could lose her freedom, her very life.

"Are you so certain of that?" Leo asked. "Surely, with your wife arrested as a radical suffragist, it would allow you the opportunity to condemn her actions. Hold her up as an example of all that is wrong with women seeking the vote. You'd have sympathy among fellow conservatives."

He glared at the suggestion but did not reply.

"And if Mrs. Stewart is convicted, it's possible she would hang," Lewis said. "If that is the case, Mrs. Bates would be rid of the obstacle standing between her and the husband she wants."

As Mr. Stewart decried the sergeant's theory as utter nonsense, Leo considered it. Porter would only remarry if his wife was totally out of the picture. Killing Geraldine would have been too risky for Emma. A murder would have been investigated, and Emma might have been found out. But if Geraldine was implicated in a treasonous crime and arrested, if she was convicted and hanged, well then... Her path to Porter Stewart would be clear.

"Mr. Stewart, we need to find your sister-in-law," Jasper said. "Where was she going from here?"

He again pressed his fingertips to his temple. "She did not say where she was going, nor did I inquire. Now, I am sending for my solicitor. I demand you all leave at once."

He turned on his heel and left them. Jasper and Lewis exchanged a victorious glance.

"Let's go back to her home," Lewis said. "She'll probably be there by now. We can bring her in for questioning."

"She'll never admit to anything," Leo said. Not with so little tangible proof that she was involved. "Mr. Stewart has proven that he is easily persuaded and spineless. She isn't, not if she's orchestrated all of this."

And for what? Emma's plan had been to step into Geraldine's shoes, to easily transfer Porter Stewart's love from his wife to her. But he didn't seem to be living up to her expectations.

The floorboards creaked behind them. Silent, the maid stood within the entryway.

"Betty?" Leo said.

The maid hadn't appeared hesitant the few times she'd previously encountered her. Quite the opposite, in fact.

"Is there something you'd like to say?" Leo pressed.

She came into the room, still cagey. "When it comes to that woman," she said quietly, "Mr. Stewart has the wool pulled over his eyes."

The maid had been listening to their conversation. Leo imagined she'd listened in on plenty of other conversations too. Jasper stepped closer, his interest clear.

"Is there something you know about Mrs. Bates?" he asked.

"She's barmy, that one." Betty tapped the side of her head with an index finger. "I keep an ear to the door whenever she's about, and she was furious earlier when he told her to leave. I didn't see anything, mind you, but I heard a scuffle. Him, pushing her away, telling her it'd been nothing but a mistake. You should've heard her howling."

"Did you know they were carrying on together?" Leo asked.

The maid gave a short nod. Servants usually knew everything that happened in the households in which they worked.

"What happened after that?" Jasper asked.

"Mr. Stewart had had enough. He hardly ever shouts, him. But his voice came clear through the door, saying that he would never love her, never choose her, even if his wife were lost to him. And then, that barmy lady says back to him: 'She will be lost to you sooner than you think.'"

Leo's stomach dropped. "'*Sooner than you think.*' She said those very words?"

The maid nodded. "Then came a loud smack, and Mrs. Bates stormed out."

An ominous thought drifted through Leo's mind. Emma Bates had gone to great lengths to secure Porter Stewart for herself. For her family too. How desperate and furious might she be now, faced with the knowledge that he would never love her, never marry her, even if Geraldine were out of the picture permanently?

"I don't like the sound of that," Jasper said. "Lewis, return to Mrs. Bates's home and see if she is there. If she is, take her into custody. If not, gather some constables and come to Holloway Prison. It's where I'm going."

Leo thanked the maid and followed the two men out

onto the front walk. Lewis peeled off at a run in the direction of Mrs. Bates's street, and Jasper hailed an oncoming hansom. As it approached, Leo waited to be told that she could not accompany him to the prison. But he only opened the cab's door and extended a hand to help her up.

"Nicely done with the newspaper article," he said as she slipped her hand into his. A burst of pleasure helped propel her into the cab.

Chapter Twenty-Two

Jasper had instructed the driver to be aggressive and move along as quickly as possible, but though the cab rattled toward Holloway Prison with noticeable speed, it wasn't nearly fast enough to put him at ease. A rock sat in his gut, growing larger as a premonition of what they would find at the prison took shape in his mind.

"The chief warder allowed us in before, but you're a police inspector. I got the impression he wouldn't have permitted me inside if you hadn't been there. He won't allow an unaccompanied woman to visit Mrs. Stewart," Leo reasoned, sitting rigidly on the opposite bench. She rubbed the center of her right palm with her thumb, massaging the scars through her glove. She did it without noticing, a habit whenever she was tense.

"It sounds like Mrs. Bates can be quite persuasive," Jasper said. "If she is desperate, there's no telling what she might do."

If she'd orchestrated this entire situation—everything

from convincing Porter Stewart to turn political, to arranging for Geraldine's implication in a bombing scheme, to protecting Porter from Niles Foster's blackmailing attempt—then she might very well feel it all unraveling. Months of work, of carefully laid plans being carried out, had come down to one remaining barricade: Mrs. Stewart herself.

"How can he profess to love his wife and then betray her as deeply as he has?" Leo asked. "And not just by taking up with her sister-in-law, though that is wretched enough. He sabotaged her work with the WEA and doesn't seem the least bit remorseful."

Jasper had met men like Porter Stewart before. Shallow men with shallow hearts. Easily persuaded, led by compliments, and lavished with doting attention, all to instill a confidence in themselves that they lacked.

"He's intimidated by his wife's strength. By her depth. He probably feels emasculated by her," Jasper replied.

Fierce annoyance flashed in Leo's eyes. "So, she must be weaker than him? Pretend to be incapable so that he might feel more manly?"

He sat forward, arms on his thighs. "I didn't say that. Your argument isn't with me; it's with Porter Stewart. Who is, I'll add, a vain man and a fool."

She dropped her shoulders. "I'm sorry. I'm not angry with you. In fact, I should say thank you for not telling me to return to the morgue."

Jasper sat back and crossed his arms. "If I had, you would have just hired a cab for yourself and followed me to Holloway."

She shrugged. "That is true."

Still, he wasn't exactly eager to take her into the

prison. His best guess was that Miss Hartley, the cell warder, had been the one to alert the Angels to their visit and questions the other day. If that was the case, she would likely report back to the Angels that he'd ignored their warning.

"Don't ask me to wait in the cab while you go in," Leo said a mere second before he opened his mouth to do just that.

"And if the Angels learn that you were there when I apprehended Emma Bates?" he challenged.

"If you won't bow down to threats made by a criminal gang, then what makes you think I will?"

The stubborn woman drove him mad. Jasper scrubbed a hand over his jaw, forgetting to be cautious of his split lip. He had no reply for her, so he let the jarring throb of pain ebb in the silence.

Their driver delivered them to the outer gate of the prison, and Jasper helped Leo down. Once they'd come through the gate in the porter's lodge, the chief warder was summoned. Mr. Vines remembered them.

"Back to see Mrs. Stewart?" he asked, his walrus mustache twitching in displeasure as he glanced at Leo.

"Has anyone else come here today to visit her?" Jasper snapped the question without a care for civility.

The chief warder frowned, taken aback. "Today? No." He eyed the gate warders. "Correct?"

The two uniformed men shook their heads in answer. Then one said, "Haven't seen anyone here for a prisoner. Just a sister, for one of the lady warders."

Alarm shuttled up Jasper's spine at the mention of a female cell warder. Jasper stepped forward. "For Miss

Hartley?" At the guard's surprised nod, he then asked, "When was this? What did the sister look like?"

The guard looked flummoxed. "It were ten minutes ago or so. The lady were pretty. Blonde hair."

"What did she want with Miss Hartley?" Leo asked eagerly.

The guard appeared even more baffled. "I didn't hear. They just talked for a short stretch, then Miss Hartley went back into the prison."

Jasper turned to the chief warder, his pulse rising with suspicion. "We have reason to believe Geraldine Stewart is in grave danger. I'll ask you to take us to her now."

"Danger from whom?" he asked.

"From her cell warder. I don't have time to explain. Just take us to Mrs. Stewart at once."

The man didn't move. "I will take you, Inspector, but the lady stays here. I cannot have female civilians in my prison if you think there is a serious threat of danger afoot."

There was no time to argue, and Leo seemed to understand as much.

"Go on," she said. "I'll wait by the front gate for Sergeant Lewis. I'm sure he'll be arriving shortly."

Jasper nodded, and the chief warder, summoning one of the guards to accompany them, started immediately toward the prison's main entrance.

They hastened across the gravel courtyard and entered the prison through the wicket gate. In the reception hall, Mr. Vines snapped his fingers at the receiving warder, Mr. Smythe. "Have you seen Miss Hartley?"

Mr. Smythe gestured toward the back of the hall. "Just now. She went back to her station."

Jasper picked up his pace, outstripping the chief warder. When he reached the receiving cells, the door to Mrs. Stewart's cell wasn't open. Miss Hartley wasn't anywhere to be seen.

A faint cry of alarm sounded from within the cell, and Jasper ran forward. "Miss Hartley!" he shouted, reaching for the door handle. It was locked. He pounded on the steel. "Open this door now, Miss Hartley!"

The chief warder arrived, the key on his iron ring already out. "Step aside," he commanded, and a moment later the door to the cell swung open.

Miss Hartley had Geraldine Stewart in her grasp, holding her as she would a shield. Though shorter than her prisoner, the cell warder was plainly more powerful. Her eyes were wide and wild as she realized she'd been found out. She held a small, handcrafted shiv to Mrs. Stewart's neck.

"Stay back!" she said, her voice high and cracking in fright.

"We know Emma Bates ordered you in here to kill Mrs. Stewart," Jasper said, entering the cell with his hands raised.

With the shiv, easily crafted within prison cells, her murder could have been made to look like a suicide.

"Emma?" Mrs. Stewart's eyes glistened with tears and stark terror as the cell warder's brawny hold kept her pinned in place. "She wouldn't."

"Miss Hartley, stand down at once," Mr. Vines commanded, no longer blustering with irritation. He'd gone calm and focused. "Think about what you are doing. If you harm that woman, you will be charged with murder. You will hang."

Miss Hartley shook her head, the hand holding the small blade moving erratically, much too close to Mrs. Stewart's throat.

"I didn't have a choice," she said, her voice pleading as the shiv trembled. She was young, no more than twenty-five years old. And if she'd received an order from Clive Paget's relation, she was correct: She hadn't had a choice at all.

"Because you are associated with the Angels," Jasper said. "And Emma Bates is Clive Paget's…what? Daughter?"

A pack of prison warders, mostly men with a few women, had arrived at the receiving cell. Some streamed inside, while others crowded the open door.

Miss Hartley hesitated. Then gave a nod to Jasper's question.

"Where is Emma now?" he asked. The warder wasn't going to harm Mrs. Stewart. The cracks in her determination were already showing. She would turn her over and surrender. "Emma Bates. Where did she go?"

"She…" Miss Hartley spluttered. "She's waiting."

As Jasper had speculated, the warder lowered the blade. She deflated, letting the weapon fall to the floor with a clatter. Mrs. Stewart was relinquished next, and she let out a sobbing breath of relief as she stumbled away, lost the strength in her legs, and landed on her knees. Mr. Vines ordered Miss Hartley cuffed and locked in a cell, and three male warders closed in on her.

"Waiting where?" Jasper asked as they pulled her arms roughly behind her back. "Miss Hartley, answer my question. Where is she waiting?"

She hung her head in submission. "The Chaplain's House."

Jasper stood aside as Miss Hartley was led away. The Chaplain's House was outside the gate, where Leo had said she would wait for Lewis. A prickling of disquiet crawled along his skin, and he turned for the exit.

The porter's gate closed behind her with a resounding clang. Leo exhaled a shaking breath. There had been no point in staying within the lodge, which had smelled of cooked onions and damp clothing, but she hated walking away from the prison when she knew that inside, Mrs. Stewart was in imminent danger.

As much as she had wanted to go with Jasper, arguing with Mr. Vines would have been petty and useless. It also could have dire consequences for Mrs. Stewart's safety. Ten minutes had passed since Miss Hartley and her 'sister' parted ways, the guard had said. It was certainly enough time for the warder to access Mrs. Stewart's cell and kill her, if she had gone in to carry out the task straightaway. How did the warder possibly believe she was going to get away with such a thing?

Leo crossed her arms, clasping her elbows as she walked swiftly toward the entrance gate and main road. As soon as Sergeant Lewis arrived, she would direct him inside…and try to follow. By then, Miss Hartley might have been detained, the danger gone.

Leo walked between the governor's and chaplain's homes, the residences matching in their towering, crenulated design. They looked medieval and austere, which wasn't, she supposed, entirely unfitting for a prison. A ripple of movement at the back corner of the Chaplain's House snagged her attention. Leo slowed as she caught sight of a wine-red cape fluttering as it disappeared behind a tall hedge planted close to the house.

It was the same wine-red hue of the velvet cape hanging in the front hall of the Stewarts' home the other day, when she'd called on Emma Bates.

With a skip in her pulse, Leo started for the hedge. If it was Emma, she wasn't about to let the woman disappear.

The chaplain's home had the shuttered, serene air of disuse. No sound came from within as she rounded the hedge and entered a small yard. The same tall brick wall that ran the perimeter of the prison grounds also bordered this side lawn. Leo took a few steps into the yard, where several young fruit trees were budding. But there was no one in sight.

She turned to retrace her steps—and jolted to a stop.

Emma Bates, her expression stony, stood less than an arm's length from her. "Why are you here, Miss Spencer? Have you followed me?"

Leo blinked rapidly, her reply delayed by incomprehension. Emma had lingered here on the secluded side of the chaplain's home. But why? Awaiting word from Miss Hartley, perhaps?

If that was the case, she might not have seen Leo's arrival earlier in the company of a Scotland Yard detective.

"No, I…I wanted to call on Geraldine, but the warder turned me away," she lied. "Did he deny you as well?"

The young widow quizzed her with a sharp look, as if weighing whether to believe her. But then, she sighed. "He did. Apparently, women are only allowed inside if they have committed a crime."

After an awkward pause, Leo gestured toward the main walkway. "Perhaps if we apply to the warder together, we can convince him."

Being here alone with Emma on this side of the chaplain's home, out of view of anyone passing on the walkway, suddenly felt perilous.

Emma smiled tightly. "Optimistic thought, but I don't believe that will persuade him. I think I'll try my luck another day. Good afternoon, Miss Spencer."

She turned on her heel and started swiftly for the front of the house and the walkway that would lead to the road. She was going to run. Leo hurried to stay with her.

"There is a coffee shop just down the road that we passed on the way up. Perhaps if you'd like—"

Emma whirled to spear Leo with a glare. "*We*? Did you not come here alone?"

Leo bit her tongue and cursed herself for the asinine blunder. Before she could concoct an explanation, a commotion of clattering wheels and whinnying horses sounded beyond the perimeter wall, coming from the direction of the entrance gate. Then, the voices of men. Sensing danger, Emma latched onto Leo's arm and hauled her close with surprising brutality.

"What have you done?" she seethed as the men's voices carried. A handful of them dashed along the walkway, which was just within their view. It was Sergeant Lewis and a few uniformed constables on his heels. Close enough to signal.

"Serg—!" The sharp point of something hard dug into Leo's waist, and she gasped, her voice cutting off.

Emma pushed Leo back toward the secluded side of the chaplain's yard. The woman's fingers clutched her arm in a bruising grip. A shock of pain lanced through her side as the blade of what appeared to be a penknife jabbed her.

"Quiet or this goes straight into your liver," Emma hissed.

Briefly, Leo considered attempting to wrest the penknife from her hand. But with the knife blade still poking into her skin, there was a steep chance of failure. She knew her own strengths, and physical prowess was not one of them.

"Actually," she said, trying to breathe evenly and not cause the blade to lodge any deeper, "the liver is on the right side of the body. As this is my left, you'd likely pierce my spleen or descending colon."

Emma shrieked in frustration, and hot pain flashed along Leo's side.

"You think you are clever, do you?" she spat out. "A clever woman would have left well enough alone, not pressed her luck."

She dragged Leo toward the corner of the house again to check if the path was clear. It wasn't. Just outside the entrance gate was a police wagon and a constable in uniform standing guard.

Emma slowly backed them out of sight.

There was no more point in lying. "Inspector Reid knows you ordered that female warder to kill Geraldine," Leo said. "He knows you are behind the bombing involving Constable Lloyd. Porter Stewart told us everything. They are here to arrest you."

Inflaming the unhinged woman's temper might just result in the blade being plunged deeper into her body. But Leo would not be cowed by fear or pain.

"Shut up," Emma ordered. Then, with a twisting tug on Leo's arm, she said, "You and I are walking out of here, and you're to do so without drawing attention our way."

Arm in arm, they would look to be bosom friends to the constable at the gate—should he not see the knife between them. A fine sweat erupted on Leo's chest and back as Emma rushed them toward the gravel path.

"And where will we go from there?" Leo asked. "You are only going to kill me afterward."

"That is your own fault. You and your inspector have ruined everything," she said, sounding petulant and desperate. "I should gut you now. It would be kinder than the punishment my family will show you."

"Ah yes, the Spitalfields Angels. Is Clive Paget your father, then? And is Miss Hartley truly your sister?"

Emma startled, surprised that her connection to the Angels had been uncovered. She glanced toward Leo, distracted. On Leo's next stride, she swung her ankle out and brought it back against Emma's in a sweeping motion. Emma tripped and, in her stumbling, the knife slid down the side of Leo's torso in another blaze of pain. Her leg tangled with Leo's, and they both landed hard on the ground, the agony in Leo's side debilitating. In a blink, Emma was on top of her, pushing her onto her back. Leo kicked and thrashed, but the woman's weight was more than she could combat.

"Oi!" the constable at the gate called out before starting toward them.

The tip of the penknife came to rest underneath Leo's chin.

"Stay back!" Emma screamed. He did, holding out his palms in surrender.

Emma's mouth twisted into a deranged expression of loathing as she loomed over Leo.

The blare of a police whistle came from within the prison walls. It shivered up Leo's spine as she lay on the cold, gravel path. Emma's face went stark white.

"You have no chance of escaping," Leo said, her heartbeat threatening to rip straight out of her chest. "Put down your knife and turn yourself over to Inspector Reid."

Emma looked toward the constable with a truncheon in his hand. He'd come closer. The knife touched the underside of Leo's chin. "I said stay back!"

He obeyed, taking a few steps in reverse. It wasn't the first time Leo had been held at knifepoint. In March, Andrew Carter had pressed his knife just below her eye, demanding that Jasper relinquish a suspect he'd arrested so that Andrew could kill him. Andrew Carter's hand had been steady with deadly intent, while Emma's was now trembling with panic. Oddly enough, it was Emma, not the East Rip, who struck Leo as more dangerous with a weapon. However, Jasper had his revolver. If he came through the porter's gate and saw Emma Bates with a knife to Leo's throat, he would use it.

Even as unstable as Emma was, even with all the pain and destruction she had wrought, Leo did not want to see her killed. She was a disturbed woman, a woman who had fallen in love with the wrong man and gone to extremes to attain him. A woman who'd been raised by criminals. Perhaps there had never been any hope that she might break free from a life of lawlessness.

None of that, however, excused what she'd done.

"You stole that valise. You arranged for the bomb," Leo said as shouts within the prison wall grew closer. Emma's rattled gaze clapped onto the porter's gate as it began to groan open.

"I'm sure your family even selected Constable Lloyd to deliver it by means of coercion. He was on the take, after all, indebted to the Angels. What did they do? Bribe him? Threaten his family?"

"He was a rotten copper, with no allegiance to anyone," Emma sneered. "He was just supposed to plant the bomb. It wasn't supposed to go off when the fool was carrying it. But I'm not sorry."

The void of feeling in the other woman's eyes left Leo feeling cold pity.

"I imagine you're not sorry about Niles Foster either. He tried to blackmail Mr. Stewart, so you tapped your family again to eliminate the threat he posed to the man you love. You will be found guilty of both murders, Mrs. Bates. But if you do not lay down that knife, I swear to you, the Inspector will shoot you as soon as he has you in his sights."

Leo knew this as keenly as she knew the moon would rise that evening, and the sun would chase it come morning. Jasper would stop at nothing to protect her.

The resounding commotion cleared the porter's gate and flowed into the courtyard.

"Drop your weapon!" Jasper's deep-throated command

rang out, and from her peripheral vision, she saw he had, in fact, aimed his Webley at Emma Bates.

"Don't shoot her! Please!" Leo called out.

"Get off Miss Spencer," Jasper commanded as several uniformed warders fanned out around him. "Now!"

Emma bared her teeth in a grimace—and then held out her arm and opened her fingers. The knife fell onto the ground, and Emma released a sob as she collapsed to the side. Leo sucked in a breath and rolled to a sitting position, her side stabbing with pain.

"Cuff her," Jasper ordered the constables as he holstered his revolver and rushed toward Leo. He crouched to grasp her arms and help her to her feet. His eyes slid over her, his honey-blond brows pulling taut as he peered at her side. "Christ, you're bleeding."

She put a hand to her waist. Her palm came away with blood, though less than she'd anticipated. Pulling up the hem of her short coat, she opened the ripped fabric of her shirtwaist and saw just how shallow the wound was.

"I'm all right," she said. "It looks and feels worse than it is."

He crouched again, this time to look closer at the wound. Worry still etched his brow. "Are you certain?"

"Positive. It's just a slice, nothing deep," she said. "But what happened inside? How is Mrs. Stewart?"

"Miss Hartley was in the cell when we arrived, but she didn't have the chance to harm Mrs. Stewart. She's been taken into custody." He grasped Leo's hips and pulled aside the sliced and bloody fabric. "This isn't shallow. I'm taking you to the prison's doctor. You need sutures."

"I am *fine*." She took hold of his wrists. As if realizing

the intimacy of being on bent knee, her hips in his palms, Jasper got to his feet and released her.

"You are sure?" he asked.

Leo nodded. "Although it might have been better for me to come into the prison with you, after all. Do you see what happens when I'm forced to stay back?"

He laughed, a grin trembling over his lips. "I don't know why I even bother."

Chapter Twenty-Three

In the hall leading to the detective department, several passing constables peered at Jasper with notable alarm before darting their eyes in another direction. They moved swiftly along as if trying to put distance between themselves and the detective inspector.

Jasper had a decent idea why.

Shortly before Mrs. Bates had been subdued, Sergeant Lewis had arrived at Holloway Prison with news from her home on Rupert Street. Her maid had nervously insisted yet again that she could not tell him anything about her mistress. Mrs. Bates was a dragon with the worst temper, and the maid provided an example of her wrath.

"Her first day on the job, the maid was cleaning in Mrs. Bates's bedroom when she found a leather case stuffed under the bed," Lewis explained, a grin pulling at his mouth as he spoke. "She took it out and was going to set it with the other luggage stored away when Mrs. Bates saw her and flew into a rage, telling her to put it back or she'd be sacked. I asked the maid to describe the case."

Jasper had caught on. "Let me guess. Brown leather with floral embroidery and a monogram that did not match the initials of her mistress?"

At Lewis's nod, Jasper knew they had her.

The detective sergeant was tasked with bringing their new prisoner to Scotland Yard to be booked and held for questioning. Meanwhile, Jasper would deliver Leo to her uncle, so that Claude could determine whether the gash along her side needed sutures.

Leo resisted, of course. "You should go with Sergeant Lewis. I'm perfectly capable of seeing myself to Spring Street."

"Get in the cab," he'd replied, holding the door open for her. The sight of her blood-darkened shirtwaist elevated his pulse—and fortified his determination to see her safely into Claude's care.

On the drive back to Westminster, Leo divulged what Emma Bates had revealed during her hasty escape attempt.

"She didn't exactly confess that she took Geraldine's valise," Leo said, pressing the handkerchief Jasper had given her to her hip. His heart rate evened somewhat when, after several minutes, the amount of blood on the linen hadn't increased.

"She didn't say anything specific about who helped assemble the bomb, but she did mention Constable Lloyd and how the plan hadn't been for him to die. He was simply supposed to place the bomb."

Her voice cracked over the last words as she'd likely thought of her friend, Miss Brooks, and the future that had been stolen from her.

"So, he was working for the Angels then?" Jasper asked.

"It doesn't sound like he had much of a choice, given he was in the gang's debt."

The depravity of Mrs. Bates's mind sickened and infuriated Jasper. Added to that was the frustration that Leo had been harmed—and that he had not been able to shield her.

After she'd alighted from the cab onto the pavement in front of the morgue, Leo held out her arm to stay him when he'd tried to walk her to the door. He bounced his chest off her palm before stepping back.

"I am perfectly well, and you are needed at the Yard." She swung out her arm, pointing in the direction of Whitehall Place. "Go."

She was right. So, he'd assented with a nod and climbed back into the cab. Now, as Jasper reached the CID, he braced himself for impact.

It came at him like a runaway train.

"What the devil have you done, Reid?" Blood infused Inspector Tomlin's cheeks and lit the tips of his ears red. "I told you to keep your nose out of my investigation."

The room went silent. Constables and detectives hung back to view the brewing altercation and give it plenty of room to unfold. Jasper could understand Tomlin's reaction. His slapdash work, which had led to a hasty arrest, was about to be thrown out. It was a bad look and a black mark on his reputation.

"I've brought in the woman who arranged for Niles Foster's murder and the bombing that killed PC Lloyd," he replied as he removed his coat and tossed it over his chair. "It will all be in my report. You're welcome to look through it once it's finished. But for now, I have an interview."

Lewis stood near the closed door to the interview room, a pane of frosted glass obscuring the sight of Mrs. Bates seated inside.

"You have nothing solid," Tomlin said, sticking to Jasper's heels.

"In fact, I do. A witness who saw Mrs. Bates with the valise in her home, and a confession Mrs. Bates made to Miss Spencer." He'd gotten damn lucky. Without the maid and Leo, Tomlin would have been correct. Jasper would have been able to implicate her in the bribery scheme involving Mr. Stewart and Sir Elliot but not the bombing.

Tomlin scoffed loudly, emitting a snort. "Miss Spencer? As I said, you have nothing. Neither the chief, the superintendent, nor the commissioner will trust a single word out of that deluded, interfering cow's mouth. The woman belongs in Bedlam."

Jasper reacted without thought. He whirled around and grabbed ahold of the belligerent detective. Grasping Tomlin's collar in his fists, he slammed him against the wall just outside the interview room. The tense quiet surrounding them shattered.

"If every woman who proved herself to be smarter than you was sent to Bedlam, they'd be spilling out the bloody windows." Jasper's broken ribs burned as he held a thrashing Tomlin in place.

"Guv," Lewis said, barring a few other officers who'd scrabbled forward to peel the two men apart. "Coughlan's on his way. Let him go."

Jasper tossed Tomlin aside, who then immediately lunged for him. The other officers intercepted, holding him back with hands and arms to his chest. Jasper readjusted his tie and threw open the door to the interview room. Mrs. Bates, seated at the table in handcuffs, peered at him coolly.

"What was that commotion?" she asked as he and Lewis stepped inside and closed the door.

"That isn't your concern." Jasper pulled out the chair across the table and sat. Lewis remained standing.

She arched a thin blonde brow as she looked Jasper over. "My, that is a considerable amount of bruising, Inspector. Whatever did happen?"

Her goading smirk failed to have the effect she desired. The brief scrap with Tomlin had been enough to work out the knot of frustration coiled within him. The release of tension in his arms and back put a grin on his face.

"Porter Stewart is expected shortly, along with his solicitor. I'm sure he will be relieved to hear that his wife is safe," Jasper said, still grinning.

Her brittle smirk cracked.

"How long do you think he and Sir Elliot will hold out before throwing you to the wolves? Their reputations are at risk, after all," he added.

Mrs. Bates hitched her chin. Her hands were folded demurely on the table before her. "They can accuse me, but they have no proof."

Jasper nodded, giving the question some thought. "You did well at first, keeping yourself in the background. Directing matters with an artful hand. You certainly concealed your involvement in the bombing well enough. That is, until your new maid told my detective sergeant here about finding a certain valise under your bed."

Her nostrils flared, her eyes flicking toward Lewis. "She is lying."

"I'm sure the magistrate will consider that possibility. But I doubt he'll be convinced."

The smugness drained from her face.

"We know you colluded with the Spitalfields Angels. You're a Paget by birth, and your staff will testify that your family are known visitors to your home—only by way of the back door, of course." Jasper drummed the table with his fingers. "To whom did you give the valise after procuring it from the Stewarts' attic?"

Mrs. Bates said nothing.

"Which Angel?" he pressed. "Was it Clive? Or Lester Rice? We know he has ties to Clan na Gael. He would have had access to materials for a bomb."

Her lips remained sealed. She'd as good as turned to stone.

"You wrote a letter to Clive Paget about a month ago. Your maid—whom I imagine you're wishing you hadn't hired—can attest to that as well. The warder, Miss Hartley, confirmed Clive is your father."

When she remained stoic, Lewis said, "The information's easy enough to get through birth records."

It was true, though it would be a hassle.

"I see. You're afraid of them," Jasper guessed. "Give up a name, and you'll likely be dead before you go to court."

She withdrew her hands from the table, the chains on the iron cuffs clanking. "I will confess to nothing. If you're determined to charge me with a crime, then do so."

"With pleasure," he said, then stood. He would get nothing more out of her, but there was enough circumstantial evidence and witness testimony, not to mention the attack on Leo outside Holloway Prison, for a jury to convict her.

Lewis opened the door, and Jasper turned to leave.

"You will want to keep an eye on Miss Spencer, Inspector."

He spun back around and glared. "Pardon?"

"There are whispers," Mrs. Bates said with an easy shrug.

He returned to the table and braced against it with his knuckles. "What whispers?"

She hedged. "What is it worth to you?"

"She's playing with you, guv," Lewis warned. "Let's go."

Jasper pushed off the table, but he wasn't convinced Lewis was right. With her connection to one of London's most notorious gangs, it was possible Emma Bates had heard something about Leo, whose family had, after all, been slaughtered by one of the Angels' enemies.

But Jasper wasn't going to give her an inch. He would keep an eye on Leo as he always had. There were other ways of finding out if something was being *whispered* about her.

"Worry about yourself, Mrs. Bates. Leonora Spencer isn't your concern."

As he closed the door behind him, he thought he heard a stifled sob.

Chapter Twenty-Four

Leo had built a fire in the hearth, and though it had warmed Jasper's study, she couldn't stop shivering. The house had been dark and quiet as she'd climbed the front step earlier. Belatedly, she remembered Mrs. Zhao had gone to stay with her sister. Without her presence, there had been a hollowness to the house when Leo unlocked the door and let herself in.

Lighting a few gas brackets and making her way to the study, she thought about the last time she'd employed her key to enter 23 Charles Street. The Inspector had given it to her long ago, but she hadn't used it until that early morning visit when she'd barged in on Jasper as if in a daze.

She blushed remembering the image that had, like every other, been trapped in the amber of her mind. Jasper, lying on his stomach in bed, unclothed. The expanse of his muscled back on display, the bed linens resting at his tapered waist. Perhaps that was the state in which he slept every night, but she imagined that he'd been airing out the gash inflicted from the previous day's explosion at a wallpaper factory. The wound had been the only blemish on his back's otherwise pale, smooth skin.

Leo was slightly ashamed of how often she'd summoned that image in the months that followed. Thinking of it had been a betrayal of her own pledge to loathe him forever. But she could not deny the truth. He was handsome, ruggedly so. Now, as it did then, thinking of him in any romantic way left her feeling turned upside down. And slightly breathless.

After he'd left her at the morgue, Leo had entered the postmortem room and utterly sidetracked Claude and Mr. Quinn from the corpse they'd been attending. At the sight of her bloody shirtwaist, they'd swarmed her in alarm.

"It is a shallow cut," she said to calm them.

"My God, Leonora, have you been mugged?" Claude asked.

"It's a long story," she said, and after closing herself in the supply closet to partially undress and clean her wound with carbolic acid and surgical gauze, she recited the tale while her uncle and Mr. Quinn listened on the other side of the door. The light of the lamp showed that her wound was, as she'd thought, relatively minor. She wasn't in dire need of sutures.

When she redressed and opened the door, she found the two men waiting for her. Claude appeared utterly baffled. Mr. Quinn, his arms crossed over his chest, stared at her with a loose jaw.

"I thought you were a typist for the morgue, Miss Spencer, not a police detective."

He was only being sarcastic, and she shouldn't have

been irritated by the comment. But she was, just the same. "You well know I am not a detective. Nor can I be."

"Then why would the inspector allow you to be present?" he'd replied. "I think it's damned irresponsible of him, in fact."

Leo had pushed past him. "It is a very good thing then that what you think doesn't bear weight on the situation."

It had been harsh, and she hadn't looked to see how he'd reacted. Nor had she much cared. Leo announced she was going home to change her clothing, and she spent the quarter-hour walk in a thunderous mood.

She wasn't a morgue typist or assistant any longer, thanks to the arrival of Connor Quinn. She couldn't be a detective or anything having to do with the police at all. Apparently, because she was a woman, she wasn't qualified to do the things at which she was quite good. She found herself on the edge of uncertainty. The last several days, the investigations had occupied her mind, but now, with Mrs. Bates having been taken into custody, there was no avoiding the question: What would come next?

She hadn't yet settled on an answer, or anything close to one.

The fire in the study now blazed. Leo uncapped the bottle of cherry liqueur she'd given the Inspector in January. But eyeing the cut crystal decanter of whisky beside it, she capped it again. Jasper had once poured her a glass of the amber liquid in his office after they'd thwarted Mr. Benjamin Munson, a deputy assistant-turned-murderer who'd tried to kill them four months ago. Drinking it had been like swallowing fire. She poured herself a splash with the hope that it might douse her shivers.

The hinges on the door to the study squeaked. Leo turned to see Jasper aiming his Webley at her. Her heart stuttered.

"Jesus, Leo." He immediately lowered the revolver. "I thought the Angels were in my house again."

She frowned. "I hadn't thought of that. I'm sorry to have alarmed you."

He holstered his revolver, then as he came into the room, shed his coat and hat. He tossed them onto the Chesterfield, his attention hinging on the drink in her hand.

"No Grants Morella?" he asked, arching a brow.

Leo swirled the shallow pour of whisky, the sharp fumes reaching her nose. "I decided I needed something stronger tonight."

He joined her at the sideboard and poured himself a heavy splash, then tapped his glass against hers.

"Cheers," he said before taking a sip.

Fire coated her throat as she drank, and she was grateful she didn't cough this time.

"So," Leo began, her voice tellingly hoarse. "What happened with Mrs. Bates?"

Finding out how things had gone at Scotland Yard was why she'd come. Partially, at least.

Jasper went to the Chesterfield and eased down onto the corner cushion so as not to jar his aching ribs. He looked worn to the bone. "She'll be arraigned tomorrow, charged with conspiracy to commit murder, attempted murder, and bribery. It appears Mrs. Bates was with Porter Stewart when he met with Sir Elliot to bribe him; Payne is admitting to the meeting. He claims he rebuffed the offer and did not attend the WEA meeting due to discomfort with Mr. Stewart."

Leo settled herself in the opposite corner of the Chesterfield. The worn leather creaked softly.

"Did Mrs. Bates name any of her accomplices?" she asked after a moment of quiet. "Lester Rice, for example?"

"No, though we did bring him in, along with the Olaf fellow from Bloom's casino room. Both are claiming innocence, of course. But Mrs. Bates will stay quiet. It won't matter that she is a Paget by blood; if she turns on them, she'll be dead. So, she's keeping names to herself."

He swirled his whisky and took another sip as a question continued to nag at her.

"How did the Angels get the idea to put Mr. Foster's body on Lord Hayes's property? Clearly, they meant to implicate the viscount, but Mrs. Bates couldn't have known about their family connection."

Jasper raised his pointer finger from his glass. "I'd thought of that too. Sir Elliot introduced his aide to Mr. Stewart and Mrs. Bates before their meeting, and when I pressed the subject, he admitted to explaining to them that Foster was a sympathy hire. A favor to his friend, Lord Hayes."

That would account for it then. Not only had Emma wished to silence Mr. Foster, but she'd also wanted to arrange for a suspect in his murder. Oliver Hayes had been the perfect scapegoat.

"And Lord Babbage?" Leo asked, recalling the anti-women's suffrage MP whom Geraldine was accused of targeting at the Yard. "How did he play in?"

"He didn't," Jasper replied. "His appointment at headquarters that day seems to have been a useful coincidence. On the surface, at least."

Like Jasper, Leo didn't wholly believe in coincidences.

"What did Porter Stewart know about all of this?" she asked. "Earlier at his home, he seemed utterly oblivious to Mrs. Bates's machinations."

Jasper released a long and weary exhalation. "I think he is trying to convince himself of his own obliviousness, though anyone with even half a brain should have been able to work it out." Shaking his head, he went on. "When I interviewed him at the Yard, he added to his statement that he'd turned to Mrs. Bates after Foster's visit to the bank. Allegedly, she told him not to worry, that she would take care of things."

"And did he ask how she intended to help?"

Jasper sent her a bemused look. "What do you think?"

Leo knew the answer. She eyed her drink. The whisky had warmed her chest and alleviated her shivering. Or perhaps that could be attributed to something else entirely. The shivers had subsided after Jasper's arrival.

"I think Geraldine Stewart should have married a better man."

He chuckled. "No arguments there."

"What will happen to her?" she asked. "Will the charges against her be dropped?"

"As the only evidence against Mrs. Stewart was her ownership of the valise, Tomlin won't have a choice but to rescind the charges. Superintendent Monroe has already ordered him to do so."

Leo well imagined Inspector Tomlin's resentment and fury that his own sewn-up case had been picked apart and correctly solved by another detective. She also knew

Jasper would suffer a fair amount of enmity from Tomlin and his team for having interfered with their investigation.

"Her reputation won't recover quickly. There's a chance it might never," Leo said, thinking of the ladies who had attended the WEA meetings. Most were wealthy and well-connected, and though they supported suffrage, they might not wish to be associated with someone who'd had scandal attached to her name.

"At least she'll have her freedom," Jasper said. "Besides, something tells me she isn't going to be dissuaded from her mission."

Leo agreed. It was nice to know Jasper could see that determination too and didn't seem to dislike her for it.

She drew her legs up onto the sofa cushion beneath her, though the motion pulled at her bandaged waist. She tried to mask her gasp of pain by bringing the glass to her lips, but he still heard it.

"Did Claude place any sutures?"

"I was right; I didn't need them."

He made a face that said he didn't believe her. "He didn't even look at your wound, did he?"

"How is your head?" she countered, wishing to get away from the topic of her injury.

He muttered under his breath and slouched further into the couch. "Fine."

Leo didn't believe him either. But he was too stubborn to complain. She supposed she was too.

"When will Mrs. Zhao be home?"

"I'll send word tomorrow that it's safe for her to return."

The pop and hiss of the coal grate filled the next drop

of silence. Then, Jasper looked at her from across the sofa. "Are you going to tell me?"

The light from the gas wall brackets and the glow from the coal fire cast his face in changing shades of golden yellow.

Leo had put off telling him about her visit to Striker's Wharf, the things Eddie Bloom had told her, and what she'd found in the steamer trunk that had inspired her to go there in the first place. What could Jasper do to resolve or change any of it?

"I'm not sure it matters." She turned her gaze toward the coal grate.

He shifted on the sofa to face her. "You wanted to tell me something earlier, and it was important. It still is."

She bit her bottom lip, hesitant. However, even if nothing could be done, she didn't want to be alone with the things she had learned.

"I found the letters Aunt Flora sent to my mother. Something was happening with my father, something dangerous. Flora never wrote anything specific, but she was afraid for us."

"Your mother knew what your father was doing?" Jasper guessed. "That he was working for the Carters?"

"Something more, I think." Leo turned toward him. "You said he was an accountant for them. That would have given him access to sensitive information regarding their income and expenses. What if he discovered something while doing their books?"

Jasper bobbed his head as if to say it was a possibility. "The Inspector thought it most likely that your father was targeted for that reason. Something having to do with his accounting work for them. But he went through all your father's papers and ledgers before giving them back to Claude, and he never found anything untoward specifically, nothing about the Carters."

It was a reminder that Jasper had always known the truth of who had killed Leo's family and had been play-acting ignorance while the Inspector worked tirelessly to discover answers to the tragedy. Leo hardened her spine and faced forward.

"Five months before the attack on my family," she began, ignoring the break in the tenuous peace between them, "my father began to receive five pounds a month. He recorded the addition in his personal ledger, marking them only with the initials BR."

There was little chance the Inspector had not seen that pattern. And there was no avoiding it any longer: She would have to go through his file on the murders, even if it made her ill and gave her nightmares.

"You think someone was paying your father to pass along information about the Carters' false accounts?"

She nodded and closed her eyes, suddenly exhausted. "I need to go through my father's things again. I might be able to find someone with those initials, or some business perhaps, listed somewhere. And then, of course, I'll have to look through the Inspector's private file."

When Jasper stayed silent, she wondered what he might be thinking. She took a guess. "Or, as I said before, maybe it doesn't matter."

"Why wouldn't it?" Jasper asked quietly.

"Does it truly matter *how* my father betrayed the East Rips? The fact is, he did. And they killed him for it. My mother and brother and sister too. None of that will change by learning the details."

In fact, discovering them could revive the danger her aunt had mentioned in her letters. Eddie Bloom had made it clear that Leo was to let sleeping dogs lie and not stir up old troubles. She considered keeping her visit to Striker's Wharf a secret. But in the end, Jasper would likely learn of it, and she'd rather it be from her.

"Don't get angry, but I went to Striker's Wharf."

He set his jaw. "When?"

"Last night."

The glow of the burning coals seemed to leap from the grate and ignite his pupils. "By yourself?"

Leo sighed. "Please don't chastise me again."

"Why did you go there?" But then, comprehension darkened his already fulminating glare. "I see. You went after you found the steamer trunk."

"It was impulsive, I admit," she said.

"*Impulsive*?" Jasper thundered. He shot off the sofa and paced away, running a hand through his golden hair, the strands already mussed. "How many times must I tell you before you understand: Eddie Bloom is a criminal. He is dangerous."

Leo braced herself against his anger and got to her feet, hitching her chin in defiance. "I agree. But I believe he tried to help me."

He slowly came back toward her. "Help you how?"

"He wouldn't let me finish my questions," she answered. "We were being observed, he claimed, and so he...showed me the door, so to speak."

"Observed by whom?" Jasper bellowed.

"He didn't explicitly say, but he indicated that my presence there could be noted by those who see me as a..." She took a jagged breath. "As a loose thread."

He swore under his breath, and a muscle ticked along his clenched jaw.

"Is Mr. Bloom correct?" she asked. "Am I a loose thread?"

He met her gaze, his temper still simmering. "After the article that bloody idiot wrote, drawing attention to your past, and now, with you beginning to ask questions, then yes. I worry they won't like it."

"They? You mean the Carters?" she asked to clarify.

Jasper gave a barely perceptible nod. "In certain circles, it must be known who was responsible for the Spencer murders. The East Rips won't like that their past failures are being brought up."

"Is that why you always hated that the Inspector kept digging into my family's deaths?" she asked. He'd been disapproving of Gregory Reid's dogged pursuit of the truth. A sudden thought numbed her. "Tell me you didn't interfere with his file."

The folder the Inspector had given to Leo shortly before his death was at least two inches thick, with interview notes, reports, photographs, documented theories, and leads.

Jasper jerked back his head. "You're asking me if I sabotaged his investigation?"

"You couldn't have wanted him to solve their murders, not if his answers led him to you and your family."

He let out a chuff of air as if she'd pummeled him in the stomach. Insult filled his stare, softening it just enough to send a coil of regret through her. She didn't want to believe he willfully would have done such a thing, knowing how important it was to the Inspector.

She faced the fire and crossed her arms over her chest. "I'm sorry, but I don't know what to think anymore."

Staring into the low flames in the grate, she sensed him coming up behind her. He then joined her at her side. Leo glanced over, but he was staring into the fire too. The glow from it shimmered on the brass buttons of his tweed waistcoat. Jasper scrubbed his jaw and knit his brow, frustrated. As he ran the back of a knuckle gently over his swollen bottom lip, her attention was drawn there in unexpected interest. Though, only until he began to speak.

"When we were first here in this house, I didn't sleep a full night for months. I thought they would come in the middle of the night to finish the job they'd left undone."

Leo held her breath. *They*. His family. Even though she now knew the truth, it still boggled her mind that Jasper's past wasn't the one she'd always assumed and envisioned. And that it was so closely linked to her own.

"I'd sit in the hallway in the dark, pinching myself to stay awake," he went on, his gaze fixed on the flickering, red-gold flames. "I believed they would come, but the only person I ever saw was the Inspector. He found me a few times. He didn't say anything. Just clapped me on the shoulder." He touched the spot lightly, as if it helped him to remember and feel, once again, the affection of the man he'd come to call Father. "I think he knew what I was doing there, even if he didn't understand why I was doing it."

Her heart swelled at the image of a young Jasper, sitting sentry outside her bedroom door, ready to stand up to the people he'd run away from. What had he been feeling to do such a thing? Shame? Or had he, too, felt wronged by his family?

Tears pricked the backs of her eyes.

Jasper met her watery gaze. "I wasn't going to let anything happen to you then, and I'm not going to let anything happen to you now."

The vow shot through her, straight into the center of her chest. A sense of safety wrapped itself around her, but it was nothing new. It had always been there, inherent between them. He would protect her, and she would do the same for him. Even so, the reason why troubled her.

"I don't want to be your responsibility," she said. "I don't want to be your punishment."

The idea that he might have stayed a part of her life all these years because he felt the need to *atone*—and not because he wanted to be there—utterly speared her.

Jasper shifted his footing toward her. "You aren't either of those things to me."

"Aren't I? I can't help but think that if you didn't feel guilty, you wouldn't still be here." She'd been tamping down that thought for months. Only now did she recognize how much it pained her.

He reached for her hand. Leo held her breath as he brought it to his chest. "Guilt isn't keeping me here."

His grip was strong, his palm coarse and warm, and at the steady beating of his heart, a shiver raced through her. It wasn't the brittle shaking she'd been plagued with earlier. This shiver was electric and hot, and it pulsed through her with a sweet ache. Slowly, Jasper lifted her hand to his mouth. That charged shiver raced to every part of her body. Holding her stare, he brushed his lips against the ridge of her knuckles.

"I can only imagine what you think of me now." His voice had turned hoarse and, to her ears, vulnerable. "But I care for you. That is why I'm here, Leo."

Her head went light at the sudden prancing of her heart. All thoughts swirled away except for the one that radiated through her mind: He cared. For *her*.

Jasper released her hand, but she did not lower it. She didn't pull away. Leo grazed her fingertips against his cheek, touching the scruff that he would shave come morning. Her fingers drew down, lightly over his healing split lip, to the tip of his chin. He remained motionless as a statue, his dark green eyes locked on hers.

He closed the scant inches remaining between them, and with a heady rush of wonder, Leo raised her mouth to meet his. Gently, Jasper's lips touched hers. He paused, lingering against her mouth, leaving her a chance to change her mind. For the barest moment, she considered it. But at the first true stroke of his lips, at the pressure of his hand at the nape of her neck, Leo leaned in.

She'd once endured an unskilled and uninvited kiss from a police constable, whom she had escaped by promptly stomping on his foot. But *this*… This kiss was poles apart from that. Jasper's mouth moved slowly against hers, the spice of whisky on his lips and his familiar scent of oakmoss and cedarwood enveloping her. Leo wanted to sink into it, let it consume her.

Why hadn't she kissed him before now? Why had it taken her so long to realize she wanted to?

With a desperate tug, Jasper drew her body flush against his. The hard wall of his chest and abdomen set off a firestorm of sensation inside her, and the sparks were as exhilarating and dangerous as their kiss. The tender nudge of his mouth became more persistent, and a faint warning struggled to be heard from the back of her mind. Such a galvanizing kiss wasn't proper. Not when they were in his home, entirely alone. Before, it hadn't mattered if they were unchaperoned. But now, the impatient fusion of their lips changed everything. Especially since Leo did not wish to end the kiss at all.

It was the very reason why she pushed against his chest and broke away.

Jasper's unfocused eyes snapped to attention, and he blinked, clearing the banked desire from them. "I'm sorry," he said reflexively. "I've offended you, I'm—"

"No." Leo backed up, colliding with the arm of the Chesterfield. Her mouth felt swollen and hot. She touched her lips with her fingertips and found her hand was trembling. "You haven't, not at all. I just…I didn't realize…"

At her hesitation, he took a stride toward her, bringing him close enough for her to touch again. Leo, however, kept her hands behind her, braced against the arm of the sofa. "What didn't you realize?" he whispered. "That I wanted to kiss you?"

She lost her breath, and the momentary lack of oxygen was surely the reason for her shameless reply. "No. I didn't realize how much I wanted you to, until you were."

Jasper reached for her, but with a hard thud of her pulse, she moved to the side. "I can't. We shouldn't."

Disoriented, she turned to find her coat and hat. Her legs had the odd feeling of being attached to her body incorrectly.

"I'm sorry, Jasper. I need time to think," she said haltingly, her voice trembling in an unfamiliar manner. "I want to forgive you, and a part of me already has, but…"

But she'd just barely reopened the door to him as a friend, as someone she could trust again.

"Of course. I understand," he said, his voice hoarse as she collected her things from the chair behind the Inspector's desk. *Jasper's* desk. This was his home now. The urge to stay, to set aside her uncertainty and kiss him again, was both foolish and perilously enticing.

"I'll hail you a cab," he said, but Leo shook her head on her way toward the study's door.

"I'll be fine on my own," she replied, her heart racing and her lips tingling.

"Leo." He followed her into the corridor where he gently took her elbow. "Wait."

After a steadying breath, she turned to face him. Her mutinous eyes went straight to his mouth. He pressed his lips together, then softened them in hesitation.

"You may not know what to think right now, but I do. Kissing you wasn't a mistake." Jasper's fingers slipped lightly from her forearm to her hand. "Take whatever time you need, but may I ask one thing?"

Leo's resolve flagged under the ache of his yearning gaze. Her pulse continued to sputter, and when she nodded, the motion was stilted.

"These last few months not talking to you, not seeing you have been hellish. Can you find it in your heart not to take as long this time around to speak to me again?"

A small grin teased the corner of his mouth, and she met it with a bashful smile of her own. She tensed her fingers around his in a reassuring squeeze. "I won't, I promise."

When Jasper released her hand and took a long step

backward rather than closer to her, she didn't know if she was relieved or disappointed.

"Goodnight, Leo."

Releasing her pent-up breath, she walked swiftly to the foyer and out the front door, shutting it behind her. Spring evening air cooled her flushed cheeks as she hurried in the direction of the cabstand, her mind whirling.

Exactly how to feel about Jasper Reid eluded her, but she knew one thing for certain: She'd never again be able to set foot inside 23 Charles Street without reliving that kiss.

Thank you for reading Courier of Death, the third book in the Spencer & Reid Mysteries!
Please leave a rating and review on Amazon to help other readers discover the series.

Leo and Jasper's next book, Cloaked in Deception, releases in September 2025.

Also by Cara Devlin

The Spencer & Reid Mysteries

SHADOW AT THE MORGUE

METHOD OF REVENGE

COURIER OF DEATH

CLOAKED IN DECEPTION

The Bow Street Duchess Mysteries

MURDER AT THE SEVEN DIALS

DEATH AT FOURNIER DOWNS

SILENCE OF DECEIT

PENANCE FOR THE DEAD

FATAL BY DESIGN

NATURE OF THE CRIME

TAKEN TO THE GRAVE

THE LADY'S LAST MISTAKE (A Bow Street Duchess Romance)

The Sage Canyon Series

A HEART WORTH HEALING

A CURE IN THE WILD

A LAND OF FIERCE MERCY

THE TROUBLE WE KEEP

A Second Chance Western Romance

About the Author

Cara is the author of the bestselling Bow Street Duchess Mystery series. She loves to write romantic historical fiction and mystery, especially when the romance is a slow burn and the mystery is multi-layered and twisty. She lives in rural New England with her husband and their three daughters. Cara is currently at work on the rest of the Spencer & Reid Mysteries. The fourth book, CLOAKED IN DECEPTION, releases September 2025.

Printed in Dunstable, United Kingdom

67988045R00170